NOT EVERY RIVER

Robbi McCoy

Bella
BOOKS
2010

Bella Books, Inc.
P.O. Box 10543
Tallahassee, FL 32302

Printed in the United States of America on acid-free paper
First Edition

Editor: Katherine V. Forrest
Cover Designer: Linda Callaghan

ISBN 13: 978-1-59493-182-6

Also by Robbi McCoy

Waltzing At Midnight
Songs Without Words

About the Author

Robbi McCoy is a native Californian who lives with her partner and two cats in the Central Valley between the mountains and the sea. She is an avid hiker with a particular fondness for the deserts of the American Southwest. She also enjoys gardening, culinary adventures and the theater. She works full-time as a software specialist and web designer for a major West Coast distribution company.

Dedication

To my sweetheart, Dot, who remains my greatest source
of confidence and hope.

Acknowledgments

I would like to thank Norma and Carmen for their help with Spanish. Muchas gracias! To Kirsty, thank you for your interest and support. Devoted readers like you are the reason for being for writers like me. Much appreciation to Gladys for the practical and the personal assistance. Thank you, Marianne, for your continuing friendship and encouragement. I know it isn't easy dealing with my ego and its evil twin, my insecurity.

I was delighted to work with Katherine V. Forrest on this project. Her skill and insight are remarkable. An enjoyable and productive partnership.

CHAPTER ONE

Matt sat cross-legged with his eyes closed, sunlight shimmering on his silver hair, looking like a sage from any bygone culture, but mostly like a Native American shaman. His straight nose and rounded face hinted at his Quechan heritage, diluted by several generations into a negligible percentage. Still, if not for his clothes, this modern man would be indistinguishable from his distant ancestors. Set against the backdrop of the Arizona desert, he might be a twenty-first century archaeologist telling a story or a sixteenth-century medicine man on a vision quest.

"The deer," he said, continuing his tale, "downed by a single arrow through its neck, fell on the spot. The man ran up and stared for a moment at the animal's wild eye, observing the last second of its life. The deer acknowledged the hunter with a slow blink, then the glint of life was gone and the black eye saw nothing."

Randi sat motionless on her warm slab of granite, listening to the story.

"The man knelt beside the animal," Matt said, his voice assuming the slow cadence of his ancestors. "He said a prayer to the spirit of the deer, thanking it for giving its life for the man's family. Then he lifted it to his shoulders and walked east toward home."

Matt opened his eyes and rearranged his legs, glancing at Randi with a benign smile and a pronounced squint against the bright sunshine.

"That happened right there," he said in his regular voice, pointing to the bottom of the wash.

Randi nodded, suppressing a grin. "You don't say."

"Yep, right there where that triangular boulder sits. That boulder was there then just as it is now, exactly the same. That's how I saw it. That's how he saw it. Nothing has changed in four hundred years."

She was used to this. Matt told many such stories, claiming to be recalling the memories of his ancestors. He didn't want to think that all that living was lost. Randi understood the feeling. Inheriting the memories of all of those who came before was a much more direct way of remembering the past than trying to figure it out from artifacts that were left behind. Rock art and shards of pottery left so many questions unanswered and so many individuals without faces or voices. He wanted to keep those people alive somehow. That was the fundamental purpose of archaeology, after all, at least if you really felt it in your heart, to bring a dead culture back to life. Randi knew this channeling of Matt's was, in his opinion, part of his job.

And how could anybody argue? It wasn't so unlikely that a hunter had killed a deer right there at some point in history. It was even likely, given all of the hunters and all of the deer over the last several centuries.

A noisy crow cawed at them from the branch of a mesquite tree. Matt turned to look at it.

"You see," he said, "the crow heralds a new beginning. Change is coming and we have to take advantage of the opportunities it brings us. It would be a mistake to ignore that."

He's in quite the contemplative frame of mind today, Randi thought.

"I think the crow is just angry at Breeze," she said, pointing to her Doberman who was nosing around in the wash.

It didn't take a cackling bird to tell Randi that change was coming. Matt's retirement papers were more than enough to get that message across.

"I'm going to stretch my legs a little before we get going," he said, standing.

"Okay. I think I'll just stay here and soak in the view."

Randi stretched out on her stomach facing Rainbow Wash, her chin resting on her crossed arms, her hat pushed back off her forehead. This was one of her favorite spots, named for the variegated colors of its soil, a small canyon through reddish conglomerate, carrying its rainy-day runoff west to the Colorado River. At the moment it was bone dry, as it almost always was. Yuma, Arizona got only a couple of inches of rain a year, so when there was water here it was a mere trickle.

Down below, Breeze sniffed methodically from one intriguing object to the next, taking no notice of the indignant crow. Just across the wash, on a dirt road, her vehicle was parked, a white Chevy Tahoe with a Bureau of Land Management insignia on the side, same as the one on her sleeve, the upside-down triangle with its snow-covered peak, blue river flowing through a green valley, dark green pine tree in the foreground. BLM's national logo was definitely not a scene from Arizona, but it was someone's idea of a natural paradise. Not hers. Randi's idea of paradise was the view that lay before her.

It was a perfect January day, clear and mild, with a timid suggestion of wind. The views were better than usual. On the western horizon, a meandering ribbon of green marked the course of the Colorado River and the California border. Beyond that was Picacho Peak, the volcanic neck that anchored Picacho State Park, and to the north were the Chocolate Mountains. From here, they looked like bare rock jutting up from the desert floor. They weren't really bare, though. There were low-growing, struggling plants covering those mountains, living at the barest of subsistence levels, like some of the human desert dwellers that she'd come to know and respect in the last couple of years.

The desert is deceptive like that, she reflected. At first you see nothing but a desolate landscape, but the longer you look, the more you see. Life, including human life, is sparse, but it's there. As you watch, the few who live there start to materialize out of the shimmering heat waves like a mirage. That's how she had come to know the small congregation of permanent inhabitants in her territory, gradually, as they made themselves visible to her.

She glanced at her watch and sighed. Her mood would have matched the weather if not for the impending arrival of their visitor, due in an hour. As she turned onto her side, propping her head up with her hand, she slowly became aware that she was being watched. When her eyes finally found that other pair of eyes in a shady alcove only ten feet away, the hair on her neck stood up and a chill raced through her. Funny how a snake can make your body turn on all of its defenses—a rush of primordial fear grips you before you're even aware of what you're looking at.

The rattler was coiled in a dark crevice, its head slightly extended toward her so that its snout was in the sunlight, its tongue flicking. As if the snake knew exactly when Randi became aware of it, it now began to sound its chilling warning.

Her body tensed in every muscle as she slowly removed her right hand from under her head and touched it down to the rock. Then she carefully pushed herself back along the ledge, inching away from the snake. Easy, she thought, speaking to both herself and the snake, reminding herself of the need to make no sudden moves, as contrary as that was to her impulse to flee. Her stare held tightly to the snake's eyes as she increased the distance between them, inching backward until she knew she was far enough away that a strike was not possible. Then she stood and scrambled down the side of the outcrop, a little too quickly, though the danger was past. She dropped down into the wash, then ran across the gravel bed to the other side, climbing out.

Breeze, thinking they were playing, came running past and bounded up the bank ahead of her.

Randi leaned against the side of her truck as the tempo of her heartbeat returned to normal. As she reached through the open window to grab a pack of gum from the dashboard, she heard the hollow sound of a voice on the radio. It was Steve, her supervisor. "Randall, Randall, come in," he said, his voice impatient.

She left the gum where it was and grabbed the microphone. "I'm here."

"I need you back at the office. Dr. Gatlin will be here at one o'clock."

"Right. Don't worry. I'll be there."

He must think I'm going to bail on him, she thought. Oh, well, that wouldn't be totally out of character. Maybe he had justification for thinking that. Dr. Gatlin, the archaeologist from California, was here to do a survey of the Black Point petroglyphs. Randi was still angry over that decision. The best way to protect such a site was to keep it a secret. Once the world at large got wind of how well-preserved and extensive the petroglyphs were, the place would be overrun with rock art tourists, some of whom would help themselves to a piece of it.

Unfortunately, that had already happened a couple of times, even as isolated as the site was. That was why, she had been told, a detailed survey by a qualified scientist was necessary. Even without publicity, the site was in danger. So, when they had been contacted by the University of California, the request seemed like a timely one. More and more people were becoming aware of Black Point. Randi knew well enough how many times someone had come into the office asking for directions to the site. It was becoming a really tricky situation.

"Come on, boy," Randi said to Breeze, holding the door open

for him. "Time to go." Then she waved to Matt and watched his stride become more purposeful in response. Matt's thin, denim-covered legs carried him smoothly through the rocky streambed and up onto the road where Randi waited. He was smiling, his face a web of deep creases, as he held his hand out, palm up, to show her a small animal skull, bleached, intact except for two clean holes in the frontal bone where some predator had sunk its canines.

"Kit fox?" Randi asked.

"That'd be my guess."

She took the skull gently in her hand and turned it over.

"I thought you could use this for your diorama," he said.

"Yes. You're right. Nice addition. Thanks." She found a rag behind the seat and wrapped the skull in it. "We need to get back. Thanks for coming out here with me. Just like old times. I'm going to miss this."

Matt smiled a calm, sympathetic smile.

Randi normally came to Rainbow Wash alone, but when she was in a mood for company in a place like this, there would be no one she would consider asking other than Matt. He had a companionable way of blending into the landscape.

Once the three of them were in the truck, Randi eased it through loose sand and onto a solid, washboard road, heading toward town.

"You sure you don't want to come in for this meeting?" she asked, returning to a topic she had brought up during lunch. She had hoped to persuade him to come back to the office with her for the meeting with Dr. Gatlin.

"I'm retired, remember?"

"Not officially. Not until June."

"Why do you want me there?" Matt threw an arm around Breeze, who sat on the seat between them, looking content, tongue hanging out the side of his mouth.

"Just to show that we know what we're doing. I mean, you know Black Point better than anybody. You could talk about the rock art in her language, like a pro."

"She'll want to draw her own conclusions," Matt said, raising his voice over the clatter of the truck. "Don't worry, Randi, I'm sure she's qualified."

"I'm not really worried about that."

"You're worried that she'll think we're backwater bumpkins?"

Randi nodded. "Doesn't it bug you that a stranger is coming in to do this? I mean, it's yours. It's been yours for decades."

"Never was mine. That site belongs to everybody and nobody. The Pima think it's theirs too. The Tohono O'odham, same thing. Doesn't belong to anybody. Belongs to history. Besides, I'm all for anybody who can appreciate it."

"But she's going to steal the glory."

"If I'd wanted glory, I would have done the survey myself years ago. In a way, I'm a kind of lazy archaeologist. I figure I'm doing my job just watching them, keeping them safe. It's important work, though, to document them. Even if there were no vandals, time itself would take them from us, eventually. This is a good thing, Randi, despite how you feel about it."

Dr. Gatlin may be qualified, Randi thought, in the sense that she had the credentials, but she couldn't possibly have Matt's spiritual link to the land and the people of the past. In addition to her spiritual defects, Randi had also assigned her a long list of physical defects as well, imagining this Dr. Gatlin as an irritating person with a unibrow, a snorting laugh and a large, hairy mole somewhere highly visible. There was also a good chance, Randi was certain, that Dr. Gatlin would address her as "my dear" in a most condescending tone, like an imperious British dowager.

Once they made it to the paved highway and the outskirts of town, wild desert gave way to flat sandy tracts choked with miles and miles of recreational vehicles, hulking white homes on wheels inhabited by retired Americans and Canadians migrating for the winter—snowbirds, tens of thousands of them, temporary residents, all squawking and hopping about in the sunshine like a flock of ecstatic cranes.

This was the sunniest place on the planet according to

local propaganda. In winter, it was a sanctuary for all of these northerners. In summer, it forced people to seclude themselves in their air-conditioned refuges for several months. That was about all she had known about Yuma two years ago, that it was a parched desert town just north of the Mexican border and just east of California, a place you drove through on your way to San Diego or Los Angeles and got out of fast.

Having come from Phoenix, Randi was familiar enough with the Arizona sun. The heat hadn't scared her. The idea of a small town, though small only in summer, hadn't scared her either. Starting over had scared her. Being alone in a new place with a new job, being single and friendless and away from her family, that had scared her.

It had been the right decision, though, she reflected, to take the BLM job and move here two years ago. Things had worked out after all. And Phoenix was only three hours away. Parents and siblings were there when she wanted them, but not so close they were breathing down her neck. As for the others, old friends and ex-lovers, it was better not to be constantly reminded of embarrassing situations and catastrophic mistakes. Why she fared so badly in the romance department, Randi couldn't say. She seemed to always make wrong choices, hooking up with the most inappropriate people, as if there were some disaster-seeking homing device in her brain. That was one of the reasons she had steered clear of romance altogether since coming here. The other reason was that she was protecting herself, protecting her fragile state of tranquility. There was too much at stake to take chances on maybes. The next time she took a chance on love, it would have to be a sure thing.

Even if she had no lover in Yuma, Randi was happy. She had friends. She'd become an integral part of the community. Life was easy and comfortable. Nobody here knew anything about her messed up past. She was respected and trusted—owned a house, for Christ's sake! She was a pillar of the community. She liked who she was now and didn't miss her previous life with its drama and disappointments, not to mention hangovers and half-

8

remembered midnight sex-capades. She was lucky to have made it through all of that relatively intact.

Unfortunately, her last relationship had not made it through. Perhaps the only relationship that had not been a mistake. Irene. Ultimately, though, that too had ended in disaster. Not Irene's fault. Randi easily took all the blame for that. It was Irene, or the loss of Irene, that had finally driven Randi to quit drinking, to return to college for her master's degree, to leave Phoenix and embark on a new chapter in her story.

"Thanks for the picnic," Matt said as they approached his house. "That reminds me. You guys planning on giving me some kind of retirement party?"

Randi grinned and winked at him. "See you later, Matt."

"You know I don't want any fuss. You know that, Randi. You won't let them make a fuss, will you?"

"Tell Barb hi for me."

He shook his head and opened the door, stepping out of the truck. Breeze moved over to the passenger side of the seat and hung his head out the window.

"See ya," Matt said, turning to walk to his front door. Randi smiled after him, then headed toward her own house.

"Now it's your turn," she said to Breeze. She thought, as she often had, that he was sufficient companionship for now. They made a good team. She had rescued him from certain destruction shortly after her arrival in Yuma. He had been an unpredictable, damaged animal, unsuitable as a pet, a victim of stupid, irresponsible owners. Against friendly advice, she'd decided to save him, to attempt it anyway. It had taken awhile, a lot of work, but it had paid off. He was now well-adjusted and happy, and the two of them had built a deep mutual trust during their many hours of training, which would form the basis, Randi hoped, of their eventual inclusion in the local search and rescue team. From worthless animal to SAR dog was her goal for Breeze, and it seemed well within reach at the moment.

Randi identified with Breeze. It seemed like they had both arrived in this place in the same condition, beaten down and aimless. Together they had realized their potential and become a success story. She was tremendously proud of that dog and of her part in his transformation. Her feelings about Breeze paralleled her feelings about herself. She had rescued herself, too, from the brink of destruction.

As soon as she dropped him off at home, she was back in the truck and on her way to the office with barely enough time to make it by one o'clock. Just as well, she thought. I'm in no hurry to meet this gatecrasher anyway. Let her wait.

Part of her resentment, she knew, was that Dr. Gatlin reminded her that Matt would soon be gone. His retirement would be a transition from one era to the next, and she didn't see how it could be a positive one. Whoever replaced him at BLM could not possibly do justice to the legacy of the past like he had. This visit from the California archaeologist was the first step toward that new era where cultural artifacts would be treated as lifeless bits of clay, stone and bone. They would lose their spirit, their stories and their life force.

This was an odd way of thinking for a geologist, Randi knew, since her own field of study involved only inanimate objects and by its very nature was thoroughly detached from humanity. But she didn't see any incompatibility between her science and her respect for the remarkable accomplishments of the human race. After all, the human race was living on the planet, had adapted to thrive on it, and, ultimately, was made of the same stuff as the lifeless mud, no matter what theory of evolution or creation you adhered to. Randi liked the idea of that. The soil and the living stuff on it were mineralogically equivalent. I'm made of carbon, nitrogen, calcium, sodium and iron, Randi thought with satisfaction, with a little gold and uranium thrown in, just like the earth's crust.

She was in the middle of town now, waiting in a long line of RVs at a stoplight.

"Damn snowbirds," she muttered.

The only good thing about the unbearable heat of summer was that it drove away all of these lightweights. Those left behind were the hardy denizens who called this place home year-round. Like any other group of people who faced hardship together, the Yumans, in all of their diversity, came together as a community with a common foe—heat. Randi had valued this sense of kinship from the beginning. That spirit of community and goodwill was one of the most appealing traits of this town. Anywhere you went, you could be sure of a smile and a friendly greeting. Yes, it really was like that here.

CHAPTER TWO

Kim had misjudged her arrival time. She had hoped to get into Yuma by eleven, but it was already after noon when she pulled into town. Driving a full-sized pickup pulling a travel trailer had turned out to have its challenges. It wasn't so bad on the open highway, but now that she was on city streets, the situation was rapidly deteriorating. Since she had an appointment at the BLM office at one o'clock, she had decided to forgo parking the trailer first and drive directly to her meeting, dragging it along behind her. That had been a mistake. The roads in town were surprisingly congested and she didn't know her way around. Now it was nearly one o'clock and she was stuck in mid-turn at the entrance road to her destination. To make matters worse, there was a lunatic in a white pickup behind her laying on the horn. She had waved her arm a couple of times already trying to get him to go around her on the other side, but the pickup remained stubbornly behind her.

When she'd borrowed this trailer from her Aunt Jess and Uncle Paul, it had seemed like the perfect solution for a three-month stay, but at the moment she wished she'd just rented an apartment instead. Driving this thing in narrow confines felt like trying to maneuver a dead whale on a skateboard.

For the third time, she couldn't make the turn, so she would have to back up again. Backing up was the problem. Up until now, she had managed to avoid that, carefully choosing her position at gas stations and last night's hotel so that when she was ready to go, all she had to do was pull forward. Optimistically giving it another try, she turned the wheel all the way to the right and backed up a few feet. The white and tan trailer went left into the curb. So she pulled forward and turned the wheel all the way to the left instead. This time, as she backed up, the trailer still went left into the curb. There seemed to be no physical logic to this contraption. She couldn't go any further forward since the squarely-planted BLM sign was on the corner in front of her, and apparently she couldn't go backward either. She was stuck. She wanted to cry. It had been a long, tiring two-day drive from Sacramento.

The honking behind her stopped. She looked in her side mirror to see the pickup backing away and parking on the street.

"Oh, crap!" She threw her hands in the air in exasperation. "Why don't you just go around me? There's plenty of room to pass. Just go around me and leave me here to die."

Then it occurred to her that the driver might be so angry that he was going to yell at her. Or maybe he wanted to help her. It looked like he was wearing a cowboy hat. Probably some good ol' boy with a soft spot for a damsel in distress. As much as Kim didn't want to be that damsel, it looked like she was anyway, so, she reasoned, she may as well let it work for her.

A pair of long, slender legs in tan slacks swung out of the

pickup and onto the gravel of the road's shoulder. Kim, staring in her side mirror, saw that it was a woman, a tall woman in dark sunglasses and a light-colored uniform, shirt tucked neatly into pants and a wide black utility belt around her waist. The cowboy hat was white with a dark-colored band.

Oh, crap, Kim thought again, abandoning the damsel in distress plan. Now she knew why the pickup driver had refused to go around her. She had been trying to get on the road to the BLM office, which Kim was thoroughly blocking. Yep, that was it, she concluded, recognizing the triangular shape of the BLM insignia on the tan shirt sleeve.

As the woman strode leisurely up to the window on a pair of brown cowboy boots, Kim shifted her gaze from the mirror image to the real thing. The ranger was about her own age, shapely, with a significant tan, feminine mouth and relaxed features, her eyes hidden behind mirrored sunglasses. As Kim turned to face her, the frown on the ranger's face softened into a look of mild surprise. The name tag on her shirt read "C. Randall."

The ranger stood silently observing her for a moment, then said, "Having a little trouble?"

Duh! thought Kim. But she spoke calmly and said, "Yes. I seem to be stuck here."

"You're lost, are you?"

"No, not lost. Just stuck. I'm trying to get down this road."

"Really?" The ranger looked down the road as if she thought she would see something unexpected, revealing to Kim that her dark brown hair was knotted into a single braid that rested between her shoulder blades. The ranger turned back. "There's nothing down there but the BLM office."

"Yes, I know. That's where I'm going."

"Oh?" The ranger removed her sunglasses, exposing placid brown eyes that stared directly into Kim's. "In that case, is it possible that *you're* Dr. Gatlin?"

Kim was momentarily surprised, but quickly realized that everybody in the office would be aware of her arrival. "Yes, I am."

The ranger's eyes widened slightly. Whatever she was

expecting, Kim thought, I'm not it. But her look of surprise faded quickly. "I'm Randi, the district geologist here."

Randi, thought Kim, making a silent, juvenile joke to herself.

Randi offered her hand and Kim shook it through the open window. She's cute, Kim thought, much more appealing than most of the geologists she had met, usually men in shabby field clothes with ridiculously unkempt beards.

"I think I can help you out with this rig," Randi said.

She had an air of confidence that persuaded Kim to let her try.

"Oh, that would be great if you could." Kim slid over and let Randi take the driver's seat. After all, she wasn't getting anywhere on her own.

Randi took a commanding hold on the steering wheel and turned sharply to the right to avoid hitting the BLM sign, missing it by no more than an inch, while Kim's right foot pressed involuntarily and firmly against the floor. Randi pulled forward into the main road, going far enough to straighten out the truck and trailer. She then began backing up slowly, keeping the trailer straight behind them, until they had backed up beyond the side road. She did all of this without a word. She then put the vehicle into drive and turned in, coasting up to the office parking lot.

"I'm going to park right here," she said, "so you can just head out forward when you leave."

Kim laughed. "That's been my strategy so far."

They both hopped out of the cab. Kim put on her hat and slung her bag over her shoulder. "Thanks so much for that," she told Randi.

Randi shrugged. "Sorry about the honking. I thought you were a snowbird. By this time of year, I'm pretty much fed up with them. Maybe you are a snowbird of sorts, aren't you? Down for the winter. Definitely drive like a snowbird. Got your Tilley hat there. Snowbirds have those."

Randi laughed, derisively, Kim thought. What's she getting at? What the hell is so funny about a Tilley hat? It's a perfectly appropriate, stylish piece of gear for working in the field.

"Are you planning on parking that trailer somewhere," Randi

asked, "or are you just going to drive around like that the whole time you're here?"

"I have a space reserved. I just didn't have time to go there first. I have a meeting at one o'clock with—"

"Steve," Randi said. "Yeah, I know. I'm supposed to be there too. Wait here while I get my truck and I'll walk you inside."

Kim wondered briefly why a geologist was going to be at her meeting. She watched Randi walk rapidly back down to the road, her gait throwing powerful signals at Kim's gaydar. At least I'll have somebody nice to look at during the meeting, she thought. Too bad I made such an ass of myself right off the bat. Oh, well, the damsel-in-distress ploy had worked, after all.

Kim looked around at the building, the demonstration garden of native plants and the brown hills beyond. This was a nice spot. The town itself, she wasn't so sure of. Her first impression of Yuma, Arizona was that it was dusty and a little sad looking. In some ways, it looked like she'd left the United States altogether and had arrived in a third-world country. She realized, driving through town, that she had imagined a place where John Wayne might have sat on a porch with his feet on the railing and his horse tethered nearby. Something quaint. A charming old western throwback with wooden sidewalks, a general store, a saloon with swinging doors. Instead, there was a general impression of brownness. A miserable place to live, she imagined. But it was only for a few months and she was sure she could enjoy herself during that time, especially with the exciting prospect of the Black Point petroglyphs to occupy her.

The extensive Hohokam etchings, from what little she'd heard and seen, were remarkable, in pristine condition and essentially undocumented. They had been alluded to in scientific articles and there were isolated published photos, but no one had studied them in depth and no one had done a formal survey. This was just what she needed to precipitate her elevation to full professorship.

She was grateful to Dr. Braddock for securing the project and making all the arrangements for her. All she had to do was show up and get to work. And meet with the rock art stewards—BLM and the local Native American tribe—and allay their fears about her qualifications and intentions.

This was not her first fieldwork experience by any means, but for the last several years, she had been more focused on teaching, and had almost no time to be out in the field anymore. Before taking the faculty position at UC Davis, she had had many more opportunities to get her hands dirty. But the Arizona desert wasn't new. She had worked in the Phoenix area before, where the major Hohokam settlements like Snaketown with their elaborate canal systems were based. But she had never been to Yuma, had never even been through it. The Hohokam cultural centers did not extend this far west, but their trade routes did. This site marked a major intersection along the route to the Pacific Coast to the west and the Gulf of California to the south.

Randi parked in front of the building and walked over to Kim. "We're five minutes late," she said.

Kim followed her inside where she removed her sunglasses again, hooking them on her front pocket, then on to the district manager's office.

Steve McCall was a big man with a warm, outgoing manner, sandy, graying hair and a thick gray mustache. He shook her hand firmly, saying, "Oh, so you've already met Randi. She'll be taking you out to the site tomorrow. She knows that area better than anybody. Out there all the time inspecting mines."

"Oh?" Kim said. "I thought I'd be working with your archaeologist. Don't you have one on staff?"

Steve nodded. "More or less. Less, actually. That would be Matt. He's on sick leave pending retirement, but he's still on the payroll, so we're a little short-staffed."

"So he's ill, then?"

"He'll be okay. Had a triple bypass last month and decided it was time to pack it in. He wanted to put in his thirty-five years, though, so he's on sick leave until June. When he's officially retired, I'll be able to hire somebody to replace him. Hey, you interested?"

17

Kim smiled, then noticed with confusion the sudden look of horror on Randi's face. "No," she said flatly, thinking that it must be hard to get a qualified scientist to work in a place like this year round.

"Didn't think so." Steve chuckled. "It's not going to be just you, I hope, out there. Not really a good idea to be out there alone."

Kim shook her head. "My department chair arranged for a student from your school, the junior college—sorry, I forgot its name."

"AWC," Randi said.

"Oh, right, Arizona Western College. We asked for a recommendation from the science department. They were able to get a student to assist me in exchange for college credit."

Too bad she wasn't going to be working with another archaeologist, Kim thought. She reminded herself that she needed to call that student as soon as she got settled into the RV park.

"That's good," Steve said. "Let's get started." He motioned toward the door. "The rep from the reservation is waiting for us."

Kim was prepared for the concerns of the local Pima tribe. She knew the value of the artifacts. She was being allowed this intimate access with the understanding that it was a privilege being granted to her by the spirits of the ancestors. Everyone agreed on the need to document the petroglyphs, even though they were concerned about publicity and about the touchy problem of public access.

"Eventually," explained Steve, "we're going to open the site up to the public. We don't see how to avoid that. But as soon as people start visiting in numbers, there will be a greater chance of graffiti and vandalism." He frowned, his gray mustache turning up at either end. "That's just the way it is. You take the good with the bad. I just hope we never have to put it behind a chain-link fence. That just destroys the feeling of a place, you know."

Kim nodded. "That would be a shame."

The meeting was routine. Kim had correctly anticipated the questions about her methods, motives and the future of the sites, as well as her rights as an agent of the University of California to the information she would be taking away. The rules and the plan for this project had already been laid out prior to her arrival by Sam Braddock, her division chair, so this meeting was really just to meet Kim and give everybody a warm and fuzzy. She did her best to seem confident and businesslike, to show them that she took this project seriously and that she was well qualified for the job.

Kim noticed that Randi remained silent throughout the meeting, slumped down in her chair, looking bored and eyeing Kim with an unfriendly gaze. If it wasn't for Steve's jovial warmth, Kim would have thought she wasn't welcome here.

After the meeting, she was introduced to the rest of the staff, a few other scientists and some clerical personnel. The office was larger than she had expected, but when Steve showed her a color-coded map outlining the extent of BLM land in southwest Arizona, she understood why. Their range was vast.

With business done, she stood in the public reception area just inside the main doors with Randi and Steve, preparing to leave.

"You'll be wanting to get out to the site tomorrow, right?" Steve asked.

"Yes, I'm anxious to get started."

"Oh, yeah, she's rarin' to go," Randi said. "Got her Tilley hat and everything."

Randi pointed to the hat in Kim's hand, grinning. Kim still didn't get the joke, but she knew she was being mocked.

"And *your* hat," she said to Randi, nodding toward the cowboy hat. "Is that part of the BLM uniform around these parts or do you wear it just because you think it makes you look cool?"

Steve coughed nervously at that, suggesting he didn't condone Randi's deviation from the official uniform.

Randi snorted and looked at Kim with a sideways glance, standing with her thumbs hooked over her front pockets. Kim wouldn't have been surprised if Randi had spit a wad of tobacco on the floor.

Then she noticed a long, glassed-in diorama at the end of the room. It was a scene of Sonoran desert life, dominated by a saguaro and a palo verde tree. From this vantage point, she could see a stuffed coyote looking her way.

"Randi," said Steve, apparently noticing Kim's distraction with the diorama, "why don't you show Kim your project there."

Randi looked reluctant, but then shrugged and walked over to the case. Kim assumed she was supposed to follow. With a closer view, she saw that the saguaro had two occupied bird nests in it. The soil in the scene looked like real sand and gravel. The boulders looked real also. Not surprising with a geologist in charge, Kim thought. Toward the back was a pile of rocks with a dark hole in the center, a cave or mine entrance. Several species of cacti were scattered throughout. There was also a desert rat, a dozen or so birds, a tortoise and some lizards. One flat-sided boulder had a series of petroglyphs etched into it, three quadrupeds and an anthromorph holding an atlatl.

"Nice," Kim said. "Very authentic looking."

"Everything's real," Randi said.

"I hope the petroglyphs aren't real!"

The barest hint of a smile played across Randi's lips. "No, but the rock is. It's granite. Granodiorite, actually."

Why do geologists always think the type of rock is relevant to any discussion? Kim wondered.

"Did you do all of this yourself?" she asked.

"No. This is a fifth grade class project. I'm just supervising and giving them some guidance. The kids carved the rock art. Looks pretty good, doesn't it?"

"Looks great."

"We're thinking of putting in a few more Indian artifacts and some mining equipment, something to represent the human impact on the land. Maybe a pick ax, old carbide lantern, that sort of thing."

For just a moment Randi looked happy, as if she had forgotten just then that she was speaking to someone she didn't like, for it had become obvious to Kim in the hour and a half that she'd been here that Randi had something against her. Smiling and distracted by her work, though, she looked animated and extremely attractive.

"Sounds like a fun project," Kim said, then turned back to Steve. "I guess I'd better get going."

"Do you think you'll need any help getting to your RV park?" Randi asked.

"No, I think I'll be okay now. Thanks. But maybe you can suggest some place for dinner."

"Depends," Randi said, "if you want something California-style or want to eat like the locals. We have great Mexican food, if you like that."

"Love it," Kim replied.

"And there's Dolly's. That's where a lot of us go."

"Okay. How about Dolly's, then?"

Randi nodded, took a pen and paper from the counter and began rapidly sketching a map. Kim glanced at it, seeing that it was neatly drawn with an arrow at the bottom right corner labeled "North." Now that was funny.

"There you go," Randi said. "Easy enough to find, if you can make your way through the snowbirds. I'll see you here tomorrow morning, then, eight o'clock sharp." She walked off.

That didn't go very well, Kim thought. Steve, apparently reading her mind said, "Randi's a great gal. Takes a bit of getting used to, but she's good people. You'll like her."

It doesn't really matter, Kim thought, if I like her or not. As soon as the work started, there would be no reason to interact with her anyway. She to her rocks, me to my glyphs, and never the twain shall meet.

CHAPTER THREE

Kim made her way without mishap to the RV park, maneuvering through the congested streets under a clear blue sky. It was a gorgeous day with views for miles in all directions. The thin winter sunlight cast violet shadows across the barren mountains east of town. The temperature was perfect, somewhere in the seventies, a remarkably fine day for January. It was no wonder so many people came down here for the winter. When she had left Sacramento yesterday, it had been cold and foggy, and had remained so throughout her drive south through California's central valley. When she left Bakersfield, heading east, the weather had improved, the landscape changing radically from fruit orchards to bare rock, desert scrub and those engaging Joshua trees that she loved. There were none of those here.

She had passed through the Mojave Desert and was now in the transition zone between the Mojave and Sonoran.

After Kim got the trailer parked and hooked up to the power supply and had done some preliminary settling in, she called the student who would assist her on this project.

A woman answered with "*Hola*."

"Could I speak to Ramon?" Kim asked.

The woman said something in Spanish, speaking very rapidly.

"Ramon, *por favor*," Kim said, using most of the Spanish she knew.

"Okay, okay," replied the woman.

In a moment, a youthful sounding man was on the phone. After Kim introduced herself, he apologized for not answering the phone himself. "That was my mother," he said. "She doesn't speak English."

"Yes, of course," Kim said. "I just wanted to let you know that I've arrived and I've already met with BLM. We're going out to the site tomorrow morning. Will you be ready to start?"

"Oh, yes!"

"Good. We'll have a chance to talk more tomorrow, then. I think I have everything we need, in terms of equipment. You'll just want to bring your lunch, since I understand this place is not really near anything."

Kim told Ramon she'd pick him up at seven thirty the next morning. He sounded enthusiastic and a little shy, she thought.

She decided not to go out for dinner after all. She had hoped, when she'd asked for a dinner recommendation, that Randi would offer to show her around town a little, not send her off on her own with a hand-drawn map. Staying in for the evening was actually okay, though. She was still tired from the trip and there were things to do to get ready for the field, such as charging her camera, GPS receiver and phone batteries, some last-minute reading and some household organizing.

That Randi was really unpleasant, Kim thought, hanging her Tilley hat on a peg near the door and remembering her disdainful sneer. Her attitude seemed resentful, which, since they had only just met, Kim knew she shouldn't take personally. Maybe she was just naturally surly. But she did have very kissable lips. A stupid thing to think, she chided herself, even if Randi was giving off a definite lesbian vibe.

She settled on a can of soup for dinner. Despite her earlier problem with it, this little trailer was exactly the right thing to bring on this trip. It was self-contained and economical and she had everything she needed at her fingertips. She could stand in front of the tiny stove and hardly have to move to get a spoon, bowl and napkin for her meal. She had a kitchen, a tiny bathroom with shower, two narrow beds, one of which could be left made up as a sofa, and a little table to work and eat on. She'd brought her music, some books and her laptop computer, which could serve as a DVD player. She had everything a modern woman needed to live comfortably, in a compact mode.

Life wasn't much different back home. Her condo was much larger, of course, and nicer, not quite stripped down to bare essentials, but it was utterly practical in its design, a pragmatist's living space. She wasn't much of a cook or entertainer, so she devoted most of her attention to her work spaces instead. Working was her delight and her refuge. She'd been working steadily for quite a while now, working almost to the exclusion of a personal life.

There was her family, of course. Her younger brother Jackson was using her condo rent-free while she was gone, a perfect solution to her absence and his needy circumstances. At twenty-six, he seemed to be just drifting, a college dropout, his approach to life very different from his older sister. But they were close. They were one another's confidantes, and he had been the first person in her family she had come out to, some nine years ago now, when she was twenty-two and in love with Julie, the first time she'd given away her heart.

With the thought of Julie, Kim sighed. Nothing like that first love. Her only serious relationship, though. Once they had split up, after five years, she had rarely dated, had focused instead on getting her doctorate and positioning herself for future success.

The truth was that it had been easier to devote the time and energy to her career without someone waiting at home for her. The last few years had been intense. There really had been no time for a relationship. She hadn't even allowed herself the companionship of a dog or cat, opting instead for a few tropical fish that made almost no demands on her time.

Kim taped up photos of her niece and nephews on the trailer's mini-refrigerator, her sister Suzie's kids. She liked having their cheerful faces grinning at her, Delaney's toothless smile not a bit self-conscious, and the twins looking identical, except that Jaden was dressed, as always, in blue, and Justin in green.

Other than her family, there was no one important in her life right now. She thought of Trish, the art teacher who had recently become her friend. It was possible that something would come of that, later, after her return. Trish was fun to hang out with. They had some things in common. Obviously, they were both teachers at the same school, and art and archaeology were compatible interests. Yes, perhaps that would develop into something someday, but, if it didn't, that was okay too. It was always nice to have friends among your colleagues.

Maybe, Kim thought, after I make full professor, I can relax for a while and cultivate more of a personal life, get a girl and a house, and roll out of bed on Sunday morning after a romantic Saturday night to a fresh pot of coffee and French toast with real maple syrup. Whoever she is, Kim thought, I hope she's a good cook.

Once her laptop was online, she sat down to check her e-mail. She had a note from her brother Jackson asking if she had arrived safely and assuring her that he had not yet destroyed all the contents of her condo. "Give me a little more time," he warned. "Not even a dead fish yet."

Kim smiled, thinking of her tropical fish tank. She had sort of brought that with her, though, because Jackson had filmed her fish swimming to and fro for fifteen minutes, then created a screen saver out of the film for her laptop. She would get used to it, she knew, but for the time being, it was startling to see her own fish swimming about on her computer screen.

After answering Jack, she opened an e-mail from her department chairman, Sam Braddock. *As soon as you've been out to the site and have something to share, send me some pics. Am anxiously awaiting first views and first impressions. Meanwhile, see enclosed photo of our Mimbres bowl, well on its way to being whole again. As we guessed, there's an image of a frog in the center and no kill hole.*

Kim opened the attached photo to view a close-up of a shallow black-on-white bowl, partially reconstructed from dozens of pieces. The black had faded to a yellowish brown now, as expected after a thousand years. In the center of the bowl was an easily recognizable frog, stylized, beautifully rendered in a way typical of the Mogollon people. As Sam said, there was no "kill hole." That was rare. Most of the Mimbres pots were uncovered in burial sites where they had been placed with a body. The burial ritual included punching a hole through the center of the vessel to allow its spirit to escape. Pottery, like everything in that culture, was more than just an object. It contained something living, some remnant of its maker, as though the clay were infused with his or her life force. This bowl had been recovered from a site in New Mexico where an ongoing excavation was being supervised by Sam. He took a new group of students there each summer.

That was the true appeal of being an archaeology student—the fieldwork, which could be tedious, even boring, invariably hot and disappointing. But it was the essence of the science, and, for a few of the students, it became a real passion as they sifted through soil for fragments of pottery, bone, wood, stone or anything testifying to the presence of humans. Kim, despite the canned beans, lack of showers and perpetual taste of dirt, had loved the fieldwork. The camaraderie on site was something you could never get on a campus or in a lab.

Kim saved the Mimbres bowl photo to her hard drive. She had not participated in this dig, but she had been following it. This frog bowl was an excellent find. Mimbres pottery from the early period was rare, prized by archaeologists and pothunters alike, "pothunters" being the polite name given to privateers who ransacked archaeological sites in search of artifacts. For the most part, collecting was becoming harder and harder to do legally.

Gorgeous, she typed back to Sam. *Looks like you managed to find all of the pieces too. Your students must be thrilled. I'll be on my way out for my first look at the site tomorrow morning. Will be in touch.*

CHAPTER FOUR

When Randi got home from work, she had a message from Alma Mendoza, calling her from The Oasis bar. Her speech was slurred. Randi listened with disappointment as Alma asked Randi to come get her. The message was only ten minutes old. While she was listening to it, her cell phone rang. She answered to a similar message, Alma in person this time.

"Just stay where you are," she said. "I'll be right there."

She got back in her truck and drove into town. The Oasis wasn't a bar Randi patronized, but it was the type of dive that she knew well from her younger days. It was dark and cramped. As soon as she passed through the door, she felt uneasy and oddly like she had gone through a time tunnel into the past. Some rough-looking men at the bar glanced at her as she stepped inside. Besides the bar stools, there were only three tables for seating. Alma was sitting at one of them, a glass in front of her, empty except for two melting ice cubes. She was dressed in her work clothes—cotton pants and a long-sleeved shirt, a red paisley bandana hanging like a three-sided curtain from under her straw hat. She looked up as Randi approached and recognized her with a sheepish smile, then looked back down, obscuring her face with the brim of her hat.

Alma was about fifty, but looked older. Booze and the desert sun had taken a toll on her. She was a field worker, mostly lettuce, and today was payday.

"*Buenas tardes*," Randi said cheerfully, carefully avoiding any sound of disapproval. "Need a ride home?"

Alma nodded, keeping her head down and refusing to meet Randi's eyes. She stood, then followed Randi unsteadily outside and took her place in the passenger seat of Randi's truck. This was the third time Randi had come for her. Alma never called her before she drank, to be talked out of it. She just called when she had had enough. That wasn't how it was supposed to work. Randi couldn't deal too harshly with her, though, considering all the grief she had given to her own sponsor, years ago, the first time she had gone to AA.

It hadn't been her idea to go. That was why she'd been uncooperative. Between the pressure from Irene and the judge, though, she was compelled to do it. She'd been sentenced to ninety meetings in ninety days. At the time, that had seemed like an unduly harsh punishment. She had grumbled about it the whole time. She even resumed drinking and showed up a couple of times at the meeting with a serious buzz on. When the ninety days were up and her sentence was satisfied, she quit going to the meetings altogether.

Randi hadn't taken the problem seriously, then. She hadn't taken Irene seriously either. She didn't believe she would leave. She thought the threats were hollow. But the second time Irene came to the police station to bail her out, Randi learned that her second chances were over. After taking her to the doctor to have her broken nose tended to, Irene packed up and left. Just left without a word. A week later her brother showed up to take her furniture, and the best thing that had ever happened to Randi was gone, just like that.

Her response to losing Irene was to get shit-faced, of course, but after a couple of months, that wasn't really working. So she quit drinking and quit making excuses. She was as surprised as anyone to see how much she changed. At first, it was to prove something to Irene, to get her to come back. But even after it was clear that wasn't going to happen, she stuck to her new course because it felt so much better. She felt better, physically and mentally. She began to think about her future.

One of the things Irene had said to her before she left had stuck with Randi, echoing in her head. "What if I need you, really need you for something?" she had asked. "What if I have a heart attack and you're the only person there? What if I fall down the stairs and need somebody to take me to the hospital? I can't rely on you."

That had made a lasting impression because Randi had always thought of herself as somebody you could count on in a pinch. That was who she was when she was sober, which, in those days, had not been often. Irene's words had also touched on Randi's greatest fear, that her drinking would lead to some disaster, to someone else getting hurt—or worse. This was her recurring nightmare, even now, even after four years of sobriety. At least twice a month she would wake up in a cold sweat, feeling a crushing sense of guilt and grief because in her dream she had been drinking and had let someone down. Someone she cared about—her mother or father, her sister or Irene—lay bleeding to death or was hit by a bus because she was passed out or too drunk to move fast enough or think clearly enough. The sensation of failure lingered long after waking, sometimes for hours. She knew, from listening to others at AA meetings, that breaking sobriety was a common nightmare. And like the others, when she woke, she had a hard time getting over the feeling that she actually had been drinking.

Even before she had quit, she had often felt sickened and disappointed with herself. She imagined Alma felt something similar, although Alma wasn't a talker, so the only clue Randi had to her state of mind was the shame on her face. At least she wasn't a combative drunk. She was silent, resigned, even depressed, which in some ways was harder to see.

They drove to Alma's apartment house where Randi helped her up the stairs to her place, a sparsely-furnished studio with dark, heavy curtains over the windows. The air inside was stale. Randi opened the front curtains and a window. Alma blinked as the room filled with the light from the setting sun. Then she sat on her sofa, hunched, with her hands hanging limp between her knees.

Randi stood in front of her and said, "Rent's due."

Alma reached into a pocket and pulled out a wad of cash, handing it over. Randi counted it.

"Where's the rest?" she asked.

"Had a nice meal," Alma said, shrugging. "Bought a few rounds for my amigos."

Randi knew this was all the money she had, that there was no bank account, and that Alma's wages were being garnished already for a long-standing debt. Randi reached into her own pocket and counted out sixty dollars, then gave a twenty back to Alma and put the rest of the money into an envelope. She sealed it and wrote the apartment number on the outside.

"I'll pick you up tomorrow after work, at six," she told Alma firmly. "We'll go to a meeting."

She nodded, looking like a guilty child. "*Gracias*," she said, still avoiding Randi's eyes.

Randi laid a hand on Alma's shoulder lightly and said, "Get a good night's sleep."

Then she went downstairs and stuck the envelope through a slot in the manager's door, thinking that she could get Alma a couple of odd jobs later in the week. When she was sober, she was a hard worker. But she was getting older. Randi wondered what she would do when her health let her down, when she couldn't

31

do field work anymore. Alma had a couple of kids somewhere. Maybe one of them would step up.

When Randi was home at last and settled in with Breeze curled up on the sofa beside her, she ate a microwave dinner in front of the television. Although she was a reasonably good cook, it was too late to start anything and it was hard to get excited about cooking for herself anyway. The show she turned on didn't hold her interest and she found her thoughts drifting, mostly in the direction of that pretty Dr. Gatlin. Randi's original idea that she would turn out to be some sort of old hag had been way off the mark. She was about thirty, with perceptive eyes and a shrewd smile. Randi liked her hair. Short, straight and dark brown, it was thin and pixie-ish. She had a funny way of squinting a little when she looked at you which made her nose turn up.

Regardless of her appealing looks, though, Randi's first impression of Kim Gatlin was that she was stuck-up. She had an attitude. Obviously thought she was superior. Thought she knew it all already. Every time anybody said anything to her at the meeting today, she was all, "Of course! Absolutely. You can be certain of it." And never made a single joke or even laughed during the whole thing. No sense of humor. Well, there was that crack about Randi's hat, after the meeting. That wasn't particularly funny, though Randi had to admit she had that coming after making fun of the Tilley hat.

Randi had also noticed that Dr. Gatlin wore no wedding ring, but she was probably some guy's trophy girl, some big shot, university president or something. Used to being treated well, living a cushy kind of life.

Randi chuckled to herself imagining that city girl at odds with the hazards of the desert. The first time she sees a snake, Randi thought, she's going to scream to high heaven and get herself bit. She's going to die out there. Oh, well, she wouldn't be the first person to die out there.

Randi smiled to herself and gave Breeze a tight hug.

CHAPTER FIVE

Kim slept well, even though the narrow bed wasn't all that comfortable. In the morning she ate a bowl of cereal, then threw her supplies in the truck and headed across town to pick up Ramon. His parents lived on the west side of town where unpretentious houses seemed to have placed themselves in a haphazard arrangement. They weren't lined up in a row, all equidistant from the street like the residential areas Kim was familiar with. None of the houses had lawns, just bare ground, and there was a goat tethered in the front yard of the house next to Ramon's.

As soon as she pulled up, he came running out wearing a classy straw hat and carrying a backpack. Ramon was a slender young man, about twenty, with beautiful eyes and a thin, sparse mustache.

Grinning excitedly, he climbed in, saying, "Morning, Dr. Gatlin," and reached for her hand.

She smiled. "You can call me Kim, Ramon, since we're going to be colleagues on this project. But I'm still the boss."

He laughed. "Yes, ma'am!"

"We're meeting a geologist," she explained, "who's going to take us out to the site."

"It's really something," he said, "that I never knew about this place. Here it was right in my own backyard."

"These will be similar to the South Mountain petroglyphs. At least, that's what I'm expecting. Do you know anything about those?"

"I've seen pictures."

"What's really interesting about this site is that it lies on the extreme western edge of Hohokam territory, overlapping into the Patayan cultural area. I won't be surprised if we see some of each."

"This is so cool! I really want to thank you for letting me work on this, Kim."

As he said her name, he looked a little bashful. Her first impression was that she was going to get along with him just fine.

When they got to the office, Randi was standing in the break room with a travel mug of coffee, talking to a colleague. It was Colin, the wildlife biologist, Kim remembered from her earlier introductions.

"Why do they call them pupfish, anyway?" Randi asked. "Do they come when you call them?"

Colin chuckled, then said, "Characteristics of their behavior. They act playful like a puppy, from a human perspective."

"Hey, Tilley," Randi called as she noticed Kim approaching.

Annoyed by the reference to her hat, Kim gave her a cool "Good morning."

"Hi, Randi," Ramon said.

"Oh, hi, Ramon. So you're the student working with Dr. Gatlin?"

34

"Uh-huh. Mr. Dalton set this up for me."

Kim was surprised and a little annoyed that Randi and Ramon knew one another. How small a town was this anyway?

"She's lucky to have you," Randi said, slapping Ramon on the back. "You're lucky to have him," she then said to Kim. "He's a good kid. Works hard. And he's smart."

Ramon looked embarrassed.

Randi gave them a handheld radio and instructed Kim to follow her and use the radio if they got separated.

"It will take us about an hour to get there," Randi said. "Ready?"

Kim nodded. They were soon on the road, heading out of town, the BLM truck in the lead.

"So how do you know her?" Kim asked Ramon, motioning vaguely in the direction of the BLM truck.

"She was my teacher last semester."

"Your teacher? What do you mean?"

"I took physical geology from her at AWC."

Kim glanced over at him, trying to fit these various pieces together. "She teaches at AWC?"

"Yeah. It was a night class. I think she just teaches one class a semester."

"I see. So you took geology as part of your requirement for an archaeology major. You're thinking ahead. That's great to use that as one of your general ed science courses because geology will be a requirement for the archaeology degree, eventually."

"Oh, no, I'm not an archaeology major."

"No? What, then?"

"Environmental technology. It's a two-year program. When I get my associate's degree, I'll be done. I'm going to work in natural resource management, you know. Physical geology is a requirement for the two-year degree."

"Oh," Kim said, surprised. "You're not a transfer student?"

"No. I'm hoping to get on with the city as an environmental technician."

"What exactly is that?"

"A guy who collects data or does inspections. Like inspects underground storage tanks at gas stations and stuff to make sure they aren't leaking and contaminating the soil."

Kim nodded.

"Are you disappointed?" Ramon asked uncertainly.

"No, no, not disappointed. I'm just surprised. I thought they were going to give me someone in archaeology or at least a related science."

"I've taken a lot of science classes. Archaeology too. I love it. I'm very good in physical sciences. Always have been. And archaeology is my favorite. Really. I begged Mr. Dalton for this assignment."

"Then why not major in it?"

"It would take so long. This way I can be out in the job market fast. And it's more practical."

"Don't like school?" Kim asked.

He looked up, his eyes wide. "I love school. I really had to beg my parents to let me go to the junior college. It's not easy for them. But I have a part-time job. And I've arranged my hours so I can work with you during the day and still put in a few hours at work in the evenings and weekends. I wanted to do this so much that I'm doing this instead of classes. I was only able to take two classes this semester, both at night. The other nights I work at Dolly's."

"The restaurant?"

"Right. You know it?"

"I've heard about it."

For the first time it occurred to Kim that this unpaid job Ramon had volunteered for might have created a real hardship for him.

"Are your parents okay with you working with me?" she asked.

"They don't really understand it. Working for no pay, I mean. But I told them I wouldn't give up my other job. I can do both."

His voice was firm, as if he had made this argument before.

Once they left the freeway, they shut the windows to keep out the dust. Randi was driving too fast for the rough dirt road, but Kim decided against telling her so. She could no longer see Randi's truck, just her dust cloud. Since nobody else was on this road, it didn't matter. There was no problem following. Ramon sat with a topo map open on his lap, tracing their route with a neon orange highlighter.

"Right over there is the Gila River," he announced, pointing north.

"Is it a big river?"

"It used to be, before all the dams were built. Now, it's like a little creek, and usually there's no water in it at all. When the gold miners were traveling to California, the Forty-Niners, it was a dangerous river to cross. That's why Yuma was originally named Yuma Crossing. Everyone who was trying to get to California in the 1850s would travel this way, like we're doing now, parallel to the Gila River. The Colorado and the Gila meet here in Yuma. So if they crossed the river here, they only had to cross one river instead of two."

"Is this even a road?" Kim asked after turning left to follow Randi's dust cloud.

"Yes. A lot of roads are like this out here."

The landscape was flat, mainly barren, with some scrubby looking plants scattered about. There was no sign of human habitation, no houses, no cars, no telephone poles. Occasionally, a jack rabbit would dart away from the road, startled into flight by the vehicles.

After a few miles, they passed an old homestead, marked now by a collapse of timber and a rusted automobile frame. It might have been an old station wagon, the kind they made back in the Sixties. Kim wondered if that relic had been sitting out here ever since.

"How are you doing back there," came Randi's voice on the radio.

Ramon answered. "A-okay."

"I'm going to turn right up here and drive through a wash, so I'll wait for you. You'll want to follow my tire tracks pretty closely to keep out of the deep sand."

As the dust settled up ahead, Kim saw that Randi had indeed stopped and was waiting for them. When they arrived, Randi drove ahead slowly through a dry waterway and onto the other side without mishap. Kim did the same, avoiding several large boulders.

"Almost there," Randi said over the radio.

The landscape had become less monotonous now, undulating gently. They were also encountering more vegetation—cholla, barrel cactus and ocotillo. They all looked pretty lifeless at the moment. Kim knew, though, that within a month, by February, all of this would change as the desert burst forth in its springtime exultation. That was definitely something to look forward to.

The "road" took them over a shallow ridge, after which Randi parked and got out of her truck, sliding her cowboy hat onto her head. Kim parked behind her.

Randi pointed south to a dark outcrop about a quarter mile away. "That's it. It's part of a lava flow that originated about a mile to the south. The basalt overlies some older granite. We're on foot the rest of the way."

Kim and Ramon put on their hats and followed Randi, who walked rapidly, her braid swinging back and forth below her hat. "That weathered basalt makes a nice, smooth surface," she explained, not turning to look at them. "Makes a good canvas for the glyphs. See how all the rocks around here look black? Covered with desert varnish. That's a coating of manganese oxide. If you break one of those black rocks open, you'll find that it's light colored on the inside, on the unweathered surface."

"Right," Kim said, hearing the exasperation in her own voice. "I know what desert varnish is. It's what they etched the petroglyphs in."

"Oh, sure," Randi said. "Sorry. I'm used to talking to tourists. What about these broken footpaths? Do you know about those, too?"

"Yes," said Kim, resisting the urge to remind Randi that she was an experienced archaeologist with a specialty in ancient cultures of the American Southwest. The footpaths they were following toward the site were faint, narrow trails through the landscape, hundreds of years old. Periodically, the trail would simply end. At that point, the continuation of the trail would be a long hop to the left or right. "They're prehistoric trails. They're broken periodically to confuse the evil spirits, to prevent them from following."

"Matt told me about that," Randi said, hopping from one trail to the next. "He said we should stay on the paths and keep up the tradition. That way, the trails won't disappear."

"Agreed," Kim said, hopping over behind Randi. Ramon followed suit.

"You can see why the site has remained pretty much secret. Nobody would ever come out here on purpose. There are no hiking trails and the road doesn't pass close enough to reveal anything. Just a pile of dark rocks to anybody passing by. And the only passersby are either BLM employees or prospectors. There are mining claims all around us."

"Gold mines?" Kim asked, walking directly behind Randi.

"Mainly, yes."

"So there's gold out here?"

"Oh, sure. There are also a lot of old, abandoned mines. You should stay away from those. They're dangerous."

They continued following the ancient pathway to the outcrop.

"Steve said you do mine inspections," Kim said. "What exactly does that involve?"

"I make sure the claim holders pay their annual fee and follow all the rules, like working their claims, for instance. I also determine the feasibility of any new claims."

"How do you do that, then?"

"Mineral evaluation. I mean, if there's no evidence of valuable minerals, the claim is denied. There are a couple of tests you have to apply. One is the marketability test. Is there any chance of making a profit, in other words, by mining the claim. And the other is the prudent man rule."

"Prudent man rule?"

"Right. Would a man, or woman, of ordinary prudence expend his or her labor, time and money to work this claim? If you can answer yes to that, then maybe it's a valid claim. These are all really old rules, from the pioneer days, but still what we use."

"Interesting," Kim said. "Why does the government care if somebody works their claim or not? In fact, why does the government care if they stake a claim where there's no gold to be found? Their tough luck, right?"

"It all goes back to the law of eighteen sixty-two." Randi's tone was authoritative. "The government didn't want people aimlessly digging around looking for gold. They wanted the gold and silver out of the ground and into circulation. It's also to prevent speculation. If there was no requirement to work the claim, people could stake claims anywhere and everywhere they wanted and just sit back and wait for somebody to stumble on a vein of gold, then they'd sell their claims at a profit, having done nobody any good while they were waiting. In other words, no precious metals in the coffers."

"I see."

"It's also to prevent homesteading on false pretenses. The requirement to work the claim prevents people just grabbing land to live on for free."

Kim scanned the landscape. "Yeah, I can see how folks would be building like crazy out here otherwise."

Randi turned and shot her one of those you're-not-as-funny-as-you-think-you-are looks.

Kim decided to change the subject. "So, are you from here?"

"No. I grew up in Phoenix. Moved here two years ago."

Kim itched to ask why. Phoenix seemed a vastly better place to be for so many reasons. But she decided the question might be too personal for their brief acquaintance and, besides, they were nearly at the site.

Just a few feet from the outcrop, Kim could still see nothing of interest. She wasn't surprised. That was the nature of petroglyphs. They weren't easy to see, especially from any distance.

As they reached the rocks, however, her eye started to pick them out. And then they began to jump at her by the dozens. She heard Ramon whistle loudly.

"My God!" she said, walking slowly along the face of the outcrop where hundreds of symbols were etched into the coating of black patina. It was incredible. There were circles and spirals, zigzags, anthromorphs, zoomorphs, geometrics and quite a few stick figures with upraised arms that Kim recognized immediately as Hohokam. Likewise, the animals were drawn in profile with V-shaped heads ended in a pointy nose. There were also plenty of those lizard men, round-bodied figures with arms, legs and a prominent appendage between the legs, interpreted to be either a tail, for a lizard, or a penis, for a man. If the appendage was longer than the legs, it was usually considered to be a tail. Unless the archaeologist was a man, Kim thought to herself with a small snort.

Among these anticipated images, though, she began to see some individual objects that were less familiar and more intriguing. Kim had seen only a few photos of isolated glyphs. She hadn't imagined that the site would be this rich. The complexity of motifs was also remarkable. She walked slowly around the gallery, her attention riveted to the rocks. On the back side, the outcrop stood on the bank of a wash. That side was unadorned with art.

When Kim returned to the north side, she saw Randi standing nearby, watching her, her thumbs hooked on her pockets, eyes behind sunglasses, her expression giving away nothing.

"How do you like our petroglyphs?" she asked.

"Astonishing," Kim replied. "Better than I imagined."

Ramon was sitting on the ground, his legs crossed, just looking at the rocks.

"Ramon, can you take a couple of GPS readings?" Kim asked. "Then we can move on to the other site." To Randi, she said, "Is it this good?"

"Similar, but not so many."

Ramon wrote down the coordinates and they hiked back to

41

the vehicles. Then they followed the dust cloud of Randi's truck again for a couple of miles to the second site. This one was closer to the road and, like Randi had promised, similar, but not so many.

"Are you planning on publishing a paper or an article or something on these?" Randi asked at the second site.

"Eventually," Kim answered. "But for right now, it's just a standard site survey."

"If you publish something, the whole world will flock out here, you know. The potential devastation to these features is huge. Archaeological resources are unrenewable."

Kim nodded, recognizing the common ranger chant. "Yes, I know. We had this discussion yesterday. I understand the need to protect cultural heritage sites. This is my business, after all."

Kim realized that her voice had gotten harsh. This woman was treating her like an amateur, though, and she definitely didn't like that, especially since Randi was speaking outside her area of expertise. Who did she think she was talking to anyway, telling an experienced scientist that archaeological resources are unrenewable?

"I'm just saying—" Randi started.

"It won't be my decision," Kim interrupted. "You don't have to worry about that. This study remains off the map for as long as the guardians of this site want it to."

"Okay," said Randi. "But you must be expecting to get something out of this."

"Other than the reward of being the first scientist to formally study these? I think that's plenty."

There was no reason to tell Randi about that full professorship. She was apparently suspicious of her motives for being here, so Randi might see that as proof that the work was not its own reward after all. Honestly, though, Kim reflected, the work would be enough to make this worthwhile. The promotion was the cherry on top.

"But, for the record," Randi said, "Matt's known about these for over thirty years."

Then maybe *he* should have published, Kim thought, irritated. But she just nodded, suddenly realizing that Randi saw her as an interloper. She had noticed that Randi referred to the sites as "*our* petroglyphs." Interesting, since Randi had only been in Yuma for two years herself.

"Thank you for the tour," Kim said. "I think we'll be fine from here on out."

Randi gazed at her from under the brim of her hat, her expression thoughtful. "Okay," she said. "I'm going to run out and check on one of my miners, then. He's just a couple of miles down the road. Name's Flynn. Lives out here full-time, so he may be the only person you see while you're out here. Make sure you bring plenty of water every day and a first-aid kit. Watch out for rattlesnakes and scorpions. And everything you bring in, you bring out. Got that?"

Kim resented the authoritative tone Randi was taking. "Of course," she answered coolly, impatient for Randi to leave.

"I mean *everything*. You're going to be working out here every day for several weeks and you're not using this place as a toilet. Get yourself some plastic bags and a pooper scooper."

Kim glanced at Ramon, whose eyes had gotten wide.

"No, I'm not kidding," Randi said sternly to Ramon. "I'll be on the radio if you need anything, like help finding your way back out."

"I'm sure we'll manage," Kim said shortly.

Randi turned and walked to her truck. A couple of minutes later, she was heading down the road.

"Redneck!" Kim said to herself. To Ramon, she said, "Let's get started. Be on the lookout for scatter—any points, scrapers, bones or other ancillary objects that might be lying around. I expect we'll find something in addition to the glyphs, although enough people have been through here that the good stuff is probably already gone. Why don't we start by drawing a rough map of both sites and taking some general photos just to get a feel for what we have here."

Ramon nodded, clearly as excited as she was.

43

CHAPTER SIX

Randi had been right about one thing—this was a lonely place. As they worked, they heard nothing other than the occasional plane passing overhead. The only animals they saw were lizards. Not even any birds, as they were nowhere near a body of water. There was no shade except the shadow cast from the outcrop itself. In the afternoon, at least, they would be sheltered.

Ramon worked his way to the east and Kim went to the west, peering from all angles at the boulders of the lava flow. After a few minutes, Kim's eyes had adapted to the colors of the patina and etchings, getting better at picking out the glyphs. Some were less distinct than others and she began to think the site would yield rock art from more than one historic period. That wasn't unusual. The confluence of two major rivers would have been noteworthy to any population that had ever lived in the area. No doubt they would have put up their own particular type of signpost. Ancient paths, too, tended to be used over and over by different groups. Why reinvent the wheel, after all. Not that these people used wheels in those days. She smiled at that thought.

"How did it look over there?" Kim asked Ramon when they met back in the middle.

"There are so many." Ramon's eyes flashed with the thrill of discovery. "They're thick up to that tall jagged boulder right over there. On the other side of that, there aren't very many. Just a few scattered here and there. There's a really nice group of deer about eye-level on that last big boulder."

"Deer?" Kim said. "You'll see when I give you the checklist, there are no deer."

"Oh, yes, they're deer all right. They have antlers and everything."

Kim laughed. "That's not what I mean. We call those horned zoomorphs." She stepped over to the outcrop and pointed to a human figure with hands raised. "Anthromorph. The idea is to avoid interpretation while doing the classification. Opinion doesn't enter into it."

He nodded. "Because if it isn't an objective description, it might be wrong."

"Exactly. We don't interpret when we record. Interpret later. Then everybody gets to interpret from the most objective starting point possible. There's a good example over here." She led him a few steps along the face of the outcrop and pointed to a faint symbol. "What do you think?"

"Looks like a snake."

"Yes, but it probably isn't. Normally this symbol represents a spring. The head of the *snake* is the source of the spring and the wavy line coming out of it is the flowing water. Pretty important thing to record in the desert."

"Oh, okay. So it's a spring."

"Nope. That's an interpretation. The way we record this is *dot with squiggle line*."

45

He raised his eyebrows in understanding.

"Even though this is generally accepted as the symbol for a spring, we still want to avoid making assumptions. You'll get it." Kim stepped out from the shadow of the outcrop. "So how about showing me those cool deer?"

Later, as they walked back to the pickup for a lunch break, Randi drove up, returning from visiting her miner.

"How are you doing?" she called from the cab.

"Great," Kim replied.

"I'm heading back to town. See you later."

Kim waved as Randi went on her way. She and Ramon sat on the tailgate with their lunches. Kim had brought a ham sandwich. Ramon had beans and tortillas.

"That smells good," Kim said.

"Just leftovers. My mother is a very traditional cook. Do you like Mexican food?"

"Oh, yeah!"

"Do you like tamales? We've got some left from Christmas."

"Homemade tamales? Now that would be a treat."

"Okay. Tomorrow, then, I'll bring tamales for both of us." Ramon smiled, showing off his perfect white teeth.

Kim sighed contentedly, gazing across the landscape. This was going to be wonderful, she thought. It felt fantastic to be out in the field again. This was what it was all about, after all. When she'd set her sights on archaeology back in junior high, it certainly wasn't about standing in front of a class of sleepy students. It was about *Tomb Raider* and King Tut, *Curse of the Mummies*, even. Like so many other youngsters, she had equated archaeology with Egyptology. And though she hadn't ever been to Egypt to see the pyramids, she had found something equally interesting closer to home. The Southwest Indian cultures were complex and fascinating, offering lifetimes of possibility for study. Even with all the work that had already been done, the stories of the ancient cultures, the Patayan, Anasazi, Hohokam and others were still just outlines. Every find was a potential explanation, another clue to reconstructing the history of these people, of how they lived, what they believed, where they came from and where they went.

Someday she would get to see those pyramids, she had no doubt. But just as a tourist. Her imagination had been thoroughly captured by the early cultures of North America now, especially the desert dwellers who had left behind so many wonderful, visible reminders of themselves like Chaco Canyon and Mesa Verde. The more she learned about them, the more she admired them, and the more she wanted to be a part of unearthing them and bringing them back to life.

It was a shame that so little of archaeology took place in the field these days. Kim supposed that was true of most of the natural sciences. She knew that geology was also like that, that what Randi was doing, running around in the desert all day, was not typical. Most of the geologists Kim knew were either teachers like herself or worked in the environmental field, in soil and groundwater contamination. They weren't doing what they thought of as "real geology." If they were on site, they were most likely supervising the drilling of monitoring wells. Kim was sure that these scientists had not been dreaming of monitoring wells in their student days while swinging their rock hammers with gusto at some provocative outcrop.

What she was doing here in Yuma was the glamorous aspect of her science, the part that everyone imagined when they contemplated archaeology. She could see it in the eyes of her students when the subject turned from a discussion of methodology to specific examples of artifacts, of glorious finds like the Chinese terra cotta warriors or the ancient hominid fossil named Lucy. They were convinced, of course, that it could happen to them too. Why not? Chauvet Cave, for instance, with its unparalleled Paleolithic art, lay undiscovered in populated France until 1994! These were the stories that drove young people to enter the field, spurred on by their imagined thrill of finding something ancient and surrounded by mystery.

Archaeology was largely a puzzle-solving process, finding all the little bits of evidence and then trying to fit them together in space and time. She had always liked puzzles, the harder the better. She could sit bent over a jigsaw puzzle, putting together a solid blue sky for several hours and not tire of it. Her brother, however, would only work sections of puzzles with detailed images. He had no interest in examining the shape of the pieces, but only the picture on the surface. That had been their method. Kim would put together a few inches of sky while Jackson would assemble a horse, barn, some ducks in a pond and a bridge over a stream. He was still like that, she thought, industrious but impatient. He worked in construction. In a few hours, he could frame a house. In a few hours, she could find one nugget of charred wood in a grid section of earth, and both of them would walk away triumphant.

Kim knew she would enjoy the petroglyph project, despite the heat, the dirt, the lack of civilization in town. And, when the time was up, she would be relieved to get home, as was always the case when she was gone for any length of time. She would even be glad to get back to those fresh-faced students with their endearing fantasies of finding their own version of Lucy.

CHAPTER SEVEN

Thursday after work Kim finally made it to Dolly's. She and Ramon stopped there for dinner, partly because the chile verde that Ramon's mother had made them for lunch had been so fiery that Kim had ended up in tears with her nose running, unable to eat more than a bite.

"I'll tell Mama to make it gringo-style from now on," Ramon had promised, trying not to laugh as Kim stuck a tortilla down her throat to try to quench the flames. So, by the end of the day, she was ravenous.

As Ramon opened the door of the restaurant for her, she saw with a start that it was actually an old jailhouse door, right out of that John Wayne western she had been looking for ever since arriving in Yuma. Ramon saw her looking at the door and grinned, then swept his hat off his head with a flourish. "Welcome to Dolly's, senorita!"

Inside, it was a curiosity shop, cluttered with a bizarre array of dissimilar objects. The place was packed. Ramon found a table for them off to the side, near a wall covered with movie posters. There was Clark Gable and Carole Lombard, and yes, John Wayne. Peering closely and scrunching up her eyes, Kim could just make out the words "To Dolly" scrawled on the Clark Gable poster above his signature. She turned to Ramon with surprise. "All of these movie stars have been here?"

"Oh, yeah," he replied. "They've been making movies here forever. All those old road movies. You know, with Bing Crosby and Bob Hope and the girl that always had that flower in her hair?"

Kim groped her memory. "Dorothy Lamour?"

"Yeah, that's her!"

Kim scanned the wall of posters, marveling at the sheer volume of them.

"What do you eat here?" she asked, picking up a menu.

"Since this is your first time," Ramon said, "you should try the *especial.*"

"Okay," Kim said, tentatively. "It's not armadillo or something?"

"No, no." He laughed. "It's a combination hotdog and cheeseburger. Nobody else does it."

"In that case, I'll have that."

An elderly woman in green polyester pants with curly red hair styled not unlike Shirley Temple's, arrived at their table with her order book, pen poised. "Hi, Ramon!" she called. "Who's your girlfriend? Cutie pie, isn't she?"

Ramon's face rapidly reddened. Kim suppressed a laugh.

"Dolly," he said, "this is Dr. Gatlin."

"Oh, land sakes!" Dolly said, reeling backward. "A doctor? Now how did a little pipsqueak like you get yourself a doctor? Honey, I don't know what this boy has been telling you, but it's a pack of lies. This boy is a waiter right here. Gets an employee

50

discount. You'll see when the bill comes. That's why he's brought you here. And he isn't even our best waiter either. He's not that fast. I mean, I think he's a darlin', but he's no Robert Redford, if you know what I mean."

Kim looked at Ramon, who looked like he was about to have a stroke, and said, "Oh, I think more of a young Antonio Banderas. With looks like that, what more does a man need?"

Dolly cackled loudly, her eyes tearing up with glee.

Ramon stuttered. "She isn't— She's not my girlfriend."

"Whatever you say, Antonio," Dolly said. "What'll you have?"

"Two especials."

When Dolly left, laughing to herself, Ramon said, "I know you're joking, but you don't want to start a rumor like that. My girlfriend is the jealous type."

"Okay," Kim said. "Sorry. I couldn't resist. What's your girlfriend's name?"

"Sophie."

"Don't worry. Sophie has nothing to be jealous about. I'm gay. You can tell her that if you want to."

He looked startled. "Oh," he said, looking down at the table.

"Is that a problem?" she asked.

He shook his head, looking up again. "No. I'm just surprised. No problem."

"Good. By the way, does this town have a gay bar?"

"Uh, yes, there is one, just one, for both men and women. It's just down the road."

Kim wanted that out in the open between them. They were going to be working alone together day after day for a while, and she didn't want to invite any misunderstandings. Although Ramon was a student, he was not that much younger than she was, and she had already dealt with her share of student crushes. Heading them off before they had to be dealt with was much preferred.

Once the food arrived, Kim went into serious eating mode. Working in the desert all day had revved up her thirst as well as

51

her appetite. They drank a pitcher of water between them. As she ate her especial, a split frankfurter on top of a hamburger patty in a bun, Kim continued to look around, trying to take in the incredible array of stuff. At the back of the restaurant were two pool tables, continuously occupied since they had come in. A card table immediately in front of the pool tables was occupied by old men playing checkers, intent on their game. In the other back corner was a net enclosing an area with a basketball hoop. A little boy was inside with his father. The kid was three or four years old, and the father laughed encouragingly every time he managed to throw the sponge ball in the area anywhere near the hoop. In the center of the room was, of all things, a battered rowboat full of bright orange sausage-shaped floats, and on the ceiling a Schwinn bicycle hung down precariously by its rear wheel. Every bit of wall space and ceiling space was covered. It was fascinating. Kim imagined that this "décor" had evolved over time without a plan, as if this spacious restaurant were someone's personal storage locker.

"How old is this restaurant?" she asked Dolly when she came to collect their plates.

"Nineteen twelve," Dolly said proudly. "It was a saloon and flophouse back then. And, no, I didn't work here in those days. I bought this place in eighty-two."

"Eighty-two? But all these movie stars must have been here before that. Some of them, anyway. Like Vivien Leigh here. She died long before that."

"Oh, sure. The 'Dolly' she signed that to was the one before me. The first Dolly. When I bought the place, I decided to keep the name. Historic old restaurant, after all. So I renamed myself instead."

Kim nodded. "Smart."

Dolly slapped Ramon playfully on the back of the head. "So how about a slice of cherry pie, Antonio?"

"No, thanks, Dolly. Kim, do you want dessert?"

Kim shook her head. Dolly ripped the bill from her book and handed it to Ramon. "Here you go, big spender," she said.

After dinner, Ramon walked outside with Kim and pointed the way to the gay bar, a single-story white house that had been converted. In front was an old neon sign shaped like a martini glass that read "Pinkie's." Classic, Kim thought. That building looked like it had been there a while too.

"Thanks," she said. "See you tomorrow."

Ramon returned to the restaurant to begin his evening work shift.

CHAPTER EIGHT

Kim went home and showered, washing a visible coat of dirt off her legs, then changed into her good pair of jeans and a cotton shirt. She didn't expect much from Pinkie's. What kind of a gay community could there be, after all, in a small border town dominated by blue-collar families, especially for someone accustomed to the metropolitan areas of northern California. But it was a place to start, to see if she could find some entertainment, some friends to go to a movie with or just somebody to talk to.

Inside, the bar was dark. The windows facing the street were shuttered. A slight man stood behind the bar on one end of a long room. The tables in the main room were mostly empty except for a trio of young men. She could hear the sound of pool tables in an unseen area of the bar, but there were no women in sight. It was worth a try, anyway, she thought. She walked up to the bar.

The bartender smiled and said, "Welcome to Pinkie's. What'll you have?"

"How about white wine?" she said, sliding onto a bar stool. "Maybe sauvignon blanc or whatever's good."

The bartender had thin blond hair, wore black-framed glasses and a crisp white shirt with rainbow-patterned suspenders. It's a look, Kim thought.

"I have a pinot gris from Santa Ynez that's outstanding. What d'ya say?"

Kim nodded. "I'll try it. Santa Barbara area, right?"

He pulled the cork from the bottle. "Exactly. You know it, then."

"I'm from California."

"Then have a little taste of home. I'm Jeff, by the way." He handed her the glass.

"Kim," she said.

"Welcome, Kim. Passing through?"

"No, actually, I'm here for a few months working." Kim explained her job in vague terms, keeping in mind the sensitivity of her subject.

"Lots of old Indian sites around here, for sure," Jeff said.

Kim tasted the wine and gave Jeff a thumbs-up.

"There are some girls in the courtyard," he said. "Come on. I'll introduce you."

Things are looking up, she thought, following him through an open doorway to a shady patio full of greenery, climbing vines and blooming potted plants. A potbellied stove in the corner provided some much-needed warmth to the tiny space. Kim could hear Patsy Cline singing low from somewhere nearby.

At a round redwood table, under an umbrella, sat Randi with three other women. Randi was wearing jeans and the same white cowboy hat, as well as a black vest over a white shirt that made her look even more like a cowgirl than before. A highball glass containing ice and a cola-colored liquid sat on the table in front of her. Rum and Coke, Kim guessed.

Randi slouched in her chair unselfconsciously, but when she saw Kim, her mouth fell open and she practically jumped to attention. Kim was amused by Randi's obvious surprise and discomfort, but wasn't really happy to see her, thinking, is she going to show up everywhere I go in this town? But maybe Randi was thinking the same thing about her.

Jeff proceeded to introduce her to Minnie, Darlene and Blair. Minnie was a tiny thing, about ninety pounds, short and so diminutive that Kim wondered whether her name was Minnie or Mini.

As Jeff was about to introduce Randi, Kim said, "Randi and I already know one another."

Minnie looked inquiringly from Kim to Randi, and said, "Oh, really? How is that?" She sounded suspicious.

"She's working with BLM," Randi explained. She had regained her composure. "Sit down, Tilley, and get acquainted."

Since Kim wasn't wearing her Tilley hat, she had hoped that Randi would have forgotten that nickname. Apparently not. Were Minnie and Randi a couple, she wondered briefly, taking an empty chair between Darlene and Blair. Darlene was about forty, tall, thin, slim-hipped, her light brown hair cut short, her round blue eyes twinkling in what seemed a perpetual smile. Blair was somewhat younger, rounder and softer, with full lips and a freckled, turned-up nose. Her hair was reddish gold, and it looked natural, a match with her fair complexion. She wore cargo shorts, out of which flowed smooth tan legs that ended in white sandals. Kim noticed the red polish on her toenails.

"Jeff will serve any paying customer," Randi said as Jeff was leaving the courtyard. "But this is actually a gay bar, primarily. Just so you know that."

"Thank you, Randi," Kim said with deliberate sarcasm, "for that illuminating information."

Blair laughed and then smiled widely at Kim. Randi frowned. So she had been hoping this was a mistake, that Kim had wandered into Pinkie's unknowingly. I'm invading your territory again, Kim thought, with just a bit of satisfaction.

"Kim's an archaeologist," Randi said to the others. "She'll be here for a few months, surveying a Hohokam site."

"Really?" said Blair. "That's fascinating. So, Hohokam, are those the ones who built the cliff houses?"

"No," Kim said, "those are the Anasazi. The Hohokam were contemporaries of the Anasazi, but the impressive thing they left behind is an elaborate system of irrigation canals. They developed a complex method of watering their crops at a time when agriculture was a completely new concept."

"Very interesting. Is that what you do, then, go around digging up old Indian artifacts?"

"It's what I do when I get the chance, which isn't often. Most of the time I teach."

"Where do you teach?" Darlene asked.

"UC Davis."

Darlene nodded appreciatively. "Good school. I teach too, English, at Arizona Western College. That's our local community college."

"Yes, I know it. The boy who's working with me, Ramon, is a student there."

During the next half hour, Kim learned that Darlene was happily coupled, her partner Trina still at work, and Blair was unattached. Blair seemed to want to make that totally clear to Kim. Minnie, a registered nurse, appeared familiar and affectionate toward Randi, who remained characteristically reserved. Blair was a physical therapist at the same hospital where Minnie worked.

"I hear they're going to start filming that new movie soon," Minnie said. "Probably need a lot of extras like usual. Anybody interested in going with me to try out?"

"I'll go," Blair said. "*The Scorpion King* was a lot of fun. I'd like to get another part like the slave girl attendant to Queen Isis." Blair fluttered her eyelashes and put the back of her hand to her forehead dramatically, sighing.

"That was the perfect part for you," Randi noted, laughing.

"I was just over at Dolly's earlier this evening," Kim said, "and saw all of the movie posters. This is apparently some kind of movie-making mecca, isn't it?"

"Yes," Darlene told her. "Some westerns, of course, as you'd expect, but the sand dunes just outside town stand in a lot for Middle Eastern and African deserts, like the Sahara. Goes way back. They filmed *The Son of the Sheik* here with Rudolph Valentino."

"It's ridiculous," Randi said. "The Imperial Dunes look nothing like the Sahara."

"In a movie, nobody's going to know the difference," Blair said. "Just a bunch of sand, after all."

"There's more to a sand dune than just a bunch of sand," Randi said, sitting up straight. "There are actually five types of dunes. You can tell them by the patterns of deposit, the shapes of the crests, that sort of thing. It all boils down to wind, the direction and intensity of it, and how much sand is available. In the Sahara, you'll see sand mounds that radiate out and down in arms, sort of like a pinwheel. They're called star dunes and they form like that because the winds come from all different directions."

Blair rolled her eyes. "Okay, okay, so the movie's going to be ruined for a few anal geologists."

Randi frowned and took a swallow of her drink. Actually, Kim thought, that was sort of interesting about the different types of dunes.

"Remember *Tank Girl*?" asked Minnie, and the entire table burst into laughter. "I'm hoping for a real part in this next one. More than just a walk-on."

"What sort of movie is it?" Kim asked.

"A western," Minnie said. "Classic Wild West with a saloon, sheriff, horses, bad guys, the whole works. They don't make many of those anymore."

"So, Randi," Kim said, "with the boots, the hat and the vest, you look like you're ready for tryouts yourself."

Blair laughed and looked at Kim appreciatively, her smile warm and inviting. Randi narrowed her eyes at Kim, but said nothing, in true western tradition. Now, Kim thought, is where she should take her six-shooter out of her gun belt and tip up the brim of her hat with the end of the barrel.

When Randi had finished her drink, she stood, saying, "Gotta go. Breeze'll be wondering what's happened to me."

"Breeze?" Kim asked.

"My dog." Randi took off without another word.

"She loves that dog," Minnie said, sounding exasperated.

Darlene started talking about her dogs, and Blair joined in with a story about her cat, and the conversation turned to pets. Kim had little to contribute to that. Tropical fish didn't generate too many funny stories. As soon as she finished her wine, she said, "I think I'll get going."

"Oh, don't go, Kim," Blair said, touching her arm lightly. "Have another glass of wine."

Kim saw Minnie raise an eyebrow in Darlene's direction, suggestively, as though they were sharing an in-joke.

"I've got an early morning tomorrow," Kim said, standing. "It was nice to meet you all. I'm sure I'll be seeing you again."

Blair followed Kim out through the front room, saying, "I'm having a party at my ranch in a couple of weeks. We'll have a bonfire, carne asada, sing some songs. That sort of thing. Would you come?"

Kim stopped at the front door. "Uh, maybe. Will Randi be there?"

"I'm sure she will. Is there a problem between you two?"

"To tell you the truth, I don't know. I don't think she likes me."

"There will be a lot of people there. It won't matter, even if that's true, although I don't see why it would be. Randi's very easygoing. She likes everybody."

"Apparently not everybody," Kim remarked, fishing one of her business cards from her bag. "Why don't you e-mail me the details?"

Blair took the card, glancing at it briefly. "I'll be in touch. I hope you can come. If you're going to be in town for a while, you'll want to meet everybody, and they'll all be there. And I'd love to see you again." Blair's hazel eyes looked nearly green as she said this.

Blair's interest was both pleasant and inconvenient. She was a sexy woman. There was a voluptuousness about her that appealed to Kim, who had always been a sucker for a deep cleavage, and Blair's low-cut blouse proudly displayed that attribute. But she was definitely not looking for a relationship of any kind while in this town. She would tell Blair that, the next time she saw her, make it clear that all she was interested in was friendship.

The bonfire sounded like fun. She hadn't been to a bonfire since girl scout camp. With a big enough crowd, it would be possible to avoid any awkward encounters with Randi. Or maybe that was the wrong approach, Kim considered. Maybe getting to know her better was the answer. Kim didn't particularly want to be involved in a feud with anyone at the BLM office. Since she was working on their land, they needed to be partners. They were on the same side, after all, in regard to the Indian artifacts. She didn't understand Randi's attitude toward her. What could she have against me, she wondered, since we've only just met? Of course, making fun of her around her friends couldn't help much. No, that was counterproductive. Hard to resist, though. Blair, for one, seemed to have appreciated it.

Picturing Randi's reluctant, close-lipped smile, Kim resolved to try harder to be friends with her, or at least not to be enemies.

CHAPTER NINE

Flynn's shack was unintentionally airy, built of lumber and tin he had scavenged from the landscape, from old mines and old mining sheds. All of his furniture was also handmade, built for practicality, not beauty. He wasn't much of a carpenter, really, and everything was cockeyed in one way or another. The table, for instance, where they sat over their domino game, wobbled back and forth when the wood chip under one of the legs slipped out.

Randi had stopped to check on Flynn, as she did at least once a week, to make sure he was okay. There were a couple of miners like him, old guys who lived out here full time. Most of the miners rarely came around. They worked their mines only enough to fulfill the requirements of the claim, but a few like

Flynn had made this their lives. Some people would find it hard to understand why a man would choose this kind of life, but she herself saw the appeal. It was uncomplicated. There was no stress and there were few decisions to be made day to day.

Flynn had electricity from a generator, so it wasn't entirely primitive here, but he cooked most of his meals in a pot on a fire outside or ate right out of cans. He came into town to get supplies, but spent most of his time alone, speaking only to Randi for days on end. That was why her visits usually extended past the obligatory professional checklist and included at least a long conversation, often a game of checkers or dominoes, like today.

There were hazards to this lifestyle as well. If Flynn got sick, he treated himself with home remedies and hoped for the best. If he got sick enough, he would die, like any other creature in the desert. That's the way he wanted it. Randi would take him to the doctor if he ever needed it, but she didn't tell him that. He wasn't afraid of dying. It was part of the natural process. Being out here with Flynn reminded Randi of that, reminded her of what was natural and what was not, what was important and what was expendable.

Today she had brought him some strawberries. That was a luxury he jumped on with lip-smacking indulgence. She'd also brought him a five-gallon can of water which she did sometimes to save him a trip into town. She tucked one of his empties into the bed of her truck for another day.

His mine yielded very little, but over time, with hard labor and patience, he could accumulate an ounce or two of gold. He would then come into town and, after a stop at the assay office, treat himself to a steak and some whiskey, like some old-time cowhand with his week's pay on a Saturday night. Other than those little treats, Flynn's life was stripped down nearly to bare essentials. Why he lived like this, how it had come about, and where he came from was never part of their conversation. Randi knew nothing about his family or his origins. He told stories of his past, but they were always about his wanderings, as a miner and a loner.

Randi tried to make her visits predictable. Otherwise, she would find Flynn dirty and foul smelling. But if she arrived on Monday afternoons, she would find him bathed, shaved and wearing clean clothes, as if they were going on a date. Sometimes he even made lunch, which cycled among hash and eggs, chili and a meaty brown stew that varied slightly in color and texture, but not in flavor, and was always served with fresh biscuits. She didn't ask what was in it, but guessed rabbit, quail and maybe the occasional rattlesnake. The stew tasted fine, but the chili was her favorite.

Today, though, it was just the strawberries and the customary box of licorice ropes, a treat he indulged in like a chain-smoker, one after another, letting them hang out of the side of his mouth like a limp cigarette. Hands free, he bit a hunk off every minute or so and the rope grew gradually shorter until it was gone. The left corner of his mouth was often stained black from this practice. At the moment, he had put the licorice aside in favor of the strawberries.

"Have you met our two visitors yet?" Randi asked him across a growing mosaic of dominoes.

"Nope. Haven't been that way lately. I should pay 'em a visit. What do you think of 'em?"

"They're okay, I guess," Randi said. "The boy is a local. Dr. Gatlin, Kim, is from Sacramento."

"That's her name, the archaeologist?"

Randi nodded, putting down a domino. Her opinion of Kim, after finding out she was a lesbian, had softened, although she was still suspicious of her motives. And then there was just her general haughtiness.

"I don't know what her angle is," she said. "I think she's ambitious, you know. Trying to make a name for herself, most likely, like she discovered something."

"So, what's wrong with that?"

"It's just wrong. Matt's been protecting these sites for decades, through his entire career. They belong to him. He should be the one to get the credit."

"But he didn't do it. He didn't want to do it, right?"

"You mean the formal survey? No, he didn't."

"Then somebody else's got to do it." Flynn made a smacking noise as he sucked another strawberry into his mouth.

"I guess," Randi admitted. "Still irks me."

"Yeah, I can see that. How is old Matt, by the way? I miss him."

"He's fine. Bounced right back from that surgery. He's just bought himself a boat."

"A boat? Fishing boat?"

"No. Sailboat. He showed me a picture. Beautiful thing. Docked in San Diego. He's going to become a sailor."

"No kidding? Moving to California, then?"

"Yes."

"Damn. Isn't that a kick in the head?"

"Yes, it is. He seemed so connected to this land that I just assumed he would stay here until he died and get buried right back into it like his ancestors. I thought he was planted here like a cholla."

"You never can tell about people," Flynn said, putting down his last domino. "You think you know 'em, but then they go and buy a sailboat. Go figure."

Flynn leaned back in his chair, tipping it onto the back legs. Having finished the strawberries, he took a rope of licorice and stuck it in its customary perch in the left corner of his mouth.

"Nothing could ever make me move to California," Randi said flatly.

"What d'ya have against California?"

"Oh, I don't know. Californians think everything's better there—the food, the weather, the beaches."

Flynn laughed loudly. "I gotta tell ya, Randi Girl, the beaches *are* better there and I don't think you'll find anybody who'd disagree."

"Okay, I'll give them that. But, you know, they think everybody else feels the same way, like all of us would rather live there if only we could, like we should be pitied. Just a huge parking lot, that's what California is."

"I don't know. You get up there around Eureka and it's damned pretty country. Redwoods, wild coastline, crystal clear streams full of trout. Back in the Seventies, I was up there for a spell. I was a young fella then. Did some panning up in the Klamath Mountains. That's where Bigfoot lives, you know, up there in the northern California mountains."

Randi had heard this before, so she tried to steer him back to the subject at hand. "I'm not saying that California isn't all that. But every place has its good points and I'd just like to hear them admit it. I can see that archaeologist just looking down her nose at us."

"I guess I'll have to pay her a visit and see for myself. She's managed to get all over your bad side." He grinned, displaying a conspicuous gap in his teeth behind his left incisor. "Is she pretty?"

"Oh, yeah, she's pretty." Randi realized that she had said that in a slightly dreamy way, so she sat up straighter and said, "But, you know, in an ordinary sort of pretty way. Nothing special."

Flynn said nothing, just eyed her as his licorice rope dwindled.

After leaving Flynn, Randi wasn't intending to stop at the petroglyph site, but as she approached it, she was startled to see a blue fiberglass Porta-Potti standing on the side of the road beside Kim's pickup.

"What the . . . ?" she said aloud.

She pulled off the road and walked up to the toilet. Then she took off toward the outcrop, almost in too much of a hurry to follow the Indian trails. She could see Kim and Ramon sitting close to one another in their beach chairs. No doubt they had seen her drive up.

"Hey," she called before reaching them. "What the hell is that thing doing out here?"

Kim turned to look at her. "You mean the chemical toilet?" she asked, calmly.

"Yeah." Randi stopped in front of her chair.

"Go ahead and use it if you want."

Now she's just mocking me, Randi decided. "You can't just bring whatever the hell you want out here. Next thing I know you'll be building a campfire and burning up all the mesquite trees."

Kim stood, looking coolly at Randi in her ordinary sort of pretty way. "The toilet is doing no harm," she said. "And it's not your call."

"What do you mean by that?"

"Steve arranged for it. If you have an issue with it, take it up with him."

Kim turned and walked pointedly away. Randi glanced at Ramon, who pursed his lips and looked as though he wanted nothing to do with this, then turned his attention back to the computer in his lap.

Randi felt herself getting red in the face. She stood there for a moment, deciding on her next move. Okay, she thought, I don't have any legitimate complaint. I'm just a big, bossy jerk. It's not illegal, harmful or permanent. The only objection I've got is that she did it without asking me. I've just made an ass of myself.

One thing Randi had learned over the years was that the best strategy when you make an ass of yourself is to just disappear. Once upon a time, she would have blustered about and made a bigger ass of herself, but not now.

She turned without a word and walked back to the road and her truck. If Kim was watching her, she didn't know it because she didn't look back.

CHAPTER TEN

Ramon and Kim had settled into an efficient routine now, mapping, gathering coordinates, taking digital photos and cataloguing the symbols on the rocks at both sites. Ramon often sat at his panel, listening to music through earphones, bopping his head as he numbered, photographed and logged each image. Kim preferred the quiet, the buzz of insects, the scuffling of lizards, the near silence of a hot wind shifting a few grains of sand. Each day, Ramon brought lunch for both of them, homemade Mexican delicacies from his mother's kitchen. She apparently enjoyed preparing their lunch, and Kim was more than grateful, especially since the level of spiciness was now tolerable.

"If I ever get married, I hope my wife can cook like this," Ramon said, eating sopapillas.

"Me too," Kim said.

Ramon laughed.

"Is Sophie a good cook?" Kim asked.

He looked suddenly bashful. Funny how he got embarrassed so easily when it came to these matters. It was endearing. "Not as good as Mama."

Kim nodded.

"Do you have a girlfriend?" he asked, surprising her.

"No, no," she said. "Nobody for me at the moment."

They ate silently for a few minutes before Ramon said, "I've been thinking about archaeology. I mean, thinking about maybe changing my major."

"Oh, really?" Kim put her food down to listen.

"Just thinking about it," he elaborated. "It would mean transferring to a university."

"Sure. Staying in school for a few more years. I think you should do it. You've obviously got the interest. And the ability to apply yourself. No reason you couldn't do it."

He nodded thoughtfully. "I'll keep thinking about it."

After lunch, they walked back to the outcrop and continued working until Kim saw a dust cloud coming their way. Must be Randi, she thought, but when the vehicle stopped beside her pickup, she saw that it wasn't the BLM truck after all. Kim watched nervously, since in the couple of weeks they'd been working out here, they hadn't seen a single person other than Randi. She got Ramon's attention by tapping his shoulder and pointed to the old green truck as a man emerged from it, waving, and began to walk toward them, not following the trails, but walking in a straight line with a decided limp. As he came closer, Kim saw that he was short, deeply tanned, deeply wrinkled.

"Hi, ya," he called to them.

Kim stood waiting for him. When at last he arrived, she saw that he had thick white whiskers framing his mouth, about three days' growth, and his clothes, jeans and a long-sleeved cotton shirt, were well worn. When he smiled, he revealed a considerable gap in his teeth.

"Hi," said Kim.

"I'm Flynn. You're the girl from California, right, come to study these pictures?"

"Yes," said Kim. She introduced herself and Ramon.

"Randi said you were pretty," said Flynn. "She's got a good eye."

Randi said I was pretty? Kim thought. That was nice, although unexpected.

"Mighty dangerous for a woman out here," Flynn said.

"I don't come out alone," she said, indicating Ramon.

"Good thing. That Randi comes out here alone all the time and I keep telling her she's looking for trouble, but she's the orneriest thing. At least she brings that dog of hers sometimes. That animal is a natural-born killer, and it's a good thing for her."

"You're out here alone, aren't you?" Kim said, annoyed that he considered it more dangerous for a woman than a man.

"Oh, sure, but I've been living out here for thirty years and I know what's what. Newcomers are always coming out here falling down mine shafts or getting shot by coyotes."

"Shot by coyotes?"

"Smugglers," Ramon explained. "Coyotes are the thugs who bring illegals across the border."

"We'll be careful," Kim assured him.

"You do that. A month ago I saw some wire burners just over the ridge there."

"Wire burners?" Kim felt like she and the old man were speaking two different languages.

"Copper thieves," he explained. "They bring their loot out here and set it on fire, burn the insulation off it to get to the copper."

"So what have you been doing out here for thirty years?" Kim asked.

"Looking for gold," he said, grinning.

"Find any?"

"A little. Enough to keep me going." Flynn stepped over to

69

a boulder and took a seat. "But I haven't struck it rich yet. Some day, though, I'll find the Wolff treasure. Been looking pretty much the whole thirty years. I'll find it yet, you bet."

"What's the Wolff treasure?"

"You don't know about that?" Flynn asked, incredulous.

Kim shook her head. Ramon too sat down to listen as Flynn began to tell the story.

"In eighteen fifty-seven," he said, "Helmuth Wolff came out here prospecting like a lot of other folks. He found a rich vein and mined it for a season. He buried a good part of the take around here somewhere and left for San Francisco. Then he got sick and died there before he could get back. He told a friend all about it. Said, you go back and get it. It's all yours. His friend came out a year later and found the mine and took out what was left, but he never found the buried gold. Nobody's ever found it."

"So how are you supposed to find it?" Kim asked, skeptical. "How do you know where to look?"

"I got directions. Clues. Everybody knows about it. See, he buried it on the bank of Hendy Wash where the sun sets over a palm tree." As Flynn said these words, he made a slow gesture of an arc, an imitation of the sun setting.

"Good luck with that," Kim said.

"I'll find it," he said with confidence.

Kim remembered Randi's prudent man rule and wondered if Flynn's search for legendary gold would pass that test. Living alone in the desert for thirty years looking for buried treasure was an odd sort of life, no doubt. Not to mention lonely. There's nothing like isolation, they say, to make a person go crazy. Kim gazed at the old man, at his deep-set eyes and whiskered grin.

Flynn sat on his rock for a while, watching them work, asking questions about their gadgets—the laptop computer, the GPS receiver, the digital camera—which intrigued him. He didn't even have a phone, he told them. Ramon took Flynn's picture several times and showed him on the viewing screen.

"Now that's a sorry-looking son-of-a-bitch!" he said as he looked at his image.

After an hour, Flynn ambled back to the road and drove off, leaving them again in silence.

Kneeling in front of a low spiral at the base of the outcrop, Kim spotted a shiny black glint in the soil near the tip of her boot. She brushed the gravel away to reveal a small shard of obsidian. She sat down in the shade of the outcrop and held the flake in her palm, admiring it, a discarded remnant of point-making. This bit, a curved piece of glass, had been chipped off by someone fashioning a projectile hundreds of years ago.

In her mind she could see a dark-haired man sitting here in the shade of the basalt flow, hitting glass with stone while his companion scraped out an image of a deer—a horned zoomorph, she reminded herself—on the rock face nearby. With precise and deliberate movements of their hands and their stone tools, they had created a work of art, two works of art, which each of them must have shown the other. Then they had built a fire and eaten some venison and talked for a while. Told stories, maybe, about the earlier races of man or the spirits they revered or how things came to be the way they were. Or maybe they just told raunchy jokes about women like any other confederacy of men around a campfire. Then they slept here under the stars at this prehistoric crossroad, waiting for morning when they would walk east toward home or west toward the ocean, never imagining that theirs wasn't the best possible kind of life. And maybe they were right about that.

Kim heard a noise, which startled her from her daydream. She looked up to see someone standing directly in front her. Randi. She hadn't spoke to Randi since the Porta-Potti incident, but at the moment, unexpectedly, she had a relaxed smile on her face.

"Hey, there, Tilley."

"Hi," Kim said, standing and dusting herself off.

"What's that?"

Kim handed her the flake of glass. "Just found this."

"Obsidian," Randi announced. "There's none around here."

"No. They were carrying it with them. That's a piece that was chipped off of an arrowhead or dart point."

"Do you actually include something that small in your survey? I mean, it isn't even an arrowhead."

"To the extent that I'll note obsidian flakes, yes. It's a sign of human activity. Not very exciting, maybe, but it counts. And, of course, the significance of the material is that it came from somewhere else."

"And that's where the geologist comes in."

Kim nodded. "Exactly. You folks will tell us where it came from. Help to establish trade and migration routes."

Randi handed the flake back. She waved to Ramon, who was working downslope with his headphones on. He waved and then went back to his work.

"We had a visit from Flynn earlier today," Kim said. "He regaled us with stories of buried treasure."

"The Wolff gold, right?" Randi said. "That story is true. At least the mine exists. I've been in it. No reason to think the rest of the story isn't true too."

"You mean you think there's a pot of gold buried out here somewhere?"

"I think there's quite a few pots of gold buried out here, and in California, and in Nevada too. It was common practice back then. There's gold and silver. A lot of it was hidden by bandits who robbed stagecoaches or trains. Happened all the time. They'd hold up the stage transferring gold, then they'd stash it somewhere so they could run from the sheriff's posse. The bandits would get killed in the shoot-out and nobody would be left to say where they'd buried the loot."

"Sounds like something from a Wild West movie."

"This *was* the Wild West, you know," Randi pointed out. "I heard that a bag of gold coins was found out here five years ago. People do find these things once in a while. Lots of people have come around looking for the Wolff gold. I mean, Flynn may be a little odd, but he's not a crackpot. He'll probably never find it, but then again he just might."

"Why hasn't someone found it, then," Kim asked, "if so many people have been looking for it?"

"The clues, like the setting sun over the palm tree, don't lead anywhere. They may have been corrupted over time. Like the words to *Wildwood Flower*."

Kim's confusion must have shown.

"You know," said Randi. "The original words became total nonsense by the time the Carter Family had a hit with it in the Thirties."

Randi stared at Kim for a few seconds, then said, "Oh, come on, you know this song. Joan Baez recorded it again in the sixties. It's a famous old folk song."

"Not ringing a bell," Kim said, apologetically.

"You must know it," Randi insisted. Then, startling Kim, she began singing. It was slightly off-key and a little rough, but the tune sounded familiar. Kim, amused at Randi's unselfconscious presentation, glanced toward Ramon, hoping he was hearing this. But he was absorbed in his work and unaware of the show. When Randi came to the end of her performance, she doffed her hat and winked at Kim. Then she pushed her hat back on at a jaunty angle.

Kim, delighted, clapped enthusiastically.

"You know it, right?" Randi asked.

"Yes. I've heard it. Thank you so much for the performance."

"You're welcome." Randi smiled with satisfaction.

It took Kim a moment to remember what they had been talking about. "So it's nonsense, then, the clues? No Hendy Wash?"

"Oh, yeah, there is. It's just two miles east of here. It drains into the Gila just like this wash. But there are no palm trees there. There's no evidence that there ever have been any palm trees. People have gone up and down that wash for a hundred and fifty years looking for the gold. I've even looked around for it myself now and then." Randi sat on the same boulder Flynn had sat on earlier, stretching her long legs out in front of her. "Maybe somebody found it a long time ago. Could be somebody found it and ran off with it without saying anything. Legally, the gold found on BLM land would belong to the federal government.

73

Since it's raw gold nuggets or dust or whatever, who could tell where it came from? Gold like that would be easy enough to sell."

"It's an interesting story," Kim said. "Even without it, though, Flynn said he's found enough gold out here to live on all these years."

"If you saw how he lives, you wouldn't be surprised."

Randi was smiling her close-lipped smile, possibly thinking about Flynn's living conditions. She seemed friendlier today, more at ease. Kim was glad.

"By the way, what's the name of *this* wash?" Kim asked, indicating the channel on the other side of the outcrop.

Randi looked perplexed and said, "Don't know. That would be a good thing for you to have, for thorough documentation. I'll check some maps back at the office."

"Thanks. I'd appreciate it."

Yes, she was definitely friendlier. Maybe she had gotten over her initial suspicions. Or, maybe, like Kim, she had just decided that it would make more sense to get along.

"Randi, are you going to Blair's party Saturday?" Kim asked.

"Sure, I'll be there. Should be a pretty good crowd. You?"

"I'm thinking I might."

"Good. You need to have a little fun. If all you do is work out here in the sun all the time, you're going to turn into an old desert rat like Flynn. Why don't you stop by Pinkie's tonight too? A few of us will be there."

"Okay, I will."

Kim was happy to see that Randi was extending a welcome at last. Even her smile seemed like less of a sneer today, a real smile that created shallow dimples in her cheeks and made her look adorable.

Randi walked back to the road, her braid swinging back and forth between her shoulder blades as she hopped from one broken trail to the next. Kim went back to work, thinking about buried treasure. It didn't seem quite real to her, but with Randi's matter-of-fact corroboration, she guessed it must be.

74

That evening, after dropping off Ramon and stopping by her trailer to change clothes, Kim drove over to Pinkie's. As she approached the door, she could hear noise from within, loud laughter and even louder music. It was later than it had been the first time she'd been here. Maybe things picked up later in the evening. She pushed the door open and peered into the dim room. There were several occupied tables this time. Nobody was behind the bar at the moment, but a group of women was standing near it, and Randi was among them. The loud music was something twangy that Kim didn't care for.

Just as she was about to step inside, Kim saw that Minnie was sitting on top of the bar. How odd, she thought. Suddenly, Randi grabbed hold of her by the seat of her pants with one hand and took a handful of her denim jacket in the other. She jerked her into a horizontal position as the little thing screamed and waved her arms frantically. Oh, my God, thought Kim, freezing in the doorway, trying to understand what she was witnessing.

Randi flung Minnie hard, punctuating her effort with a loud "Yaaaa!" Minnie went sliding down the top of the bar like a shuffleboard puck, smashing into the wall at the end and then tumbling off onto the floor.

Kim gasped involuntarily as Minnie rolled over and sat up. It looked like she was okay. She was getting to her feet at least. Randi laughed, sat on her bar stool and took a drink from her glass, saying, simply, "Ha!" as though proud of herself.

Kim took a step back out of the doorway, letting the door shut in front of her face. She turned and practically ran to her pickup. Apparently this is still the Wild West, she concluded, with its buried treasures, hard-drinking women and barroom brawls.

As she drove to her RV park, Kim was haunted by the image of Minnie careening down the length of the bar. It was hard to believe what she had just seen. Violence between women was something she couldn't tolerate, and drunken violence was just pathetic.

She found herself lying awake thinking about it most of the

night. Was this common around here? Was this typical of Randi's drinking behavior? Would Minnie let it go? Would Minnie's friends retaliate? Maybe it had erupted into a full-blown fracas after Kim left and the whole bunch of them were in jail right now sleeping it off.

Kim debated over and over in her mind about going to Blair's party. Having witnessed Randi's attack on Minnie, she was torn. She didn't want to associate with Randi, but she agreed with her that she needed to have a little fun and Randi should not be preventing her from finding friends. Since Randi seemed to be everywhere there were lesbians, Kim didn't see how to avoid her entirely. It was too bad, she thought, not for the first time, that Randi had turned out to be such a low-class, hooch-swilling ruffian. Because, despite all of that, there was something about Randi that she liked. Yes, it was too damned bad.

CHAPTER ELEVEN

Despite the digital camera, there were times when Kim made the effort to sketch a particularly interesting image on her notepad. Drawing the glyphs by hand sometimes revealed something new about them. In this case, it was a large anthromorph wearing a headdress and carrying an indeterminate object in one hand. It stood erect with squared off shoulders, a classic design that appeared on gift shop T-shirts throughout the Southwest.

She sat on a low beach chair at Site B with her sketchpad propped against her thighs, facing the petroglyph and concentrating on the smallest of lines. Time and the elements had stolen some of the detail from the feature, so she wasn't sure she was re-creating it faithfully. This image was directly to the left of a gaping rectangular hole in the surface of the outcrop where someone had stolen a sizable chunk from the panel. At the moment, there was no way to know if the missing piece made any meaningful comment on the part that was still there. Kim was hoping that she could turn up someone with a photograph of this section taken while it was still intact. According to Randi, this theft had occurred in 1989. That was secondhand information, of course, originating with Matt. If anyone had a photo to fill in the gap for her, she figured it would be him.

It was still morning and still cool. Earlier they had seen a rare sign of life as a roadrunner sprinted away from their location. It reminded Kim of the first time she had seen a roadrunner, as a graduate student on a field trip, and she had been tremendously disappointed to discover that a skinny, drab bird was the inspiration for the Looney Tunes cartoon bird with its elaborate plumage and brilliant coloring. However, subsequent sightings of the birds had thrilled her because it was unusual to see one. It was unusual to see any animals in the desert, so their appearance was always noteworthy. Kim had still never seen a desert tortoise and had seen bighorn sheep only from great distances.

She was getting used to the quiet here and the long, uninterrupted days measured only by the lengthening of shadows on the soil and the darkening shades of purple on the distant mountains. Every once in a while a squad of fighter jets would plow through the sky on their way to or from the Marine Corps Air Station, dramatically shattering the silence. A lizard, in the characteristic pattern of scurrying and halting, would sometimes draw her attention away from the work, but there were long stretches of time where there were no distractions at all. This made possible the kind of concentration that was nearly impossible back home. With so many sights and sounds coming at you hour after hour, it was harder and harder to achieve this kind of focus, even for a short period of time. She saw that in her students. They had gotten so used to doing three things at once that they were now incapable of single-tasking. Kim wasn't sure if that was good or bad. They were quick and efficient, but they operated on more of a surface level than was sometimes desirable.

That was why Kim was sketching the petroglyph with a pencil. The process forced her to slow down and observe it more carefully, not only observe it, but follow its lines in a manner that put her in touch with the original artist's movements, perhaps even thoughts. It was as close as she could get to the experience of actually etching the image into the stone.

Ramon, wearing his headphones around his neck, came over to get a protein bar out of his backpack. He handed one to Kim.

"Thanks," she said, tearing off the wrapper. "Feels like it's going to be hot today."

"Supposed to be in the nineties." He sat down in the chair next to her and looked at her sketch. "Nice."

She took a bite of the bar, then said, "Have you thought anymore about becoming an archaeologist?"

"Yes, I have. I've been thinking that maybe I could go to the University of Arizona."

"That would be a good choice, I think, especially if you want to continue with the Southwest. It doesn't hurt to go to school on location, so to speak. And Tucson's not that far from home."

"Maybe. Not too far to come home sometimes for weekends."

"That would appeal to your parents, I suppose. Do they like that idea?"

Ramon looked evasive, then said, "I haven't told them."

"Why not?"

"I'm still thinking about it."

"Have you applied?"

"Not yet. I have the application, though. And some scholarship and grant applications too. I was wondering if you'd write me a letter of recommendation."

He made his last request timidly.

"Of course!" Kim answered. "I'd be happy to."

Ramon smiled widely, then returned to his work. Kim finished her snack, then took a swallow from her water bottle just as the sound of a gunshot rang out. She jumped out of her chair, knocking her sketchpad to the ground. Ramon spun around, a startled look on his face. Both of them found the source of the noise simultaneously. An old woman carrying a rifle was walking rapidly toward them, up over the ridge that separated their work site from the road. As she neared, Kim saw that she was scowling fiercely at them under a bare head of snowy-white hair. She wore boots, faded denim jeans and a long-sleeved plaid shirt.

"Hold it right there!" she commanded, still about fifty feet away but quickly closing the distance. "You run and I shoot ya!"

Kim stood planted on the spot, fearing for her life. Were they being robbed? She caught Ramon's confused glance, then turned back to face the old woman who had stopped ten feet away and was pointing the rifle directly at Ramon.

"I caught you this time," she said, grimacing. "I already called the sheriff and now we're going to wait for him. Sit down, both of you!"

"I think you've made a mistake," Kim suggested.

"Sit!" the woman commanded.

Kim lowered herself to the ground. Ramon did the same.

"I think she thinks we're vandals," he said quietly.

"Damn right!" the woman replied. "You've been out here all morning. You're trying to steal 'em."

"No, no," Kim protested. "Look, we're taking pictures." She pointed to the camera near Ramon. "And drawings." Kim held up her sketchpad. "Look for yourself. We haven't taken so much as a pebble."

The old woman scanned the face of the outcrop suspiciously.

"I'm an archaeologist," Kim explained. "We're here on official business. It's all above board, really. You can check with BLM if you want. Let me give you my card."

Kim opened her wallet with deliberate care as the gun barrel moved to point in her direction. She took out a card and held it at arm's length. The woman inched toward it and snatched it away, then squinted intensely in an effort to read it.

"Dr. Kimberly Gatlin," she read. "That you?"

Kim nodded.

"BLM, you say?" she asked. "They know you're here?"

"Yes."

"Does Randi know you're here?"

Randi? Kim thought, hesitating. Why Randi? Why not Steve? He's the boss. This irritated Kim because the old woman, whoever she was, seemed to be buying into Randi's own notion that she was in charge of the place. With the gun pointed at her, she didn't feel like objecting, though, so she said, "Yes, she does."

Holding the rifle in one arm, the old woman pulled a cell phone out of her shirt pocket and punched a couple of buttons, her tongue sticking out of the side of her mouth. "We'll see if I can get through," she said. "Signal's weak."

She put the phone to her ear and, in a minute, yelled into it, saying, "Randi, Randi, is that you? This is Nellie. I've got a couple of folks out here. Claim you know all about them. An archaeologist, that's what she says." She hesitated and yelled louder into the phone. "Right, County Road nine. Yeah, we'll wait right here for ya." She slid the phone into her pocket. "She's on her way. She said fifteen minutes."

While they waited, Nellie kept the rifle ready, but was no longer aiming it at them. The three of them sat and eyed one another, but did not speak. Kim felt the sun burning into her neck, so she readjusted her bandana to compensate. Finally, a dust cloud appeared a couple of miles away and then the familiar Chevy Tahoe came up the road, disappearing behind the ridge where it went silent. A moment later Randi's white hat appeared at the ridge line, and then she came over it, walking rapidly toward them. They all stood.

"Whoa, Nellie!" Randi called, waving cheerfully.

Nellie waved back. Randi approached, grinning. Apparently, she thought this was funny. She walked up to Nellie and hugged her warmly.

"What have you caught here?" she asked.

"Do you know these two? Is she really an archaeologist?"

"That's right," Randi said. "She's legit."

81

Nellie looked momentarily disappointed.

"But thanks for keeping such a good eye out," Randi told her. "We wouldn't want to lose any more of these."

Kim bristled at Randi's nonchalant attitude. "What right does she have coming in here and threatening us at gunpoint? If she had shot us, would you still be just patting her on the back?"

"Nellie knows how to handle a gun," Randi said. "She wouldn't shoot you unless she had a good reason to."

Nellie nodded in agreement, smugly, it seemed to Kim.

"You mean like if she mistakenly thought we were thieves?" Kim suggested.

Randi shrugged. She wasn't taking any of this seriously.

"When the sheriff gets here," Kim said, "I'm going to file a complaint."

"Sheriff?"

"I called," Nellie said. "Earlier."

Randi nodded. "I'll call in and tell them not to bother."

Randi turned to climb back over the ridge to the road as Kim stood where she was, angry and indignant.

"Did you hear what I just said?" she called after Randi.

Randi called over her shoulder, "No need to get all riled up, Tilley. No harm done."

She continued walking and was soon out of sight.

"Sorry," Nellie said to Kim, looking like a recalcitrant child and deflating Kim's indignation.

"That's okay," she said. "So who appointed you guardian of this place anyway?"

"These were my ancestors," Nellie said, strolling over to the rock art. "My name is Nellie WhiteOwl. My ma was full-blooded Tohono O'odham. I've lived here all my life and my people have lived here for a thousand years. This is a sacred place."

"You know this site well, then?" Kim asked.

"Sure."

"What about this?" Kim approached the rock wall and pointed to the missing panel. "What was there? Do you know?"

Nellie nodded. "Too bad I wasn't out here that day. Whoever

took that wouldn't have been walking away from here on two legs, I can guarantee you."

"Do you have a photograph?"

"No. I remember it, though."

"Do you think you could draw it?"

Nellie shrugged. "Maybe so."

Kim gave Nellie her sketchpad, turning over to a blank page. "I'd appreciate it," she said.

Nellie sat in Kim's beach chair and proceeded to sketch. Randi returned, announcing that the sheriff had gone back to town. She looked over at Nellie, who was hunched over the paper, intent on her task.

"What's she doing?" Randi asked.

"Drawing the missing panel."

"Really? That ought to be interesting. So I guess you two have made peace, then."

"I guess. But I don't think you should be so casual about lunatics running around the desert pointing loaded guns at people."

"She's not a lunatic."

"Nevertheless—"

"That's just the way it is out here," Randi said. "This isn't the city, Tilley. There's too much land, too few people. Anybody living out here has to be able to look out for herself...and whatever she considers her own."

"Does she live out here?"

"She has a ranch about three miles down the road. She has some chickens and a bunch of burros she's adopted through our wild horse and burro program."

"Are there wild horses around here?" Kim asked with interest.

"Not right here, but there's a herd over by Picacho. Gotta adopt a few out periodically to make sure the wild ones stay healthy and have enough to eat. It's a great program. A lot of 4-H kids adopt the horses and then break them."

"I didn't even know there were wild horses anymore."

"Oh, sure. Mainly on BLM land. It's an exciting thing to see, too, a herd of wild horses running across the landscape. Like a tornado. Nellie doesn't have any horses, though. She's partial to the burros, which is great for us, since the horses are easier to adopt out. You can't see it, but one of her burros is hitched up to a little cart there on the road. That's how she got here. I guess you didn't even see her coming."

Kim shook her head.

Randi walked over to Nellie and said, "I see you've got Tootsie pulling your cart today."

"She's a good little jennie," Nellie said. "Took no time to gentle her."

"Not for you, maybe." Randi laughed and turned to Kim. "Nellie here is a burro whisperer."

Nellie made a dismissive sputter, not unlike a horse.

Randi put a hand on her shoulder. "Adoption day is coming up next month. You think you want another one?"

"Oh, sure. Always room for one more."

"Good. I'll bring an application out for you next week."

Nellie went back to her drawing and Randi turned to Kim.

"Hey," she said, "I was looking out for you last night at Pinkie's. You didn't show."

"No," Kim said, hesitating while she considered how to answer. "I decided I couldn't spare the time. I needed to try to catch up on some paperwork. There's more of that than you might think on a project like this."

"Oh, that's the case for all of us nowadays, so, sure, I understand how it is. You missed a good night, though. There were a lot of people there."

Your idea of a good night, Kim thought, is knocking the crap out of a friend? Unbelievable!

"I'll see you Saturday anyway," Randi said. "You wouldn't want to miss that."

Kim forced a smile before Randi turned to walk back to her truck. Then she stepped over to Nellie to peer over her shoulder at the sketchpad. She had drawn a string of three anthromorphs similar to the one Kim herself had been copying. All three of them had their arms thrust skyward in a pose generally assumed to represent communion with the spirit world. Beside them was a "ladder" of four concentric circles bisected with a straight line, a symbol for ascension through the four levels of existence—the underworlds, the present world and the world of the ascended. The three shamanistic figures had stood to the right of the one that was still in place. The thieves had most likely taken advantage of an existing fracture in the rock face to remove their panel, which would account for why they left the fourth figure behind.

Kim wondered what had happened to the stolen panel. Was it decorating someone's yard? Had it ended up in a museum? Had it been purchased by some foreign collector and made its way in a secret transport to a far-off place never conceived of by any Paleo-Indian? Whatever had happened to it, it had lost its story by being removed. Even among archaeologists, the practice of leaving things where they were found was fairly modern. Unfortunately, archaeologists weren't the only people out looking for these things. Petroglyphs had an advantage against thieves in that they weren't easily portable, not like a clay pot, for instance. The missing hunk of rock had to have weighed hundreds of pounds and taken hours to extract. It would have required at least two men and maybe a hand truck to transport. Whoever did this had been determined. And, yes, Kim thought, too bad Nellie wasn't out here that day.

When Nellie had finished the drawing, she proudly surrendered it to Kim, who thanked her, then walked with her out to the road where a colorful two-wheeled cart stood hitched to a placid-looking burro wearing a straw hat. The cart was adorned with a yellow fringed shade, red wooden wheels and geometric designs.

"Time to go, Toots," Nellie called to the burro.

She stowed her rifle behind the seat and climbed into the cart. "Bye, now," she said as the cart began to move. "Sorry I scared you."

Kim waved, watching the cart moving jerkily off so slowly

that it raised no dust. She stood there for a moment looking at it, thinking about Randi's relationship with the locals. Kim's personal observations about Randi's character didn't seem to warrant the apparent affection and respect of these people. But there could be no doubt about how Flynn and Nellie felt about her.

C. Randall was a puzzling woman.

CHAPTER TWELVE

There was a good-sized crowd at Blair's ranch, about equally divided between men and women. Kim could imagine that the entire gay community of Yuma was here, although she was told that wasn't so. There are apparently a lot more of us, she realized, than one might have guessed by the size of the town. That was good to see for several reasons, including how easy it was going to be to avoid Randi.

The ranch house was surrounded by a lush cactus garden, and behind it the land sloped away gently down to a ravine. There were lawn chairs set out and some of the guests were building the foundation for what promised to be an enormous fire. A fifty-five gallon drum barbecue was already loaded with meat and chilies and the drinks were flowing. Speakers mounted outside of the house were blasting out rock music.

Kim was introduced to a lot of people, too many to remember names, but she did already know Minnie, Blair and Darlene. Darlene's partner, Trina, was also there. And Jeff, the bartender at Pinkie's, she knew him. Minnie, Kim noticed, stuck with Randi just as before, following her around and acting as friendly as ever. Now that was disgusting, Kim thought, vividly recalling the image of Minnie sliding across the bar. The woman has no self-esteem. It was like something you'd see on *Cops*. How could she let herself be treated like that?

By the time Kim got her carne asada off the grill and a glass of chardonnay, the sun was setting. She sat down to watch it while she ate. The sky was turning pink and orange. Someone lit the fire, and it gradually took on momentum. It seemed like the fire was taking its sustenance from the sky. The darker the latter became, the brighter the former grew.

The music blaring from the house was Cyndi Lauper singing, "She Bop!"

As Kim ate, she saw Randi approaching. She was wearing a long-sleeved salmon-colored shirt tucked into slim-cut blue jeans. No hat tonight. Around her neck was a black leather bolo tie with a trilobite slide. Now that was unique, Kim thought, and fitting for a geologist.

"Hey, Tilley, I'm glad to see you made it. It's a really nice turnout."

As Randi started to sit down beside her, Kim stood up, saying, "Excuse me, I'm going to go get some beans." She didn't see how she could speak to Randi civilly, even if Minnie had forgiven her. Randi looked confused as Kim turned to walk away.

As she ladled some beans onto her plate, she saw Darlene and Trina standing nearby, so she joined them.

"Are Randi and Minnie a couple?" she asked.

Darlene shook her head. "No. If Randi wanted them to be, they would be. But, no, they're just friends."

Some kind of abusive friendship, Kim thought disapprovingly. Poor Minnie is offering love. Gets her nowhere with a woman like that, except knocked around. Kim talked for a while to Darlene and Trina about problem students and problem administrators, which can be a never-ending source of conversation for teachers. After that, she got another glass of wine and found a chair in proximity to the fire. Randi and Minnie were now line dancing in a group of women, and both of them looked like they were having a great time. Everything flickered orange in the light from the fire. Blair came along then and slid into the chair next to Kim. She was wearing cargo shorts and another low-cut blouse. She knew her fine points.

"Are you enjoying yourself," Blair asked, speaking close to her ear.

"Very much. Thanks for inviting me. You have a really nice place out here."

"Thanks. There's a lot of space and no neighbors, so it makes a good spot for parties, anyway." Blair's freckled cheeks looked bright red in the firelight.

"So how did you end up in Yuma," Kim asked.

"I followed my heart. Fell in love with a woman who lived here. After we broke up, I just stayed. I like it here."

A surprising number of people do like it here, Kim realized.

From the house, Joan Jett was screaming, "Do You Wanna Touch Me?" Everybody around the fire was clapping in sync with the beat and singing along, including Blair and Kim.

As the crowd hollered, "Oh, yeah!" in a communal answer to Joan Jett's question, Blair leaned in close to Kim and said, "Oh, yeah!" softly, next to her ear. Kim, startled, stopped clapping and turned to look at Blair, who was grinning at her, but then she looked away and resumed singing, so Kim did the same.

After a couple more songs, the music stopped. In the absence of competing sound, the fire crackled loudly, flames and sparks leaping into the sky. Blair went to get herself another beer and was back in a few seconds with a bottle of white wine, from which she refilled Kim's glass.

After a few minutes of silence, Kim heard a guitar and looked for the source. It was Randi, seated nearly on the other side of the fire next to Minnie and some others. As she warmed up, the crowd began to settle into a quiet, listening audience. And then there were two guitars. One of the men was also playing. Kim began to recognize the tune. It was "Wildwood Flower." Randi was looking directly at Kim, then she winked, a gesture that Blair must have noticed.

"What's going on between you two?" she asked. "Friends?"

"Not really. I mean, I wouldn't go that far. We're just acquaintances. Colleagues. I doubt we would ever be friends. She's just not— Nothing in common."

Blair nodded, approvingly.

Kim noticed that Randi was playing sweetly with no mistakes. Not drunk yet, anyway, she thought.

"Who's that guy playing?" she asked.

"That's Gareth. He's good, isn't he?"

"Yes. So is she."

"Totally," Blair agreed. "They sound good together."

They were now playing "Waltzing Matilda." Kim and Blair sang along. When the song was over, Randi stood up and announced, "Breast cancer walk-a-thon next Sunday everybody! Be there for Callie!" That woman could be really loud when she wanted to, Kim marveled. "She's doing great. I stopped by the hospital on my way here. She sends her love to everyone and will be here next time, for sure."

"Who's Callie?" Kim asked Blair.

"One of our friends," Blair answered, filling Kim's glass. "She just had a mastectomy. She'll be in the hospital for a couple more days."

As Randi started playing "Ghost Riders in the Sky," Kim reflected that she absolutely did not understand Randi. On the one hand, she seemed like a responsible, mature individual. She was concerned about Black Point, concerned about her miners, had a sense of community that was strong enough to alienate her from newcomers. And yet, she was rude, hostile, even violent toward her friends. As Kim watched Randi interact with people, though, she saw no evidence that anyone had anything but affection for her.

"What's Randi's real first name?" Kim asked.

"I think it's Claudine. Don't tell her I told you that or she'll kill me. And if you call her that, she'll kill you."

Kim giggled, imagining springing that on Randi.

"I'm serious," Blair said, also giggling, slipping her arm around Kim's shoulders, and touching their heads together. "Don't tell her."

Kim and Blair gave up singing after that, except for the occasional easy chorus. Blair sat close to Kim, their thighs pressed together, keeping her glass full. Kim was feeling very hot despite the cool evening that had descended around them. Staring at Blair's mouth, she was suddenly startled to hear another voice. Turning, she saw Minnie standing in front of them.

"Blair," she said, "we're taking up a collection for Callie, to get her a gift for when she goes home. We were thinking of one of those gourmet food baskets from—"

"Okay, okay," Blair said impatiently, making a shooing gesture. "Great idea. I'll give you the money tomorrow."

Minnie frowned and moved away.

"You got a girlfriend back home?" Blair asked, turning her attention back to Kim.

"Nope," Kim answered. "Not a one."

"That's good." Blair rested her hand on Kim's knee, and then they both laughed.

Kim stared into the plunging neckline of Blair's blouse at her smooth, creamy breasts, thinking they looked like meringue on a lemon pie, and wanting to lick it off. It was with that thought that she knew she'd had too much wine. In fact, the bottle standing on the ground next to her chair was nearly empty. Kim wondered if it was possible that she'd drunk all of that by herself, not to mention the two glasses she'd had before that. She didn't think she'd drank that much wine since her first year in college.

"Maybe I should go home," Kim suggested, attempting to sound controlled. She heard the slurring in her voice with dismay.

"Honey," Blair said, "you're drunk. You're not driving yourself home tonight."

"No," Kim agreed. "I shouldn't drive."

"Don't worry. I'm prepared." Blair didn't sound all that sober herself. "I've got a room for you. You can stay here. I've got a few spending the night. For everybody who stays over, there'll be a big pancake breakfast tomorrow morning."

"Really?" Kim asked. "I love pancakes."

"Well, sure you do. Come on. Let me show you your room. In the morning, after breakfast, you can drive yourself home. How's that?"

"Sounds good," Kim said, thinking about pancakes.

Blair stood up first, then helped Kim to her feet, holding her firmly around the waist as they stumbled into the house. Inside, Blair led the way down a hallway to a bedroom at the end, a large room with a king-sized bed piled up with pillows in gold and brown satin fabrics.

"How's this?" Blair asked her, kicking the door shut and silencing the sound of guitars and singing outside.

Kim, ready to collapse, stepped over to the bed and crawled onto it, lying with her face in the pillows, her eyes closed. Any minute, she would be asleep, she knew.

"Hey, honey," Blair said, "don't pass out on me just yet."

Blair rolled her over onto her back and was lying beside her. Kim looked at Blair's cute, freckled nose and flushed cheeks. She's going to kiss me, Kim thought, and, sure enough, she did. Blair's lips were soft and seductive. Blair moved on top of Kim and kissed her again, deep and hard. Feeling aroused and forgetting about sleep, Kim kissed her back, their mouths locked tightly together.

"Ummm," Blair said, releasing Kim's mouth.

Kim pressed her face into Blair's chest, running her tongue over the exposed curve of her breasts and down between them, into the dark groove of her deep cleavage.

"That's more like it," Blair breathed, rapidly undoing the top three buttons on Kim's shirt.

CHAPTER THIRTEEN

Watching Blair drag Kim into the house, Randi felt herself becoming angry. Almost without realizing it, she stopped playing her guitar and let her hand fall to her knee, staring at the door they had gone through.

"What's the matter?" Minnie asked.

Gareth continued playing the song on his own as Randi propped her guitar against her chair and stood. "I can't let her get away with this."

"Are you talking about Blair? Looks like she's got that archaeologist right where she wants her, huh?"

"I'm going to stop her."

"What? Are you serious? Leave it alone. It's none of your business."

Minnie was right, of course, but Randi didn't seem to be able to help herself. Even after Kim had pointedly snubbed her, she had been watching her all evening, watching Blair's methodical seduction of her, and becoming more and more distressed. She had tried several times to ignore the two of them, but it had been no good.

"I just have to, Min."

Why, she asked herself, striding rapidly across the yard, why am I butting in here? Because she's drunk, she answered. Because Blair is taking advantage of her. Because she'll be sorry in the morning, especially if there's a woman back home trusting her.

Once inside the house, Randi moved quickly down the hallway toward Blair's bedroom, having no doubt where she would find them. Flinging open the door, she saw Kim lying on her back with Blair straddling her, undoing the buttons on her shirt. As Randi stepped into the room, Blair sprang off the bed, looking startled and indignant.

"What are you doing?" Randi asked her.

"Nothing," Blair said, defiantly. "Just offering Kim a place to stay for the night. She can't drive in her condition. I'm going to let her sleep here."

"But this is *your* room."

"We're going to have pancakes in the morning," Kim announced, rolling onto her side. Her unbuttoned shirt fell open, revealing a lacy pink bra. "Are you staying too, Randi?"

"I'll take her home," Randi told Blair.

"No need," Blair objected. "You just go back to the party. Everything's under control here."

"Yeah," Randi replied sarcastically. "I'm sure."

Kim sat up and swung her legs over the side of the bed.

"I'm taking you home, Tilley," Randi said, pulling Kim to her feet. Kim's body was compliant as Randi clamped a firm arm around her waist.

"What right do you have barging into my bedroom," Blair asked, "and telling us what to do?"

"I'm not going to argue with you," Randi said sternly. "If she wants to come back when she's sober, she's all yours."

Randi paused, momentarily distracted by the soft curve of Kim's breasts above her bra. She let her eyes feast on this delicious view for a couple of heartbeats. Bringing herself back to the moment, Randi carefully buttoned Kim's shirt, observing the goofy smile on her face. She then pulled her out of the bedroom and down the hall at a pace too rapid for Kim to manage. But it didn't matter because Randi was barely allowing her feet to touch the floor. She felt a sense of urgency to get her out of Blair's grasp before either of them gathered their wits enough to form a coherent objection.

"What the hell?" was all Blair could come up with.

She followed, looking confused and angry, but didn't make any physical move against Randi.

"Does this mean I won't get pancakes?" Kim asked when Randi stopped to open the door.

"Where are your keys?" Randi asked her. Kim reached into her front pocket and pulled out her car keys, handing them over.

Minnie met them as they emerged from the house.

"Take my truck," Randi said, handing her own keys to Minnie. "Follow me. I'm driving her home."

Minnie nodded. Randi put Kim into the passenger seat of her pickup while Blair stood watching, her lips held tightly together in frustration.

The bonfire was dwindling, and as they drove away, it became the only thing Randi could see of Blair's ranch, the twinkling flames in the darkness. Once she hit the paved road, Randi took a deep breath, feeling as if she'd been holding it during the entire abduction. That was the word that came to her mind, *abduction.* Kim didn't seem unhappy, though, so perhaps "rescue" was the right word after all.

"Where's your hat?" Kim asked, slurring her words. "I like you in your hat."

Randi didn't answer, noting that Kim was much more friendly toward her now than she had been earlier in the evening. Booze makes friends out of everybody.

"Not very talkative tonight, are you, Claudine."

Randi snapped her head sideways to see Kim looking pleased with herself. Although she wanted to ask who gave her that tidbit of information, she decided to remain silent and turned her attention back to the road.

Kim seemed to slump in her seat after that, and there were no more attempts at conversation.

At last, they pulled into the RV park. "Where's your space?" Randi asked.

Kim pointed to the left. "Up the next corner."

After parking, Randi came around to open the door. Kim slid out of the pickup, wrapping her arms around Randi's neck. Randi kicked the car door shut and swung Kim over to her hip, then walked her to her door, fumbling momentarily with the keys. She pushed the door open to the trailer's dark interior. Once she'd gotten both of them inside, she released her hold.

"Can you turn on a light?" Randi asked, running a hand along the door frame looking for a switch.

She felt Kim's arms slide around her neck again and the increasing pressure of her body as Kim pressed herself closer, pinning Randi against the wall. "Kiss me," she said.

She's trying to drive me nuts, Randi thought, struggling against her desire to comply. Though it was too dark to see, she could tell Kim's mouth was close to hers. There was a strong smell of alcohol on her breath. That was definitely a turnoff. Still, standing in the dark with their bodies touching, she couldn't deny the urge she felt to do more than just kiss Kim.

Randi heard the engine of her own truck arrive outside, reminding her why she was here.

"You sure are easy when you're drunk," she said, pushing Kim gently away.

Randi managed to find a light switch, then, and they were no longer in the dark. Kim stood smiling inanely at her.

"I'm putting your keys here on the table," Randi said. "You go to bed."

Randi shut the door between them as she hurried out and climbed behind the wheel of her pickup. Minnie had already moved to the passenger seat.

"Is she okay?" Minnie asked.

"She's fine."

"Blair is so pissed at you."

"No surprise there."

Randi drove away from the trailer park, still feeling the sensation of Kim's body against hers.

"I still don't understand why you did that?" Minnie said. "Especially since you don't like that woman. Stuck-up, know-it-all bitch, that's what you called her."

Randi winced at hearing that. "I may have been a little hasty."

"So, what, you mean you like her now? What did she do to change your mind?"

"Nothing, really. I barely know her. But even if she is a stuck-up, know-it-all bitch, she's our guest in town. We should be decent hosts."

"Yeah, and it's just like you, Randi, to assume responsibility for the whole damn town."

Randi's feelings toward Kim had definitely changed since her arrival. The reasons weren't all that easy to explain. The other day when she had walked up on Kim sitting in the dirt with a small chip of obsidian in her hand, she'd been surprised that Kim hadn't heard her approach. She sat there, covered with dirt, her hair a mess, a glob of white sunblock on her nose, transfixed by a sliver of glass that few people would have even noticed. When she had finally seen Randi there, she had handed over the glass as if it were an object of great importance, as if it were something precious. And on Kim's face there had been a look of child-like delight.

Randi knew right then that Kim was the real thing, after all. She wasn't just in it for what she could get out of it. She really felt it, the worth of what she was doing. After that, she could no longer dismiss her as a lightweight. And once Randi's professional objections to Kim were gone, her personal attraction had begun to assert itself.

She didn't feel like she could tell any of this to Minnie. For one thing, Minnie would be jealous, even though it had been quite a while now since Randi had gotten the point across that the two of them would never be a couple. Minnie was a great friend, and Randi had been more in need of friends when she arrived in Yuma than lovers. Minnie was, in fact, her best friend. There was no reason to hurt her feelings by talking about some vague attraction to another woman, especially since it would never lead to anything.

When they arrived at Minnie's house, Randi said, "I hope that stuck-up, know-it-all bitch appreciates what I did for her tonight."

Minnie laughed and said good-night, disappearing into her house.

CHAPTER FOURTEEN

Predictably, when Kim woke in the morning, her head was splitting, her mouth was dry and she was still wearing the clothes she'd worn the night before. She got up to go to the bathroom, drank a glass of water, and decided to lie down again. Details of the previous evening gradually drifted into her consciousness—the spectacular bonfire, singing folk songs, kissing Blair. Randi taking her home. How had Randi ended up in Blair's bedroom? And why did she drag her out of Blair's bed? Just doing a good deed, maybe, like a Boy Scout. Or the Lone Ranger. Yes, definitely more like the Lone Ranger with that white hat.

And then she remembered being home, clinging to Randi in the dark while Randi tried to escape as fast as she could. How humiliating!

Kim lay in bed with her eyes closed for at least an hour, drifting in and out of sleep, until she heard a vehicle stop outside. A moment later there was a firm knock on her aluminum door.

"Hey, Tilley," called a familiar voice.

Oh, great, Kim thought, rolling out of bed. I'm sure I look like shit. She opened the door to Randi, who came in carrying a Styrofoam box and a large cup of coffee. She set these on the table.

"Good morning," Randi said, taking off her hat. "Feel like crap, I imagine. I brought you breakfast." Randi opened the box to reveal a stack of pancakes. "Since you seemed more upset about losing out to pancakes than you did about losing out to Blair last night."

Kim took the coffee, sat on the bed, and sipped at it tentatively. "That's very thoughtful of you," she said, "considering how much trouble I caused you last night."

Randi sat on the sofa across the table. "Yeah, you were a handful, all right."

"I'm really sorry. I don't drink much. I'm not used to it. I don't know why I did that."

"You had a lot of encouragement."

"Blair?"

Randi nodded. "You were just too tempting a morsel for her to pass up."

Kim drank the coffee while Randi sat across from her, a sly, slight smile on her lips.

"You probably don't feel like eating right now," she said, "but later, just pop those in the microwave for a couple of seconds and they'll be fine."

"Thanks. I will." Kim was already feeling a little better, but the headache was still piercing through her left temple. She was definitely relieved at Randi's demeanor, which appeared friendly and relaxed, not at all reproachful.

"Are you going to show me your place?" Randi asked. "I didn't really see it last night."

Kim laughed. "What you see..." she said, twirling her arm over her head.

Randi got up and looked around the kitchen, pausing at the photos on the refrigerator. "Not your kids, I'm guessing."

"Niece and nephews. My sister's."

"And this?" she asked, indicating a slip of paper containing one of Kim's favorite quotations. "Try reasoning with a rhino, end up dead." Randi huffed. "Sounds familiar. That's Catherine Gardiner. From her poem about failed relationships. I mean *one* of her poems about failed relationships. She has many."

"You know it?" Kim was surprised.

"Yeah. I really like her. Why that quote?"

"It reminds me that there's a right solution and many wrong solutions to each problem, that you have to think it through before you know how to tackle it. Like, despite the first inclination of a geologist, a rock hammer is not the right tool for every task."

Randi laughed, then abruptly stopped. "Oh, you're not joking, are you?"

Kim laughed, then, realizing that Randi *was* joking. The self-knowing smile was very attractive.

"I have to admit I know nothing about Catherine Gardiner," Kim said. "That was just a line I stumbled on."

"So what poets do you like?"

"Oh, you know, the usual, I suppose. Emily Dickinson."

"You like her?" Randi looked uncertain.

"Sure. Don't you?"

"Personally, I think she's a little sing-songy and her preoccupation with death and the afterlife is irritating. Every other poem is longing for death or an ode to it. On and on, interminably, death, death, death."

Startled at Randi's words, Kim just stared at her.

"I mean," Randi continued, "if you're going to be a poet obsessed with death, the least you could do is kill yourself, like Anne Sexton or Sylvia Plath."

"What a horrible thing to say!" Kim said, acknowledging privately that Randi knew more than she would have guessed about poetry.

"Sure, suicide is horrible, but as a poetic gesture, it has a sort of elegance that can't be beat."

"Perhaps," Kim said, "but it isn't just a poetic gesture, of course. I mean, I know what you're saying, but they weren't just poets. They were people with families and they should have been prescribed Prozac or something."

Randi nodded. "You have a point. But if they had been, we would have been robbed of some stunning verse. Dickinson was a literary genius, just not to my taste."

Kim drank her coffee, thinking about Randi's knowledge of poetry and the fact that few people outside of academia had the confidence to criticize the iconic Emily Dickinson.

Randi leaned casually against the counter. "She was a product of her time. A woman of tremendous passion, looking for a way to express it. She found this outlet, the poetry, but even there she held back. She used poetry as a device to transform her intense emotions into something she could handle, I think. It was her way of coping."

"Coping with?" asked Kim.

"Living in Victorian New England with the restrictions of being a thinking woman in a man's world."

Kim just nodded, not really up to this conversation in her condition.

"I'd like to think that if Emily Dickinson were alive today," Randi continued, "she'd have been out there with us last night singing 'Where Have All the Flowers Gone.' Then maybe she and one of the girls could have enjoyed a sizzling night of pleasure, and in the morning she wouldn't have had a single rhyme in her head. Can't you just see her with her long hair all loose on a pillow and those intense eyes looking up at some girl?"

Kim laughed loudly. "The image that brings to mind is just too funny."

"Yes," agreed Randi, laughing too. Her eyes sparkled as she did so, crinkling up around the edges, making her look cuter than ever.

"Why do you know so much about poetry?" Kim asked.

"Believe it or not, my first year of college I debated between

102

English and geology as a major. Science won out, but only for practical reasons. I've always loved literature."

Interesting, thought Kim.

"I prefer Sylvia Plath because she's fearless. Her material is honest and ruthless."

"I guess I see what you mean. There's no real edge to Dickinson."

"Exactly," Randi said, smiling with approval.

Isn't this odd? Kim thought. The geologist and the archaeologist are discussing poetry. After a moment of silence and another gulp of coffee, she asked, "Why did you do it?"

"Do what?"

"Come to my rescue last night."

Randi hesitated before answering. "I've seen people do a lot of stupid things when they're drinking. I've done a lot of stupid things myself. I thought Blair was way out of line. I couldn't stand by— I don't know. Just did."

Kim thought of Randi throwing Minnie down the bar. Is that the kind of thing she was referring to as "stupid"?

"You drove me home," Kim began. "You were sober?"

"Yes. I don't drink. Not anymore, not at all."

"But I saw you the other day with a drink at Pinkie's."

"Just a Coke. I haven't had a drink in four years."

"Oh, I see." So she didn't even have that excuse. "That must have made me seem really unpleasant last night."

"Yep," agreed Randi. "You were extremely unappealing. At least to me. Obviously not to Blair."

Kim suddenly remembered asking Randi to kiss her. God, she thought, what must she have thought of that, especially since she finds me "extremely unappealing." Kim took a deep breath. "I guess I should say thank you. Not quite the impression I wanted to give to the community my first time out."

"Don't worry about it. Most of them wouldn't have noticed. You didn't dance naked around the fire or anything."

"But *you* noticed."

"Yeah, but I was watching."

She was looking out for me, Kim thought. Like her petroglyphs and her miners. I'm a responsibility to her, like a kid sister. Maybe she thought she was the lesbian etiquette police or something.

"Why?" Kim asked. "You're not responsible for me. I can take care of myself."

"Oh?" Randi raised an eyebrow. "Didn't look like it last night."

There was that arrogance again. In fact, thought Kim, Randi's behavior last night was about as arrogant as anyone could be. All of the sudden, seeing that self-satisfied grin on Randi's face, Kim started to get angry. "It's not like I was asking to be rescued. You just busted in and dragged me out of there like a Neanderthal claiming your property."

Randi looked unpleasantly surprised at Kim's change of tone. "You would have preferred to have been left alone?"

"Well, I—" Kim sputtered. "How would you know what I preferred? You didn't ask. Blair was right. You had no business barging in there like that."

Randi nodded thoughtfully, frowning now. "Sorry I ruined your fun. I thought you were too drunk to know what you were doing. Apparently, I was wrong."

Randi pushed her hat on and was out the door in a second.

Kim listened to her drive away, feeling stupid. Of course she was glad that Randi had intervened. She had been drunk out of her mind. If only Randi was not so pleased with herself all the time. That characteristic really grated on Kim. A little humility would be a terrific addition to her personality.

CHAPTER FIFTEEN

Randi didn't really know why, when other people got drunk, she felt compelled to go to an AA meeting, but it was inevitable that she did. So Sunday evening she spent an hour listening to stories of broken homes, shattered dreams and the slow, successful steps back toward sobriety and good health from those like herself who had once let their lives be ruled by alcohol. She didn't believe that Kim was one of these. If she were an alcoholic, she would have had more control. She'd be used to being drunk. She obviously wasn't.

Alma was here tonight. She thanked Randi for helping her out with the rent and the side jobs Randi had arranged for her. "Haven't had a drink since," she said.

Randi hugged her warmly and said hello to several of the

others before taking a seat next to Gareth. During the meeting, her mind strayed from the speakers' stories to wander over events of the last twenty-four hours.

All day long, ever since leaving Kim's trailer, Randi had been asking herself the same question that Kim had asked her. Why had she butted in and stopped Blair? It wasn't a moral imperative. Blair wasn't going to murder her, for Christ's sake. They were both adults. But for some reason, as Randi had watched Blair with her hands all over Kim, keeping her wineglass full, she had become enraged. It was likely that Kim had someone back home who was trusting her, for one thing. "But, honey, I was drunk," was not an excuse, as Randi knew well. It wasn't an excuse for anything, really.

So maybe it was just her natural inclination to be protective that had taken over. Randi didn't want it to be more than that, for several reasons, even if Kim was single. She wasn't ready to open up her heart again. Things were working for her here, working better than expected. A change as drastic as falling in love was too great a risk. It could throw her completely out of control. She couldn't predict what would happen and how she would react. So far, here in Yuma, she had weathered whatever had come her way, but she always felt she was just one tiny step away from completely unraveling. Even if she wasn't that shaky, she didn't want to test her resiliency, not yet. She couldn't afford a distraction. Kim was definitely a distraction.

Tonight people were talking about their greatest fears. Gareth was speaking, his hands clasped between his knees.

"I'm scared that I'm going to lose my kid," he said. "Lose his respect or lose access to him. He's the most precious thing in the world to me, but the fact is that there's less of a threat to our relationship from homosexuality than from alcohol."

When Gareth had finished, Randi said, "I have something to say."

Gareth turned to smile at her and she squeezed his hand tightly before speaking.

"For a long time my greatest fear was that I'd kill somebody."

She saw a couple of the others nod. "In a car accident or because of a drunken rage or something. I once shot off a gun in a crowd. I was out of my mind. It was dumb luck that I didn't hit somebody. The worst would be a child, killing a child. You'd never recover from something like that. You couldn't forgive yourself. But anybody, really. Killing someone or even failing to save someone's life because you had too much to drink... That's just terrifying. I have that nightmare all the time. Still. That fear has never left me."

After the meeting, Gareth approached her and said, "Did you get your friend home safely last night?"

My friend? thought Randi ironically. "Yes. She spent the day recuperating."

"Will I see you at Pinkie's later?"

"No, not tonight. I'm planning on a quiet evening at home."

A quiet evening at home was exactly what Randi was looking forward to, just her and Breeze and the television.

Driving up to her house, she saw a car parked at the curb, a green Jetta with a conspicuous dent in the front driver's side fender. She didn't recognize the car and decided it belonged to someone visiting a neighbor. But as she stepped out of her truck, she saw a woman standing on her walkway.

As Randi took a step, the floodlight over her garage door came on, casting a sheet of light over the front yard. Her visitor, she saw, was her old friend Danya from Phoenix. Danya smiled as the light hit her face, displaying a gaunt, tired visage that matched her gangly frame. Danya had always been thin, not lithe and graceful, but lean and scruffy like an alley cat. Randi hadn't seen her since leaving Phoenix. Her appearance here was a complete surprise, one that filled Randi with apprehension.

"Hey, Rocky, is that you?" she called as Randi approached her, using an old nickname common among her drinking buddies. She hadn't heard it for two years. Nobody here in Yuma knew about that nickname and she wanted to keep it that way. It was a name she had earned in college because she was a geology major. But, later, with the bar crowd, a lot of people thought it had something to do with her left jab. She didn't particularly want to be reminded of that. The AA rule flitted through her mind about getting away from the people who were part of the destructive lifestyle. Danya definitely was one of those, one of three or four good buddies who could always be counted on to keep her company in the bar. So this was probably bad news, after all, Danya turning up like this, trespassing on Randi's new, sober life.

"Danya," Randi said, reaching out to give her a hug. "What are you doing in Yuma?"

"I've come to visit an old friend," she said. Then she laughed awkwardly, as if she'd made a joke. "You, of course! Hey, what's with the long hair and the braid?"

"Just wanted something different. How'd you find me?" Randi wondered if that sounded rude.

"You're in the fucking phone book."

"Oh, right."

Randi led Danya into the house and switched on lights, greeting Breeze and introducing him to her guest. Danya stood turning in circles in the front room, taking it all in.

"Wow, this is nice!"

"Thank you. I'm pretty happy here."

"Are you renting?" Danya asked as she wandered into the kitchen.

"No, no, I bought it. I've got a big old honking mortgage payment and everything."

Danya looked at her and nodded appreciatively. "That college education paid off, then, didn't it?"

Randi led Danya through the kitchen to the sunroom. Since it was dark out, she couldn't see the view, but she whistled low at the room itself. "You work for the government, right?"

"Right. BLM. I'm the district geologist here."

"Cool!"

Randi felt impatient and slightly invaded. "So, Danya, what are you doing here?"

Danya, who was fingering a quartz crystal on Randi's rock

108

shelf, turned and looked at her with a questioning expression. "I told you, I came to visit you."

"I know, but why? Why now? Why come without calling?"

"Oh, you know me. I'm not much for planning things. Just got a bug and thought I'd visit an old friend. So here I am. That's okay, isn't it?"

"I guess," Randi said, not sure if it was okay. Danya sounded very matter-of-fact, but Randi didn't trust her. Their friendship went way back, so she knew what kind of manipulation Danya was capable of. And there was a current of nervousness running through her, just under the surface, that made Randi even more wary.

"So how about let's have dinner and catch up," Danya suggested.

Randi relaxed slightly. "Okay. I'll take you to my favorite Mexican place."

"Great. Just show me your bathroom, okay, so I can pee, and, oh, by the way, do you have a spare bed? Or even the couch would do me for the night. It's way too far to drive back to Phoenix tonight and I really can't afford a hotel."

This request would have sounded reasonable to anyone who didn't know Danya, but for Randi, it was an alarm going off. She didn't know what else to do, though, so she said, "There's a very comfortable guest room. You're welcome to sleep there tonight."

A wide smile filled Danya's face. "Thanks, Rocky, you're the best."

"Danya," Randi said, "I would rather you didn't call me that anymore."

Danya raised her eyebrows. "Oh, right, because you're sober. Not so much for the bar fights now. You're still sober, right?"

Randi nodded.

"That's so great... Randi. Or is it Claudine now?"

Randi laughed. "Oh, no, please no! Randi."

"Okay. I'm so glad to hear that you're still on the wagon because I am too."

"Really?" Randi was incredulous.

"Yep. Clean as a whistle. Never gonna touch that stuff again."

"Wow! That's fantastic."

Danya smiled, looking pleased with herself, and turned toward the hallway and the bathroom. "On the wagon," meant that Danya was *not* going to AA. That wasn't a phrase they used. So she must be trying to quit on her own. Randi tried not to let herself be skeptical of Danya's attempt at sobriety. People had been skeptical of her too. Understandably. You had to give people the benefit of the doubt. So Randi decided to do that for Danya. After all, they had been the best of friends back then. More than friends in the beginning.

Randi had met Danya during her freshman year on the college partying circuit, and within a couple of weeks, they were lovers. Danya hadn't been a student, but she worked at one of the local hangouts where the kids gathered and became one of the regulars in Randi's crowd. Their relationship spanned many years, not as an exclusive one, for they broke up regularly and they slept together even when they weren't officially together. It was all about the drinking, of course. Randi sometimes wondered how she had ever managed to get through college at all considering how many days started out with her head over a toilet. She had never made the honor roll, not even close. She had barely scraped by, and after graduation, it was one long summer party, and suddenly every thought she'd ever had about graduate school just floated right out of her head. In the couple of years that followed, whenever she went through a bad patch and lapsed back into heavy drinking, Danya always turned up again, as if she could smell Randi's weakness, as if she thrived on it.

And that was why Irene considered Danya the enemy, why Danya had been banned from their apartment, and why Danya's appearance here was fraught with anxiety for Randi. Danya personified so many things about herself that Randi wanted to leave behind, all of the things she was ashamed of—irresponsibility, infidelity, self-destructiveness. Danya wasn't responsible for those behaviors, but she was an acute reminder.

Randi knew that the persona she projected was confident, strong, even boastful. That was her public self. That image belied her self-doubt and regrets about the past and the way she had disappointed people she cared about, disappointed herself. She was a better person than that and she was determined to prove it, even if it took the rest of her life. Danya didn't know her any more, despite her certainty that she did, because Randi had left that person behind for good. Danya probably didn't believe that. She probably believed that old Rocky Randall was lurking there just under the surface and, given a few beers, would jump right out and start a party. Randi herself wasn't sure that wouldn't happen. To make sure it never did, old Rocky Randall was not going to get those few beers. Nobody here in Yuma would recognize the woman that Danya had known so well. Randi didn't intend to introduce them to her.

She took Danya out for dinner and listened as she dug up memories of their youth together. One of the differences between herself and Danya, Randi noticed, was that Danya didn't seem to have any misgivings about those early years. She reminisced with joyful nostalgia about the old days, about the raucous sing-a-longs at Pop's, their favorite hang-out with its retro tunes on its equally retro jukebox. She seemed happy to remember waking up in unexpected places like someone's bed or front lawn or chaise lounge poolside in an unsuspecting neighbor's backyard. There were the times they woke up together too, waking in a haze of confusion about how this had happened, neither one of them knowing for sure if they had had sex or not, but suspecting that if they hadn't, it was only because they had been incapable of it.

Just such an incident had preceded the first time Irene had left. Randi had protested fiercely that it was quite possible there had been no sexual contact at all with Danya that night. Irene said it didn't matter, and the fact that Randi couldn't even tell her for sure was even more disturbing. Randi had been argumentative at the time, but now she felt that Irene had been more than justified in leaving. And she probably shouldn't have come back.

But of all of those "good" times that Danya wanted to revisit, none were as bad as the time that Randi had knocked out Danya's two front teeth. She had a bridge now. You couldn't really tell. While "Blueberry Hill" had played on the jukebox, Danya and Randi had drunk beer and played a game of checkers. Oddly, as drunk as she'd been, that was one night she could recall vividly.

"Do you remember how that got started?" Danya asked.

"Yeah. You were telling me how you had a dream in which your dead grandmother told you to move to Peru and raise llamas. So you were going to go. And I said you were a fucking moron."

"Yes, you did." Danya laughed. "We sure did get out of hand that night."

"Sure did. Neither one of us was ever allowed in that place again."

"Can't blame Pops. We made a pretty big mess."

"On each other too."

"Right." Danya pointed to her false front teeth. "And your nose, of course."

"I was so stupid," Randi said, touching her nose.

"Both of us were stupid." Danya directed her thin smile at Randi and looked thoughtful. "Irene left you after that, didn't she?"

Randi nodded. "For good that time."

"I've run into her around town a couple of times, but she's really cold toward me. Doesn't talk to me. From what I hear, though, she's happy in her new life. Moved on."

"Yes, I knew that. Me too."

"No woman here, though, is there?" Danya asked.

"No. I'm busy with my job, both of my jobs. I also teach a class at the college one night a week."

"You're a college professor? Woo-hoo!" Danya slapped the table, then nodded appreciatively. "Irene would be impressed by that."

Randi shrugged. "Doesn't matter. That's over."

Randi tipped up her glass, letting the ice cubes clunk against her top lip as she finished the last of her soda.

After a silent moment between them, Danya said, "Maybe we should get back together."

Randi couldn't tell if she was serious or not. That was most likely her intent. Now there's a disaster waiting to happen, thought Randi.

"Maybe we shouldn't," she said, pulling a couple of bills out of her front pocket and leaving them on the table as she shoved her chair back and stood. "Let's go."

Danya shrugged and followed Randi to the truck. She climbed into the passenger seat while the engine turned over. As Randi shifted into reverse, Danya's hand slid suggestively across her thigh. Randi froze.

"It's okay if you aren't looking for anything serious," Danya said, adopting her bedroom voice. "Maybe we could just fool around a little. You always did know how to make me purr."

"Nope," Randi said, "not going to happen." Then she lifted Danya's hand by the wrist and moved it off her thigh.

"Why not?" Danya asked. "At least neither one of us has anybody else this time. It would do you good. You seem all tense. Let me make you feel better."

"I feel fine. Drop it."

Is that what she's here for? Randi wondered, backing out of her parking space. She had no residual attraction left for Danya. In fact, those years she was with Irene, even then she was way over Danya. The couple of times she'd slipped up, that wasn't due to any real attraction. That was just a self-destructive dive into the cesspool of impersonal boozy lust when Danya happened to be the woman near at hand. And there was definitely no attraction now, as Danya's alley cat demeanor had become even more scruffy and desperate since Randi had seen her last. If Danya had come here hoping to reignite their romance, she would be disappointed.

CHAPTER SIXTEEN

Six kids were working on the diorama today under Randi's supervision. One of the girls, Emma, was carefully nestling the kit fox skull into the sand at an angle of precision an engineer would have envied. The other kids were planting tufts of deer grass at irregular intervals. Natalie was sitting at a worktable drawing a design for the clay pot they were making, a replica of a Hohokam olla. Kim would like that, Randi thought with an involuntary smile. And then she frowned, feeling annoyed with herself. Who cares what Kim likes, she reprimanded herself.

Emma stood, encased behind glass, standing over the partially buried skull, looking triumphant. She waited for Randi's declaration. Randi gave her a thumbs-up. The girl broke into a big smile and then proceeded to back out of the case, covering her footprints as she went.

"Ten minutes, people!" Randi told them. "Let's start cleaning up."

Emma stood beside Randi looking at the tiny skull through the glass.

"What do you think?" Randi asked her.

"I think it's perfect," she said in the adult manner she customarily took with Randi, as though they were colleagues.

"Sure is. It's one of those things you won't see right away, but if you stand here awhile, you'll start to see all of these details. That's what we're aiming for, something like the real desert where there's a lot going on, but you don't notice unless you're paying close attention."

Randi became aware of an adult presence nearby and turned to address her, thinking it was the class teacher. But it was Kim, standing a few paces away, watching the activity. As Randi caught her eye, she smiled tentatively.

"It's coming along great," Kim said.

"Randi!" called Natalie.

Randi walked over to look at Natalie's drawing. It was a series of rust-colored diagonal zigzags that faithfully imitated a jar they had photographed in a museum.

"Beautiful job!" Randi said.

"Can I see it?" Kim asked.

Natalie nodded vigorously and moved aside so Kim could stand directly in front of the drawing. "It's for a pot," Natalie told her.

"Hohokam red-on-buff," Kim said.

"Yes!" Natalie sounded surprised. "You know."

Kim held a hand out to Natalie. "I'm Kim," she said.

Natalie shook her hand. "I'm Natalie."

"I'm very familiar with these pots, Natalie. I actually have a couple of them in my house."

"Really? So, can you give me some tips, then?"

"No, I don't think I can. Your design is flawless. This is going to be an exciting artifact."

"After we paint it, we're going to put it in a fire and everything to get soot all over it."

Kim nodded. "Exactly right. Randi knows how it's done."

Kim turned to look at Randi then. Looking into her eyes with their slight, characteristic squint, Randi felt the residual anger from Sunday draining out of her.

"Okay, kids," Randi said, "let's go."

After they had all filed out the door into the custody of their teacher, she returned to Kim, who stood waiting in front of the diorama.

"Randi," Kim began, "I want to apologize for the way I acted Sunday. It was stupid and I didn't mean it."

"Okay," Randi said, softening even more.

"I'm grateful that you intervened with Blair. Obviously, I was incapacitated and needed the help."

"No hard feelings," Randi said, thankful for Kim's change of heart. For the first time, she seemed vulnerable. Randi always responded positively to that. Kim looked really cute today, she thought, remembering how she had pressed herself against Randi and demanded a kiss. Sloppy drunk, she had not been the least bit kissable, but today, sober and apologetic, smiling with an edge of timidity, Kim seemed more attractive than she ever had.

"That makes me feel a lot better, thanks." Kim sounded genuinely relieved.

Briefly, Randi considered asking her to dinner. But then she thought better of it. She didn't want her to think she was being asked on a date. And, more importantly, Randi had to resist thinking that way about Kim. She was an interesting woman, but she was only in town for a short time, and Randi wasn't interested in a short-term relationship. She wasn't sure that she was ready for any kind of relationship, but when she was, it would have to be a serious one. Besides, she thought, there was no reason to think Kim was interested in her, despite her behavior Saturday night. Randi knew well how alcohol affected the libido.

Kim was an ambitious academic who held herself above the place and people that were integral to Randi's life. Randi was sure that she looked down on everyone in Yuma. In her eyes, the town probably looked squalid and the people seemed pitiable. No doubt she was anxiously looking forward to the day she could leave this place behind. If she really knew all about me, Randi thought, she'd be contemptuous. I'm just another one of the low-lifes in a low-life town. That's how she would see it. I definitely don't need anybody looking down their nose at me. I've done enough of that myself.

So Randi gave up the idea of dinner. Besides, Danya was waiting at home for her to provide some evening entertainment. That was a lot harder to do now than it had been a few years ago. In the old days, any bar would have provided all the diversion they required.

"Anything else?" Randi asked.

Kim shook her head. "No. Just that."

"Okay. See you later, then."

When Randi arrived home, she was surprised to find the place sparkling clean and smelling of something tomatoey and cheesy. Danya didn't cook. At least she never had in all the years that Randi had known her. But she was in the kitchen peering into the oven. The dishes were all washed and put away. The floor had been mopped. The place looked great.

"You're making dinner?" Randi asked.

Danya beamed as she pulled a large foil tray from the oven, her hands in quilted mitts. "It's a frozen lasagna. I remember how you like Italian food. This is a good one."

At first Randi felt threatened by this gesture of domesticity. She didn't want Danya to make herself at home, to find a role for herself in Randi's domain. But she was hungry, the lasagna looked good, and Danya was just trying to be helpful. She'd been home all day while Randi was at work. It was no surprise that she'd done some chores.

"Looks great," Randi said. "I'll go change."

"I'll set the table."

As Randi changed out of her uniform and into shorts and a T-shirt, she felt an old warm feeling of comfort having someone

117

greet her when she came home with a smile and an offer of food. It had been a long time since she'd been greeted by anyone other than Breeze. He was an excellent companion, but he had never produced a lasagna.

CHAPTER SEVENTEEN

Tuesday, while working at Site A, Kim reflected on her latest conversation with Randi and another failed attempt at friendship. She was disappointed that Randi seemed anxious to get rid of her. There was no hint that once the business at hand was taken care of, there might be any further reason for the two of them to spend any time together. At least she was consistent. Randi had never shown the least bit of interest in socializing one on one. Kim thought again of the Lone Ranger. "Lone" was a big part of that image, after all.

What difference did it make, anyway? She had now met quite a few people in this town. It wouldn't be long before she had some regulars to dine with. Darlene and Trina, for instance, were interesting and pleasant to be around. A couple of the others she had met at Blair's ranch, before getting drunk, held out some potential as friends.

So why am I not convincing myself, she wondered.

Midmorning, Flynn stopped by for a visit, sitting on his rock to observe. He asked Kim now and then for an explanation of one of the petroglyphs. He was particularly taken by one of the more distinctive designs on a boulder detached from the main outcrop. It was more detailed than most, comprised of several nested geometric shapes.

"We can't be sure, of course," Kim said. "But it might be the Thunder God. These concentric squares are the eyes, you see, and the jack-o-lantern style mouth here, full of pointy teeth, that represents the mountains."

Flynn knelt in front of the boulder, peering at it. "No kidding?"

"No kidding."

"How did you figure that out?"

"An interpretation like that comes from seeing a lot of similar images and from the mythology. Old stories that were passed down through the generations. They tell us that the Thunder God lived in the mountains because the people thought the mountains were the source of rain. So this god was extremely important."

"And stingy too," Flynn said, standing with an audible creak of his knees.

"Yes!" Kim laughed. "And that may be why this image is here, an homage to the Thunder God, a way of requesting rain or saying thank you for it."

"Never really thought about these much. Just old graffiti, I thought."

"In a way, they are. But they're more than that. Nobody really knows what these things mean. The idea of the Thunder God, for example, is just a guess. Usually, I try to avoid forming any opinions about what they mean because that would get in the way. I like to just let them speak for themselves."

He nodded, thoughtfully. "So, if this is a prayer to the Thunder God, then you could say this place is a kind of temple?"

"Yes, you could say that. Obviously, it's a sacred place. But all of these images are not necessarily spiritual. They could be much more practical. Like signposts of some sort, marking the way to a water supply, a food supply, an astrological observance. Some people think they're territorial markers. Or they tell a story, like a historical tableau. Or they could just be doodles. Whatever they meant to their creators, they're centuries old, and therefore very valuable."

"The older the better," said Flynn. "Like me, eh?" He winked at Kim, his gap tooth showing prominently.

She smiled. "Right. The older the better, although there are two inscriptions from nineteenth-century Europeans. Those are interesting too, to historians."

"Show me," said Flynn, jumping off his rock.

Kim took him around the east side of the outcrop and indicated where somebody named C. E. Hendy had neatly carved his name and the date, 1860. A similar inscription in block letters was nearby, Julius Salvatore, 1879.

"Nineteenth-century graffiti!" Flynn pronounced. "So these are worth something too?"

"Yes, they're a record of at least two people who came through here early on."

"So, who were those guys?"

"No idea. I haven't done any research into that. Settlers or prospectors."

"Suppose that Hendy guy is the one the wash over there is named for?" Flynn gestured toward the east.

"I'm assuming that. Maybe he worked a mine over there. Might have even tried to homestead if he had a crazy streak in him."

Flynn grinned knowingly, then returned to his rock where he remained until the three of them walked back to the road for lunch.

"We've got something for you," Kim said, retrieving an eight-by-ten color print from the pickup. It was the best of the photos Ramon had taken of him. It showed him grinning, his head uncovered, his bald spot shining brightly, standing in front of a symbol-covered panel of the outcrop.

Flynn took it, grimacing with bashful delight.

"I'll hang this up," he said. "I don't think I've seen a picture of myself since I was a kid."

Flynn left with his photo. After lunch, Kim and Ramon returned to their methodical routine. Although she had told Flynn that she tried not to apply an interpretation to the symbols, it was hard not to speculate to some degree. The naturalistic images, like birds, people and animals, were obvious, not so much for why they were there, but at least for what they represented. The other symbols, though, were the ones that sent her mind wandering. There were things that looked like ladders, meandering lines, circles, shields, fish bones, links in a chain. If these were maps of some sort, a zigzaggy line could be a boundary or a river. What appeared to be random dots might be celestial objects, a constellation, for instance, that could be used for night travelers to orient themselves. These were the kinds of thoughts Kim allowed herself while cataloguing the symbols. These speculations, though, didn't make their way into the official reports.

This place was full of mysteries. One of the biggest mysteries, and one that she would not even attempt to answer, was what had happened to the Hohokam. By 1450, they had disappeared from the Sonoran Desert, had abandoned their cultural centers completely. Nobody could really explain that. After more than a thousand years of living here successfully, their story simply ended. That was even before the Spanish arrived. There were several hypotheses, but none of them, alone, was convincing. That's the thing about these ancient civilizations, Kim thought, they left so little of themselves behind. Reconstructing their history was largely a matter of conjecture, using the few shreds of evidence there were. These people had no interest in leaving any clues for some future investigator to find. This rock art, for instance, wasn't put here for Kim to translate six hundred years into the future.

Modern societies, by comparison, were perpetually thinking about the legacy of the human race with their time capsules and written histories and messages broadcast into the furthest reaches of the galaxy with the hope that someone might someday answer. It was becoming more and more true that nothing humans ever did or said would be lost, that every story of every person would be told and recorded for all time. That impulse extended back in time as far as human beings could make it go. It was retroactive. Even now, there were people all over the globe transcribing or scanning every document ever written, from ancient tax lists to royal decrees to the last will and testament of an ordinary citizen who died in a Scottish village in 1622, everything, in fact, that anyone could lay their hands on.

And she, of course, was doing the same thing right here. Someone in the fifteenth century had stood in this spot scratching stone against stone to convey some message to other members of the tribe. Kim and others like her were attempting to preserve that message for all time. Why? Whatever the purpose of the message had been at the time, it was no longer meaningful to anyone. If it said, for instance, here is the way to California, nobody needed it anymore. Now they had Interstate 8. But everything she had ever been taught told her that preserving this message was valuable, even if, ironically, they never could figure out what the message was.

Some people hypothesized that these symbols were used in vision quests, that a shaman would draw them or just look at them to lead him through the spiritual journey. Sometimes Kim thought that if she stared hard enough at them, they would somehow come to life and reveal their tale, like a cartoon. The snakes would slither and the dancers would dance and the deer would bound out of the scene. But such a thing never happened, of course, except briefly in her mind.

Kim noticed that she was no longer in the shade, that the sun's position had shifted and she would need to move. She looked up to note the position of the sun. Just there at the edge of the outcrop was a person, kneeling and facing her. A wave of adrenaline surged through her. Staring up, she held her hand to her forehead to shade her eyes, but the figure was in front of the sun, so she could see only a profile, no details.

She looked around to see Ramon several feet downslope, concentrating on his laptop screen. He had his earphones on and wouldn't hear her if she called out. She stood up and moved into the shade so she could get a better look. As she did so, the figure changed shape, moving from a kneeling to standing position. It was a girl, she saw, a dark-haired girl of about eleven or twelve.

"Hey," she called up. "What are you doing here?"

As soon as she spoke, the girl disappeared over the back edge of the rocks. Kim followed quickly, running around the end of the outcrop and down into the wash, then up the other side. The girl was running away from her across the open desert. Kim ran after her. Her hiking boots, though great for walking in the desert, were not well suited for this chase.

"Stop!" Kim called.

The girl didn't slow or turn, but Kim was running faster than she was, so she kept up pursuit, thinking that she would overtake her if she could do it before she got winded. As the girl ran up a slight rise, Kim hit a hole, an animal burrow of some kind, and flew forward into the ground, her hands slamming hard into the gravel. She cried out in surprise and pain, looking up to see the girl halting at the top of the rise, looking back at her for a few seconds. Then she disappeared over the other side.

"Shit!" Kim exclaimed, wincing and pulling her left hand up to see that it was scraped and bleeding. Noticing a stabbing pain in her right leg, she sat up and found that there were several cactus needles stuck in her shin. The culprit, a large prickly pear, stood inches away. She carefully moved away from it, then sat still, looking at her injuries. She pulled tentatively on one of the cactus spines, which sent a searing pain through her leg. She immediately stopped tugging. The stinging in her leg seemed to worsen as the pain in her hand diminished. She finally got to her feet and scanned the horizon. Nothing stirred.

Then she heard Ramon calling her name, sounding slightly

panicked. He came into view on the bank of the wash.

"Here!" she hollered, waving. He saw her and started walking rapidly toward her. She walked toward him as well, limping, since each step she took caused a series of shooting pains in her leg.

"What happened?" he asked.

"I saw a girl watching us. Just up on top of the outcrop. She ran and I chased her, but I fell and lost her." She pointed to the needles sticking out of her leg. "Hit a cactus."

Ramon whistled at the sight. "I think there's a pair of pliers in the truck," he said. "We should pull those out. Can you walk okay?"

"Yes. Just a little painful."

On the way back to the road, Ramon said, "You saw a girl? You mean a little girl?"

"Right. About eleven, twelve. When I called to her, she took off."

"Are you sure you didn't imagine it? You know how far we are from any houses. Are you getting overheated?"

It wasn't that hot, Kim thought, but she had been daydreaming at the time, thinking about vision quests. Could she have imagined it? Could she have been chasing a mirage? The girl, from what she could see, could have been an Indian. She had straight, dark hair and a round face. Had her mind summoned up some ancient spirit who had gone through a ceremonial rite of passage here hundreds of years ago?

Once they reached the truck, Ramon took the lid off the water jug and instructed Kim to immerse her leg in the water.

"Soften up your skin," he explained, "so they'll come out easier. Usually we use olive oil, but we don't have any here."

Kim leaned against the tailgate with one leg in the water jug. Ramon cleaned her wounded hands, which didn't look as serious with the blood and dirt removed. He then applied antiseptic and a bandage to the left hand, the one that had taken the biggest hit. He worked silently and methodically, touching her with unhurried gentleness. Once her hands were tended to, she removed her leg from the water jug and sat on the tailgate while he pulled the spines from her shin with a pair of pliers, extracting them smoothly and cleanly one by one. She sat with her eyes closed and her teeth clamped tightly together, determined not to yelp.

"These aren't so bad," Ramon said. "Lucky you didn't run into a cholla."

When the last of the needles was out, Kim sat looking at the red welts on her leg while Ramon packed up the gear.

He drove home, tuning the radio to his favorite pop station, while Kim sat looking silently out across the landscape, watching the dancing heat waves and wondering who or what she had been chasing.

CHAPTER EIGHTEEN

"What do you want to do tonight?" Danya asked Randi as they put the dishes in the dishwasher.

"I thought I'd go to an AA meeting," Randi said. "Why don't you come with me?"

"Oh, I don't think so." Danya shook her head and scowled. "Why do you still go? You haven't had a drink in four years. When are you going to be done with that?"

"Never." Randi laughed. "It's an ongoing commitment."

"But at some point you ought to be able to say, Hooray for me. I did it! I'm a success."

"Sure, in a way. I don't go to the meetings just for me anymore. There are always new people, the ones who struggle with it every day. They need the moral support and they need to see examples of people who've made it through the worst part."

"Oh, so you're a role model." There was a mocking tone in her voice.

"To some people. Somebody needs to be there for them, to have faith in them. That's what did it for me. I couldn't have done it without those people, without their trust. Now, it's just good reinforcement. As long as I go to meetings, I know I won't drink."

"And that's another thing," Danya objected. "What's the big deal if you do have a drink? You twelve-steppers act like if you have one drink, you've ruined everything and you have to go back and start all over again. Why not just have a drink, enjoy it, and go on being a fine, upstanding citizen? It's not like one drink is going to hurt you as long as you don't let it get out of hand."

Randi looked at Danya for a moment, realizing how little she understood about sobriety, Randi's type of sobriety at least. "How long since you had a drink?"

"Couple of weeks."

"What made you stop?"

Danya averted her eyes. "Oh, you know," she said evasively. "All the usual reasons. Tired of feeling lousy in the morning."

There was something that didn't feel right about this picture. Danya was hiding something, Randi thought, which wasn't like her. "Why don't you come to a meeting with me," she said. "See what it's like."

"It's like going to fucking church. It's not for me. I'm doing just fine on my own."

"Okay," Randi relented. "This works for me, but it's not the only way."

"Right. It isn't." Danya had become defensive.

Randi grabbed their water glasses from the table and placed them in the top rack of the dishwasher.

"Hey, why don't we go bowling?" Danya suggested. "I'm no better at it than I was before, but it was always fun anyway. Maybe I can even keep the ball in the lane when I'm sober."

Before Randi could answer, the phone rang. She picked it

up in the kitchen while Danya finished loading the dishes. It was Kim.

"Hey, Tilley," she said. "What's up?"

Randi saw the look of suspicious curiosity on Danya's face before she turned to wipe down the sink.

"We had a little incident at the site today," Kim said. "Ramon thinks I'm hallucinating, but I saw a girl of about eleven or twelve out there. She ran and I chased her. Unfortunately, I fell and she got away."

"Are you okay?"

"I am now. Ramon had to pull some cactus spines out of my leg, but I think he got them all."

"Ouch!"

"Oh, yeah, that put an end to our work day."

Kim laughed, so Randi laughed too, figuring it was okay.

"Did you see any vehicles out there?" Randi asked.

"No. Nobody came out today."

"There's no way a kid could be out there unless she was seriously lost. She would have had to walk for twenty or more miles. I can ask the sheriff if there are any reports of missing children in the county. I haven't heard of any, though, and normally we would know about something like that. It would be a big deal."

"I didn't get a great look at her, but she could have been Indian."

"Even the closest reservation homes are too far for a kid to wander. Maybe Ramon's right. Maybe the glyphs are getting to you."

"I don't know. I've never been prone to hallucinations."

"No, I wouldn't expect you to be. So coolheaded."

Randi walked into the living room to escape the proximity of Danya, whose hackles were up. Randi easily recognized that old look of suspicion.

"Do you think so?" Kim asked, sounding flirtatious. "Do you think of me as coolheaded?"

"Absolutely. As together as they come. Like a scientist."

"That's good, because that's what I am. You too."

"Me too, what? Coolheaded or a scientist?"

"Both."

She doesn't know me very well, Randi thought, hasn't seen beneath the surface. "Thanks."

As if she were reminded then to be coolheaded, Randi returned to her professional mode and asked, "Anything else going on out there?"

"Did you know that there are a couple of eighteenth-century names on those rocks?"

"Sure, I knew that. One of them's Hendy, right?"

"Yes. The same Hendy, I suppose."

"One and the same. I checked that out a while back. C. E. Hendy. That's Charles Edward. There isn't much information on him. Just another fortune seeker, I guess, whose name got stuck on a wash. That would have been sometime before Wolff came through and made that wash all famous with his buried treasure."

"What about Julius Salvatore?"

"Checked him out too. An Italian con artist. He got into quite a bit of trouble over in California, swindling folks out of their pocket change. Must have had a big head too because he carved his name in quite a few places in Nevada, California and Arizona."

"Salvatore was here," Kim said with a pronounced Italian accent.

Randi laughed, then they said goodbye. Danya was leaning against the kitchen counter, a pouty look on her face.

"That was a colleague," Randi said, feeling like she had to explain. "Just business."

"Didn't sound like business. Sounded like you were having a nice friendly chat."

Randi cleared her throat, not happy about the irrational feeling of guilt that was coming over her, then said, "I think we need to talk. About your plans."

At that, Danya looked disappointed, as if she had been hoping to postpone the reckoning indefinitely. She sat in one of the kitchen chairs, then asked, "What do you want to talk about?"

"For one thing, when are you going home?"

"Uh, I was hoping to stay here a while. If you want me to pay you rent—"

"No, that's not what I'm getting at. You can't stay here permanently. When you showed up, it was just for a visit, remember? You need to go back home."

Danya gazed silently at the table for a moment, then said, "I can't go home. I don't have a home to go to. I was living with someone. We broke up. It was her place. I don't have anywhere else to go."

So you came here to be rescued, Randi thought, trying to steel herself against the puppydog look that Danya gave her. "What about a job? Don't you have a job to go back to?"

Danya shook her head.

"Then you'll need to get one," Randi said, "unless you've become independently wealthy since we last met."

"Oh, yeah, that's a good one!"

"Get online and search the want ads in Phoenix." Randi heard her own voice and thought she sounded stern, like an unhappy parent.

"What about around here?" Danya asked, looking hopeful.

Randi stiffened, realizing she wanted Danya out of her space. She didn't want her staying here, letting the old life seep into the new life. They needed to remain distinctly separate. "There's nothing here for you. Very few opportunities. You'll have a lot more options in Phoenix. You can stay here a while longer, but you've got to find yourself a job and get back home. You're clean and sober now, so holding a job shouldn't be the challenge it used to be."

Danya smiled, stood, and came over to Randi, kissing her on the forehead. "Thank you, Rocky. You've always been so good to me. I know I don't deserve you."

Randi wasn't happy with this situation, but the truth was that Danya wasn't causing her any real trouble. She wasn't drinking and she wasn't stealing anything. After the first night, she had given up the idea of reconnecting romantically with Randi. At least, she had not made another move like that. Danya was being unpredictably well behaved. And Randi was enjoying the company, which surprised her. She'd been alone here for a long time and had gotten used to it, had thought she preferred it. Everything was under control, her control. She needed that kind of control, or thought she did, to keep herself safe. So far, Danya hadn't threatened that security, but Randi was wary of her just the same. In her experience, there was no one more messy and destructive than Danya. Of course, Randi knew and admitted her part in that. In a way, she owed her a chance at redemption. If Randi could make a new life for herself, maybe Danya could too. If she needed a little help on her way to that new life, why not help her?

"So," Randi said, "put on your bowling shoes. Let's go out and have some fun."

CHAPTER NINETEEN

Kim and Ramon worked steadily and quietly side by side for the next day and a half without incident and without seeing anyone. Each time Kim heard a sound, she looked around, half expecting to see the mysterious girl again. But there was no sign of anyone, not even Flynn or Randi.

"Let's break for lunch," she said around one o'clock, and they walked together back to the road. When they got to the truck, they discovered their lunch tote was missing.

"Are you sure we had it?" she asked Ramon.

"Yes. I remember putting it in this morning. I know it was here."

While looking for the lunch tote, Kim realized that their water can was also gone. They always kept a five-gallon plastic jug of water in the back and refilled their water bottles from that.

133

It was cinched in place with a canvas belt that now lay slack where the can had been.

"The water's gone too," Kim said, trying not to sound as alarmed as she felt.

"We've been robbed!" Ramon stood scanning the landscape as if he might get a glimpse of the culprit.

There was no other explanation, which meant that there was someone out here, someone they hadn't seen who had managed to slip in, take their things, and slip out again unnoticed. Since they were a quarter mile from the road, that would not have been so difficult, but if there had been a vehicle, they would have known it. The thief had been on foot. Kim inspected the rest of their belongings, but found nothing else missing. Whoever it was had only been interested in the most essential of items, food and water.

"I think we need to get out of here," Kim said. "Let's get our stuff and go back to town."

After treating Ramon to a restaurant meal, she dropped him off and swung by BLM to consult with Randi. Once she explained what had happened, Randi looked worried and said, "That sounds like a dangerous situation. If there's somebody out there desperate enough to steal your food and water, then it may not be safe for you to be working out there. Tomorrow's Saturday. I'll take Breeze out and we'll see if we can track them down."

The next day, Randi picked up Kim in her truck and they drove out to the site. If there were people nearby, Randi assured her, Breeze would locate them.

While they were waiting for Breeze to turn something up, Kim snapped some photos of the emerging wildflowers and a brilliant blooming ocotillo. Every day now the desert became more colorful as spring unfolded across the landscape with swaths of red, yellow, purple and white. She had been waiting for this. There was nothing like the desert in bloom. She took a few pictures of Randi as well, a lovely woman sitting on a rock in the sunshine, one knee tucked under her chin, her eyes shaded by her hat brim, appearing to be lost in thought.

Breeze returned at last, ready to lead them to his discovery. Randi hooked his lead on and then, to Kim's horror, took a pistol out of her pack and tucked it into her belt. Kim heard herself gasp aloud.

"I just want to be prepared," Randi said. "There are some dangerous people out here and they're all carrying guns."

"Maybe we shouldn't be doing this," Kim suggested, terrified at the thought of a shoot-out.

"If it looks like there's going to be trouble, we'll get out fast. I'll call the sheriff."

They followed Breeze across the open desert for a quarter mile, further away from the road and the safety of the truck. He led them to a shallow ravine and an open mine adit, a dark entrance about three feet high and two feet wide. That's where they stopped.

"I know this mine," whispered Randi. "It's abandoned."

"How far in does it go?"

"About thirty feet." Randi swung her pack off and fished out a flashlight. Leaving her pack on the ground, she moved toward the mine opening. "Hello!" she called loudly. "Anybody here?"

There was silence. At the edge of the opening, she sent Breeze in, letting go of his lead, and then shined the flashlight inside.

From inside the mine, they heard Breeze bark and then they heard a flurry of Spanish, a woman's voice. Kim felt the hair on her arms stand at attention. Randi called Breeze, her voice urgent, and he came running out of the mine to sit beside her. She glanced at Kim and pulled her gun out of her belt. "Stay here," she said.

"Oh, God, Randi, you're not going in there, are you?" Kim whispered frantically. "Let's call the sheriff."

Randi hesitated and might have agreed, but just then a girl came running out of the mine, the same girl Kim had seen a couple of days before, her clothes and face grimy with dirt. From inside, they heard the woman's frenzied voice crying, "Nita! Nita!"

The girl stopped in front of Kim and stared at her, her eyes dark and wide. "*Puede ayudar?*" she asked, her voice insistent.

Kim glanced at Randi, who quietly translated. "She's asking if you're here to help."

"*Sí*," Kim said, turning back to the girl and smiling as benignly as she could. Then she reached out and took hold of the girl's hand. The girl didn't smile, but she hung on tightly.

Randi called into the mine. "*Todos afuera! Nadie les hará daño!*" There was no response. Randi called into the mine again, more emphatically this time. A moment passed before a teenage boy appeared at the opening, emerging into sunshine and blinking his eyes, his hands raised above his head in surrender. Randi, who had been aiming her gun at the mine entrance, now lowered it. She spoke to the boy in Spanish and he answered, lowering his hands and pointing to the mine's dark entrance.

"His parents are inside," Randi said. "His father is hurt."

With that, Randi went inside, Kim behind her, and at the far end of the tunnel, in the near darkness, they found a man lying on the ground with a woman sitting beside him. The woman looked frightened and angry at the same time. The man was barely conscious, one leg of his trousers stiff with dried blood. His head was lying on a bunched-up piece of clothing, his eyes half-open.

Randi put the safety back on her gun and returned it to her waistband, then she knelt beside the man and felt his forehead with the back of her hand. She spoke to the woman gently, but her voice was full of authority. Gradually the woman's defiance diminished and gave way to quiet sobs. Now, Kim realized, she had really given up. These were tears of grief. Whatever hope she had been holding out for a way to salvage their dream of America, she let go of in that moment. Kim felt a heaviness descend on her heart. She held the hand of the little girl more securely.

Randi took out her pocketknife and cut the man's trouser leg open. Kim saw her wince when she saw what was under the cloth. "He's been shot," she explained to Kim. "The operation must have gone bad somehow. They're not going to tell us what happened, but their *pollero* is long gone. They've been left out here to die, basically."

"*Pollero?*"

"Chicken handler. It's what they call the guys who take the illegals to their destination. The illegals are the chickens. It's a really ugly business. These people pay a lot of money to get led through here, to get to a safe house, then on to somewhere else to get a minimum wage job, if they're lucky. The truck breaks down, something else goes wrong, they end up stranded in the desert and they die. Since they've tightened up the border so much around San Diego, we've been getting more and more of this here. But, here too, the danger is greater than it's ever been."

"Danger of getting caught, you mean?"

"No. Danger of dying. These people are literally running through here with nothing—no food, no water, no money. And they're afraid. They get lost, they get left behind. Sometimes the *polleros* just abandon them once they get them over the border. People are found dead out here. Happens every year."

"How long have they been here?" Kim asked.

"She says three days right here. I don't know how long since they crossed the border. This wound is infected."

As Kim's eyes became adjusted to the dimness, she saw Ramon's lunch tote and their water jug in the back of the mine.

Randi spoke again to the man's wife, who was still sobbing. By her tone, Kim could tell that Randi was trying to reassure the woman that things would be okay. Kim was struck again by Randi's competence, her ease at taking control of a situation. There were times, Kim thought, that she wore that white hat very well.

Recalling the image of Randi tossing Minnie down Pinkie's bar and laughing about it, she shook her head. She couldn't reconcile these different characters. There was obviously something she didn't understand about what had happened that night.

Randi led the way out of the mine and Kim followed, the girl still clinging to her hand.

"We'll need to get him to a hospital," Randi said. "Let's go back to the truck and call the sheriff."

"Can we leave them here? They won't make a run for it?"

"That guy is going nowhere. The boy may be able to carry a five-gallon jug of water, but he can't carry his father. And I don't think little Nita here is going to leave your side for a while."

Randi smiled at the girl, whose expression remained passive as it had been the whole time. The three of them walked back to the road.

"What's going to happen to them?" Kim asked.

"Eventually, they'll be going home, back to Mexico."

Kim knew very little about this kind of situation, but she imagined that the family had paid a lot of money to be smuggled over the border, money that was gone, money that might represent their entire savings. "It's sad," she said.

"Yes, it is," Randi agreed. "But at least her father isn't going to die now, thanks to you."

The places Kim had worked before had never been this remote, this untamed. It was beautiful and alluring, but also scary, all of a sudden.

"Randi," Kim asked, tentatively, "have you ever seen a dead body out here?"

"Once," Randi said. "I was out here with Matt last year and we came across one, a young man who must have died of heat stroke. He'd been dead about a week."

The two of them walked silently the rest of the way to the truck.

"Thanks for coming out," Kim said, "I was a little afraid to come back here after our stuff was stolen."

"I don't blame you." Randi gave Breeze a treat and patted his flank.

"Seems like you're always coming to my rescue," Kim said.

Randi grinned. "Seems like you always need rescuing."

Two hours later, the Mexican family was gone, taken to town by the sheriff, and Kim had collected her containers from the mine. The little girl had been reluctant to give up Kim's hand when the time came, for some reason feeling safe in her care in this world of great unknowns. Perhaps she had seen something while watching her at the petroglyph site that had reassured her that Kim could be trusted. Kim gave her back to her mother in the sheriff's car and gave her a parting smile, her only real means of communicating with the child.

It was just around lunchtime when they got back to town. Kim knew by now that there was no point sitting around idly waiting for Randi to ask her to lunch. The thought didn't seem to occur to her.

"Let me buy you lunch," she said, "to thank you for all your help."

"I can't really spare the time today," Randi said. "I have papers to grade and a bunch of chores that I won't have time for tomorrow because of the walk-a-thon. That's going to take up a good part of the day. Busy weekend. But, thanks."

Kim was disappointed. "You know, I sort of forgot that you teach."

"This is my third semester at AWC."

"How do you like it?"

"I love it. The students are really interested, most of them. We have a good time. Most of the students are older than what you get at the university, I'm sure, but they're enthusiastic and I get to talk about rocks."

"I'd settle for enthusiasm any day. If my students stay awake, I feel lucky, but part of that's due to the size of classes. Too many students to interact very closely with them. It's more of a formal lecture type of setting. How many students in your classes?"

"They start out about thirty, thirty-five, but the drop rate is high. I end up with about fifteen by the end, the fifteen good ones, so, yes, it's very personal. Conversational by the end of the semester. Right now, though, we're just starting, so I have quite a few papers to get done."

Kim nodded. "No TA's, I guess?"

"No, nothing like that."

"How did you get started doing that?" she asked. "Sounds like you weren't here long before taking that job."

"No, I wasn't. One thing I've discovered here is that a professional person with a willingness to get involved is really in demand. If you want to contribute to this community, there are more opportunities here than there are in a lot of other places, Phoenix, for instance, and I'm sure to an even greater extent in Sacramento. I was asked one time to speak to an environmental technology class, as the BLM geologist, and the next thing I knew, the department chairman called me and asked me if I wanted to teach. I guess he thought I was okay."

Kim said nothing, thinking about what Randi was saying, thinking too that she sounded rather humble for a change. That was definitely refreshing.

"There are other things like that, too," Randi continued. "I never felt so much a part of a place as I do here. I drive through town and always see people I know. I feel connected to the land, even. I suppose that's because of my job. After all, most of it is BLM land, so it's natural to feel some responsibility for it, but that feeling extends to the town and the people. It was less than a year after I moved here that I started to feel that way, and it's just grown ever since."

Randi stopped the truck in front of Kim's trailer.

"That's really nice," Kim said.

"Yes, it is. I like the feeling of being a part of something, not just an anonymous cog in the machine."

Suddenly, Randi didn't seem much of a hick. She seemed, in fact, like an intelligent, interesting professional woman with an admirable sense of community. It's the place that misled me, Kim thought, the strange environment of the desert and a border town, a place she had not understood very well and had made a lot of assumptions about. Well, that and the cowboy hat and boots, too. Those were not things she was accustomed to seeing on the sort of woman she would consider her type. Where she came from, women didn't dress like that unless they were going to a rodeo. By "her type," she cautioned herself, she meant the type of woman she could be friends with.

Randi didn't seem that interested in being friends, though

she seemed more than willing to be helpful. She showed up when called, yes, just like the Lone Ranger, and when the danger had passed, she was long gone before you'd gotten a clue about who it really was under that mask. And, Kim thought with dismay, *I'm not even Tonto. I'm that hapless woman with the long skirt who falls down in the dirt when she tries to run away from the bad guys.*

Kim got out of the truck and shut the door. "Thanks again," she said through the open window.

Although Randi just nodded, Kim's imagination had her touch the brim of her hat in one of those subtle cowboy-style salutes and say, "You're mighty welcome, ma'am."

Kim sighed, watching Randi drive off.

CHAPTER TWENTY

A voice mail message from Randi asked Kim to stop by the office when she got back to town after work.

When she arrived, she found Randi at her desk with a yellowish map spread out on top of it.

"Hi," Randi said, looking up and smiling brightly. "Thanks for coming by. You remember asking me the name of that wash behind Black Point?"

"Sure," Kim said, noting the undercurrent of excitement in Randi's voice.

"I've been doing some research. On the new maps, that wash doesn't even show, or when it does, it has no name. So I decided to try some older maps. You'll never guess what I've discovered."

Randi motioned Kim to come around the desk, then pointed

to a spot on the map, an obviously old, not altogether formal looking map. "Here's Black Point. Right about here is where your Site A would be. So, this drainage beside it is the wash in question."

Randi pointed to a thin line that ran crookedly down toward the Gila River. That line was labeled Hendy Wash.

Kim looked up, connecting with Randi's eyes. "I don't understand."

"This map is dated 1888. I've checked several already, some older, some newer. Most of the maps after this date show this other wash as Hendy Wash." Randi pointed to another thin line draining toward the Gila. "That's the one we know by that name today. But all of the older maps consistently identify the Black Point wash as Hendy."

Randi waited for this news to make sense to Kim, a look of expectancy on her face.

"Wow," Kim said, finally.

"Uh-huh." Randi grinned.

"Wow," Kim said again, the impact of Randi's discovery becoming clearer.

"Wow is right! It's not uncommon for these kinds of things to happen, especially in places like this where people didn't form settlements. No locals around to verify place names. The real Hendy Wash, the original one anyway, is the one behind the petroglyphs. That wash runs about five miles north to south, starting a mile up from Black Point and draining down to the Gila."

"That makes the inscription even more understandable, the C. E. Hendy."

"Right. That could even be the reason it was named Hendy Wash in the first place, because his name was there by the time people started coming through in numbers."

"So the gold, the Wolff gold, is buried there, right there in our wash?"

Randi flashed her an amused smile. "If the legend is true and nobody has found it, yes. All of these fortune hunters have been looking in the wrong place all these years." Randi folded the map.

"Incredible!"

"You can't tell anybody about this, you understand?"

"Why not?"

"Everybody who's been out here for the last twenty years to find that gold would rush back to look in your wash, which would bring them right to the petroglyphs. They'd be swarming all around there. We can't let that happen. That site has remained protected because there was nothing around it of interest to anybody. Buried treasure is of interest to just about everybody."

Kim nodded. "I understand. Are there any palm trees in this wash, the real Hendy Wash?"

"I don't know. I haven't looked."

"But you're about to, aren't you?" Kim asked.

"How could I not?"

"Right. And you're going to take me with you."

"And why would I do that, Tilley?" Randi asked, obviously teasing.

"It's because of me that you figured this out. I should get a cut of the spoils."

"You know, if we did find the gold, it belongs to the government."

"Oh, sure, I know that. I just meant that I should be a part of it, the fun. Imagine finding a buried treasure. It's just so cool."

"Meet me at my house at seven tomorrow morning. We're going for a hike."

Just then Steve stuck his head in and said, "Hey, Kim, I thought I saw you come in. How about doing us a little favor? When you're done here, I need an archaeologist up front."

Kim laughed. "Really? Like, is there an archaeologist in the house?"

He grinned. "Something like that."

"Okay. I think we're done here."

Randi nodded.

Steve ducked back out. Kim whispered, "I'll see you

tomorrow," to Randi before following him to the reception area where a woman and a girl stood waiting.

"Here she is!" Steve announced heartily, his ruddy face beaming as if he had just pulled a rabbit out of his hat.

He introduced her as "Dr. Kimberly Gatlin, an archaeologist from the University of California." The woman was Beverly Thompson and her daughter was Constance, but the girl, who looked about fourteen, informed Kim politely that she was called Connie.

"How can I help you?" Kim asked.

"I found an arrowhead," the girl announced, losing her composure completely and wriggling all over.

Steve handed Kim a piece of paper covered with an image. "Thought you might be able to tell her something about it. Connie and her mother have been extremely responsible. They left the point where it was and took photos."

"That's what Mr. Mendoza told us to do," Connie said.

"Mr. Mendoza?" asked Kim.

"That's Matt," Steve explained. "Matt Mendoza."

Kim nodded.

"He went with us on a field trip to Casa Grande over a year ago," Mrs. Thompson explained. "Connie loved it and she has been looking for Indian artifacts ever since. This is the first one, though, that she's found."

"I came in here to show him," Connie said.

"Lucky for you," Steve told her, "you get Dr. Gatlin instead."

"Casa Grande is quite a place, isn't it?" Kim said, recalling the crumbling walls of pink caliche. "Do you remember what Indians lived there?"

"Hohokam," Connie replied instantly.

"Yes." Kim studied the image on the printout for a moment. "This point is probably a dart head, not an arrowhead. How big is it?"

Connie held her fingers about two inches apart and looked expectantly up at Kim.

145

"If it's that big, it is most certainly not an arrowhead. The arrows were small and light. Their tips were much smaller. Otherwise, the arrows would have been too heavy to travel very far."

"A dart?" Connie repeated. "Like a blowgun dart?"

Kim shook her head. "No. They threw it, like a small spear. This looks like a very fine specimen."

"Did they kill people with it?" Connie asked.

Kim smiled. "No. They hunted animals with it." She was fairly confident about the projectile. It was cream-colored rock, narrow and long with smooth edges, not serrated, so not the early period. "This is Hohokam and I'm guessing it's made of chert. But I can't be sure without looking at it in person."

"Do you want me to show you?" Connie asked excitedly.

"Sure." Kim turned to Steve. "I'll go take a look."

"Thanks," he said with a wink.

Good PR, that's what this was about, Kim understood, especially when someone actually obeyed the rules and left their find in place.

Kim followed Beverly's car to the site of the discovery beside a dirt road just outside the city limits. Connie leapt out of the car and ran to the spot, standing impatiently over her find. As Kim approached, Connie stood pointing at the ground. Kim knelt and picked up the object. She smiled up at Connie and said, "Now that is a beautiful specimen." Connie beamed.

Kim took a GPS reading and digital photos of the point. Then she took photos of Connie holding the point, and had Mrs. Thompson take a couple of pictures of the two of them. Then they put the point back where they'd found it and Kim thanked them both for being good citizens. Her mother seemed especially grateful for the attention and thanked Kim for taking time out for them.

"I'm so glad she got to meet you," Beverly Thompson said as Kim prepared to leave. "To see a woman in a professional position, I mean. She was already excited about archaeology, but you're the first female archaeologist she's met. It's just that much more inspiring."

146

"That's really nice to hear," Kim said, thinking about how important it was for everyone to have that one mentor or role model that sets you on your course, the pursuit of your lifelong passion. For Kim, that person had been the famous archaeologist Mary Leakey. When Kim was in high school, she had had a rare opportunity to hear Leakey speak. Her science teacher offered extra credit for anyone who attended the lecture, so several of them did. Listening to Leakey's description of her work at Olduvai Gorge, Kim's imagination was sparked. With an example like Mary Leakey standing before her eyes, what might have seemed like an impossible dream before became an attainable goal. But it didn't require someone as impressive as Mary Leakey, Kim knew, to inspire a child.

The next day Kim made an eight-by-ten print of one of the photos. In it, she stood beside Connie, her arm around the girl's shoulders. Connie was holding the dart point and beaming with pride. On one corner of the photo, she wrote, "Connie, congratulations on your first important discovery. Welcome to the profession. Kim Gatlin."

It would be something, she thought, if this girl actually did become an archaeologist. Kim hoped that she was going to cherish this photo, frame it, and hang it on her bedroom wall. And maybe some day she would show her grandchildren and say, "This is how it all began."

Kim slid the photo in a mailer and addressed it. It wasn't very likely that she would ever have children of her own. And her students were a little old, most of them, to inspire with awe in quite this way, with such a pure delight.

Perhaps I'll hang this photo on my own bedroom wall, too, she thought.

CHAPTER TWENTY-ONE

Danya carefully turned an egg with a spatula in gently simmering cooking oil. "You're going hiking?"

"Yes," Randi answered. "It'll be an all-day thing. If you didn't have that job interview, I'd ask you along. Do you have something to wear to that?"

"Sure. I have a nice blouse and some slacks. That'll work."

"What time is your interview?"

"One."

"So you'll need to leave here by ten, maybe a little earlier, to get to Phoenix by one. You should give yourself some leeway."

"Yeah, I know how long a drive it is." Danya sounded irritated as she removed the egg to a plate. "You want one egg or two?"

"Two, please. I'm going to be burning some energy today."

Danya cracked another egg into the pan. Randi pulled on her hiking boots and laced them tight.

"I hate to ask," Danya said, "but do you think you could give me a few bucks for gas?"

Randi stood and took a couple of twenties from her wallet, laying them on the table, thinking that Danya must have let herself get pretty close to bottom before turning up here if she couldn't even buy herself a tank of gas. Then she was reminded of Danya's offer the other day to pay rent and wondered if that had been completely hollow. She took another twenty out and laid it over the others. "Buy yourself lunch while you're there," she said.

Danya flashed her a grateful smile. "Speaking of lunch, should I pack you something for the trail?"

"No, thanks. Tilley's bringing lunch."

"Tilley? Isn't that the woman you were on the phone with the other night?"

"Yes, that's her. Her name is actually Kim. Tilley's just something I call her. Sort of a joke." Talking about Kim to Danya made Randi nervous. "She's an archaeologist I've been working with. There's something out there near her worksite that we need to check out."

"Is she a lesbian?" Danya asked this without turning away from her pan, obviously trying, but not succeeding, to sound nonchalant.

"Yes," Randi said, also trying to sound nonchalant. "But there's nothing between us."

Why do I feel like I have to say that? Randi asked herself with irritation.

Danya gave her a suspicious look as she slid the second egg from the frying pan onto a plate.

After breakfast, Randi wished Danya good luck with her interview and went out to get the truck ready. She didn't want to introduce Kim to Danya, especially since Danya was clearly about to go all jealous on her, so when Kim showed up at the curb, Randi met her there, ready to go. Breeze was ready too, jumping in and out of the front seat of the truck in anticipation. Kim looked cute in hiking boots, shorts and a T-shirt. She wore a sky blue handkerchief around her neck to protect herself from the sun.

Breeze sat between them as Randi drove and Kim applied sunscreen to her arms, legs and face.

It took them over forty-five minutes to reach the Gila River where Hendy Wash, the real Hendy Wash, emptied into it. Both of them wore light jackets against the morning chill. They pulled on their backpacks and hats, Randi her cowboy hat and Kim a straw one. With her sunglasses and hat on, she looked even cuter.

"Wolff Mine is just down river less than a half mile from here," Randi said. "That gives even more credence to this new information. From the mine, this is the nearest side stream. He wouldn't have wanted to carry the gold too far, but with a mule he could have taken it any distance up the canyon to bury it."

"So we're looking for palm trees, right?" Kim asked.

"Yes, but I'm not really expecting to see any. Native palms are pretty rare here. There's a grove of them to the northwest in Kofa Wildlife Refuge, and those are the only ones I've heard of. If there were ever any palms here, they would have been tucked away in some shady spot, something sheltered from the worst of the heat, near some reliable water source. The particular tree that Wolff mentioned would be long gone, so we're looking for a spot palms might have been able to inhabit, once upon a time."

Randi pulled a portable metal detector from her truck. "If we do find a likely spot," she said, "we can use this."

"Oh, good thinking."

The Gila River, lined with cottonwood and tamarisk, was dry, but still supported a fragile riparian habitat. Birdsong surrounded them as they started up the canyon. Even without the excuse of treasure hunting, Randi thought, this was going to be fun, a relaxing hike in the desert. They walked up the wash, following its turns as it headed up and away from the river through loose gravel and boulders.

Wherever the wash curved, they looked into protected corners for evidence of water, not necessarily visible water, but green plants to indicate the presence of water. The wash was shallow and didn't offer much protection for plants. The flora here was the same as it was outside of the wash—mesquite, brittlebush, cholla and beavertail cactus. So far, nothing of interest had revealed itself. The day was beautiful, though, with some wispy cloud action above and blooming wildflowers all around.

Kim had brought a camera and stopped occasionally to take pictures of flowers or an attractive vista. Randi looked up from searching the stream bed once to see Kim standing ahead of her with the camera aimed in her direction. She snapped a photo and smiled self-consciously before turning to continue up canyon.

Along the way, they scared up a roadrunner that took off straight down the center of the wash ahead of them. Breeze started after it at full tilt until Randi called to him sharply. He stopped and sat immediately, waiting for them.

"That's a good dog," observed Kim.

As the sun rose, Kim took off her windbreaker, rolled it up, and stuffed it in her backpack. Randi did the same. Their hike was mostly silent except for an occasional observation about an interesting rock or plant. There was nothing awkward about the silence. Randi was enjoying the peacefulness of the trek and the comfortable companionship. Kim seemed to be having a good time too.

About halfway along, Randi stopped to pull her rock hammer out of her pack and crack open a rock. She positioned it carefully and, with a single swing, broke it in half.

"Something of interest?" Kim asked.

"Yes," Randi said. "This rhyolite has unusually large feldspar phenocrysts. Very nice specimen."

Kim shook her head, obviously disappointed. Maybe she'd been expecting gold. Randi stood in the shade of the canyon wall to take a drink from her water bottle. "How far have we gone?" she asked.

Kim glanced at her GPS receiver. "Three miles."

151

"You've got your petroglyph site plugged into that, right?"

"Yes. It should be another mile up the wash."

"Let's stop there for lunch, then."

Kim nodded and they continued. Just a couple of minutes beyond that, Randi stopped again, for a plant this time. "Here's a cereus, I'm pretty sure."

Kim came over to look at the plant as Randi knelt beside it. There were three of those remarkable plants clustered together at the edge of the wash, just slender bare stems now, but, come summer, for one night only, a beautiful, fragrant white flower would bloom on that nondescript plant. Since first hearing about it from Bill, the BLM botanist, Randi had made a pact with herself to catch it blooming, to see for herself that single, ghostly bloom open in the dark and then close forever at sunrise. Few people ever witnessed that in the wild, she'd been told. Things like that happened in the desert. There was a lot of space. A lot of life went unobserved, quietly unfolding in its own private way, unobtrusive, but miraculous.

"There's another place I've seen them," Randi said, "west of Yuma in Rainbow Wash. This thing supposedly only blooms one night in the summer."

"For a rock girl, you know an awful lot about plants." Kim said.

"I hang around with a botanist," Randi explained. "They get pretty excited about this plant. People hardly ever get a chance to see its flower."

"Sounds like something worth waiting for. What did you call it?"

"Its common name is Arizona Queen of the Night."

"How romantic."

They continued walking. At a wide turn in the wash, they stopped to examine the debris at the outer edge as they had been doing at such spots. Randi switched on the metal detector and ran it over the gravel. A moment later it started beeping. She followed the signal to the spot of its loudest alarm. Kim came closer to watch.

"See if you can find anything there," Randi said.

Kim shoved some of the gravel aside with her boot, digging a shallow depression until she turned up a rusted tin can. She pulled it free of the gravel. Randi passed the metal detector over the spot again. It was silent.

"Oh, well," Kim said, leading the way forward.

At last Randi saw the familiar shape of the Black Point rock outcrop up ahead. They stopped to have lunch, sitting in the shade of the symbol-covered rocks.

"That's it, then," Randi said, "No palm trees here. This canyon is too shallow for a palm grove. There's no protection."

"There's still about a mile left."

"We'll finish it out, but Wolff wouldn't have needed to go that far from the river to bury his treasure. I don't think we're going to find anything." Randi was disappointed. She realized that she had really wanted to find the treasure, not just for the obvious reasons, but because pulling out a trick like that for Kim, to delight her, would have been fantastic.

Kim removed her hat and opened the lunch tote to produce a thermos of lemonade and two colorful salads—roasted chicken with tomatoes, basil and mozzarella, and a corkscrew pasta with steamed asparagus and olives, both from a downtown deli.

"Whoa!" Randi said when she saw them. "I was expecting PB & J."

Kim smiled a self-satisfied smile and poured two cups of lemonade. She then spooned a portion of each of the salads onto a plastic plate and passed it to Randi along with a plastic fork. Breeze lay down next to Randi, resting his head on her leg.

For the next few minutes, they were silent as they concentrated on lunch. Kim sat with her legs folded in the lotus position, holding her plate with one hand. A light sheen of perspiration coated her legs and arms. She wasn't looking at Randi. She was gazing at the rocks, at the petroglyphs. Randi took the opportunity to look at her unobserved, admiring her delicate neck and the crease on the left side of her mouth, more than usually pronounced as she chewed her food. Randi liked the way Kim's hair stuck to her forehead where her hatband had been. She liked the nearly straight line of her eyebrows. When she arched one or both of them, it made a considerable impact on an observer. Just then the left one did arch slightly as Kim looked at Randi and said, "You're not eating. Don't you like it?"

"Oh, no, I love it." Randi took a big forkful of pasta as if to prove it, realizing that she had almost been caught staring with what had to have been a stupid look on her face.

"This is such a peaceful place," Kim sighed.

"Yes," Randi said. "How is your survey going, by the way?"

"Good. Slow and careful."

"How much longer do you think you'll be out here?"

"Hard to say. I can leave whenever we finish, but I have to be back by the end of April. There's a conference I'm scheduled to attend. Actually, I'm one of the speakers, so there's no choice about being there. I don't think it will be a problem to finish by then. Besides, it will be too hot here to stay any longer than that."

"Right. Nobody's going to want to be out here after March. Other than Flynn. He's like a lizard. The heat doesn't seem to bother him. I guess he's adapted." Randi hesitated. "At this conference where you're speaking, is your subject going to be this site?"

"Yes. I've started putting the presentation together already. There are several of my colleagues who are anxious to see what's here, as you can imagine."

"I thought you were going to keep it under wraps?"

"These are all professionals. This isn't the general public we're talking about. They'll understand, and my department knows I'm here, of course. This isn't a secret mission I'm on. Besides, I think BLM is planning on opening this up sooner than you imagined. I wouldn't be surprised if they do it next winter. They were just waiting for a thorough survey. That's my guess."

"Too bad." Randi glanced up at the petroglyphs. "There's something in it for you then, after all, isn't there?"

"I hope so. I'm not going to apologize for wanting to advance my career. I've worked really hard to get where I am. But like I told you before, I'm not going to publish until the site goes public. I'm keeping that promise."

Randi nodded thoughtfully. "Good. Must be hard to resist."

"It is. This is just such a rich resource."

Randi wasn't going to argue any more about it. It wasn't Kim's fault. Kim must have recognized Randi's change of attitude because she looked at her with a sympathetic and grateful smile.

"If you really take to heart the idea that this is public land," Kim said, "then you have to give the public access to it when that makes sense, and you have to involve the public in caring for it."

"Theoretically, yes," Randi said. "It only takes a few jerks, though, to ruin it."

"A girl and her mother came into the office yesterday. That was why Steve was looking for an archaeologist. They brought in a photo of a dart point the girl found. She left it where it was and reported it because she'd learned that from Matt."

"Really?"

"Yes. I mean, it does work. The girl was full of respect for the relic. She'd been to Casa Grande. It had impressed her. Some kid's going to come here, to this site, and feel the same sense of awe. Develop a sense of responsibility for protecting these resources."

"That's really encouraging," Randi offered.

"Yes, it is. Matt did a good job getting the message across, I guess. I really believe that ignorance is the biggest threat."

"You make a good point," Randi admitted, not feeling the least bit like arguing.

"That reminds me, I'd like to talk to Matt before I'm done here. He must have some ideas about these glyphs, and I'd be interested in hearing them. I'd also just like to meet the guy. I keep hearing about him. It sounds like he's going to be hard to replace."

Randi smiled. "Yes, he will. He's quite a talker, so I'm sure he can be coaxed into it. I'll put you in touch."

"Thanks." Kim took a long drink of her lemonade, then asked, "Why geology?"

Randi, noticing that one of her legs had gone to sleep,

shifted position. "Lots of reasons. Always liked rocks. I had a rock collection when I was just six, just things I'd picked up that I thought were pretty. And then I had my first geology class in high school. I discovered that the laws of geology were not only things I could remember, but things I could understand, unlike physics, for instance."

"You mean the law of uniformitarianism, things like that?"

Now that they were talking science, it was clear to Randi that they were both on easy, familiar ground.

"Right. And the law of superposition. The things on top were deposited after the things underneath 'em. Oh, boy, doesn't take a rocket scientist for that one, does it?"

Kim grinned. "Which physics often does."

"Exactly."

"But geology gets much more complicated than that."

"Oh, sure, but I didn't realize it in high school. Later, taking all that calculus and chemistry, well, then I did realize it, but it was too late to back out. I was in love with geology by then. The thing that really did it for me, really captured my imagination, was the concept of deep time."

"Deep time, yes," Kim said, nodding, "how human history barely registers on the time scale of the planet."

"Right. Rock sequences and convection and plate tectonics are all fascinating on their own, but behind every topic in geology is the idea of deep time. It's always about millions and billions of years. You archaeologists are going to dig down a few feet into the earth's crust through at most ten thousand years. For most people, that length of time is comprehensible. But in geology, we cover billions of years and we don't dig down through time, at least not billions of years. Hang around long enough, though, and the Earth has turned itself all inside out like a giant plow and a clam is freaking sitting on top of Mount McKinley!"

Kim laughed. "I know what you mean. It's just astonishing, the whole long, amazing process."

"I don't think most people can comprehend a billion years. I know I can't."

"Wouldn't it be something to be able to hang around for a billion years to see what develops? Don't you think about that?"

"Lots of times." Randi nodded. "It's funny how our two sciences are almost mutually exclusive. I've got the time before humans and yours doesn't even start until they show up."

"Geology doesn't stop with the appearance of humans."

"No, but geologic processes are so slow that nothing much has changed since people showed up. All the good stuff happened before that. For instance, this lava flow occurred ten thousand years ago, probably before the first human stepped foot here. So every person who has ever been past here has seen this outcrop looking a lot like what it does right now. That's a comforting thought, don't you think, that something could stay the same so long?"

Kim smiled, an easy, genuine look of friendship.

"Not so many rules like that in archaeology, I guess," Randi noted. "Not like superposition."

"No," Kim agreed. "Laws of nature don't help a lot where people are concerned. But they're not irrelevant. There are things about nature that every culture must have known to survive."

"Like what?"

"Like the knowledge that a river always flows to the sea, eventually."

"Well, not every river..."

Kim laughed and slapped a hand on her knee. "I knew you were going to say that! You're such a *geologist*."

Randi smiled and fingered a pebble, her eyes focusing on a small freckle on Kim's wrist where it creased when flexed. Sometimes she found it hard to look Kim in the eye.

"But, you know what I mean," Kim said. "Long before Newton described it as gravity, millions of people had known about it, a force of nature they understood, even if they didn't have a name for it. They knew that a river would follow the path of least resistance, head downgrade, that sort of thing. The kind of rule that, although there are exceptions, would serve them well. A truth they could live by. There aren't too many of those, certainties. Near certainties."

"No, not too many certainties. Even now."

They lapsed into silence again and finished eating.

"Too bad we didn't think of parking your truck here," Randi said. "Then we wouldn't have to walk all the way back."

"That's okay. I don't mind hiking. Besides, it's all downhill on the way back."

Leaning against a rock, Randi felt thoroughly relaxed. She was feeling more talkative than usual and told Kim about some of the characters she'd run into in the desert.

"There's a miner named Potter," she said, "lives on his claim and never wears clothes. Doesn't see the point. Most of the time, it doesn't matter. Nobody ever sees him. He lives in his tunnels like a mole, but the couple of times that I've gone out to inspect his place, it's been a little awkward, believe me."

"He doesn't put on clothes even when you come to visit?"

"He doesn't know I'm coming. It's not like I can call him. These guys are living in a world of their own. They like being cut off from everything. He doesn't seem to care, or notice. I had to ask him to put on pants, both times."

Kim laughed. "Some strange people live in the desert, don't they?"

"Yes. It seems to breed rare folks like rare flowers." Randi laughed too.

Kim glanced at her watch. "Wow! We've been sitting here over an hour."

As if they were both feeling somehow guilty for losing track of time, the rest of their hike was focused and nearly silent, a rapid, no-nonsense trek to the end of the wash where it became just flat desert floor, and then five miles back to the river. There was no looking at flowers or rocks on the way down, nor was there much need to look for places where gold might be buried. If the gold was buried in this wash, finding it was going to be sheer luck. There didn't seem to be anything to tie it to the few clues Helmuth Wolff had left behind.

CHAPTER TWENTY-TWO

As they made their way back to town, Randi calculated that even if Danya had driven straight back after her interview, she wouldn't be home for at least an hour. Randi felt herself struggling with the idea of inviting Kim in, of being alone with her in the house and maybe even kissing her. The image kept floating through her mind, growing more vivid the closer they got to home. I don't even know if she's single, Randi reminded herself, wishing she could think of a way to ask.

Pulling up in front of her house, she saw no sign of Danya's car. "Let me show you around, if you have a minute."

"Sure," said Kim, then transferred her stuff to the back of her own pickup.

Randi led the way into the house, noticing as soon as she stepped inside the unexpected, distinctive sweet smell of marijuana smoke. She stopped in the front room and turned to look at Kim, wondering if she smelled it and if she knew what it was. Miss Straightlaced Academe probably had no idea what marijuana smelled like. At the moment, Randi was grateful for Kim's ivory-tower lifestyle. She wanted to back out the front door and send Kim away, but how to do that without looking nuts was a puzzle she didn't know how to solve.

Breeze trotted past them on his way to his food dish.

"It's an old house," Randi said, regaining her composure. "But I've done a lot of updates."

"It's darling," Kim said.

Randi led the way to the sunroom where Breeze was drinking from his dish with noisy slurps. Both of the ceiling fans were on, turning slowly, and there were two glasses on the coffee table, beads of condensation surrounding their lower halves. Randi wanted to walk over and smell them to see what they contained, but stood where she was, smiling at Kim instead. *What the hell is going on*, she thought silently, realizing that she needed to get Kim out of the house and on her way as quickly as she could without seeming rude.

"This is gorgeous," Kim said, looking out the windows to the cactus-covered slope behind the house. "So tastefully decorated. I love the Southwest style. It flows into the landscape. That always seems so important to me, to blend yourself into your natural surroundings if you can."

"It's important to me too. I added this room after I moved in. I needed a place to sit and look at the desert without having to actually be in it. This room's air conditioning runs on solar energy. There are panels on the roof here."

Kim nodded. "That's terrific."

"I basically had to give up my backyard to put this in, but I think it's worth it."

"Absolutely! Your house is really great. And I love the fact that your yard is natural, even in front, landscaped with native plants. No lawn. Ecologically sound."

Kim strolled over to a shelf where Randi displayed some of

160

her favorite rocks. She turned and smiled an adorable, knowing smile at Randi, as if to say, "Of course!"

"Could I have some water?" Kim asked. "Kind of thirsty."

"Oh, sure. Come on into the kitchen."

Randi took a pitcher out of the refrigerator and poured Kim a glass of water, noticing that there were new, dirty dishes on the counter. It was becoming clear to her that Danya must have bailed on her job interview and spent the day here.

"I had a great time today," Kim said, sounding sincere. "Even if we didn't find any buried treasure."

"Me too," Randi said.

As Kim set her water glass on the counter, Danya's voice reached them from another room. "Hey, Rocky, are you home?"

Randi winced at the nickname. She glanced at Kim, noticing her expression of confusion. "Friend of mine," she explained. "Visiting for a few days."

Kim nodded. Randi pushed through the door into the front room where Danya was toddling down the hallway in her bathrobe, looking disheveled and bleary-eyed, as if she had just rolled out of bed.

"Yes, I'm home," Randi said. "Kim, this is my friend Danya."

Kim smiled and nodded in Danya's direction.

"Have a good hike?" Danya asked.

"I'm surprised to see you here," Randi said. "I thought you'd be in Phoenix."

Danya tossed her hand through the air and sputtered. "Decided not to go."

"Where's your car?"

"Nicki took it to go get some tacos."

"Nicki?" Randi felt herself getting angry, but, under Kim's gaze, she held back.

"You know Nicki," Danya said, sounding drunk or high or both.

Randi did know Nicki. She was a loser, as far as Randi was concerned, a woman who reminded her of people she had known well in younger days—hard-edged, defiant, living on the fringes of society, the sort of woman she and Danya would have welcomed

161

into their circle at one time. The sort of woman she and Danya had been at one time. Randi was surprised that Danya had gotten to know Nicki well enough to party with her. She apparently didn't spend all of her time playing housewife to Randi while she was at work.

Randi turned to Kim and said, "Uh, look—"

Before she could say anything else, Kim said, "Hey, I need to get going."

Kim strode to the front door, Randi right behind her.

"Thanks for a great day," Kim said as she pulled the door open.

"Why don't you stop by Pinkie's tomorrow," Randi suggested. "A bunch of us are going to be there. They're having a Valentine's Day party. For singles too, not just couples. Just an excuse to get together."

Kim looked startled. "Oh, I hadn't even noticed it was Valentine's Day."

"So you don't have one, do you?" Randi asked.

"One what?"

"Valentine. Back home, I mean."

"Oh, no!" Kim looked surprised. "I'm definitely single. I thought you knew."

"Okay, then," Randi said, realizing how relieved she was to hear that, "you may as well come by."

"See you there."

Randi watched her walk to the curb, then turned her attention back to Danya, who was draped across the couch, looking uninterested in Kim, Randi and the world in general. She was combing at her hair with her hand.

"So why didn't you go to the interview?" Randi asked.

"Such a long way to drive. And it was a lousy job anyway."

"It doesn't seem like you're in a position to be all that choosy. How would you even know it was a lousy job?"

Danya shrugged.

"So you decided to stay here and party instead?"

"A girl's got to have a little fun. I ran into Nicki at the store

162

and we decided to come back here. We had a nice time."

"You embarrassed me in front of Kim."

"Embarrassed you? How?"

"The pot, for one thing. You've been smoking pot in my house!"

"Damn, Randi, when did you become such a prude?"

"Have you been drinking too? If there's liquor in this house—"

"No, no liquor. I told you I quit. That's the truth."

Randi sighed. She recognized that she felt threatened. Her need for order was being trampled on.

Danya slid off the couch and came over to Randi, touching her cheek gently. "Thanks to you," she said, "I'm still okay. You're the best friend a girl ever had, Rocky. You've always come through for me. You're the one person in the world that I know I can count on."

That kind of endorsement meant a lot to Randi. It was the exact opposite, in fact, of those stinging words that Irene had left her with. She felt herself soften.

"Sorry if I embarrassed you," Danya said, looking contrite. "That Kim's really cute."

Randi shrugged. "I guess."

A car pulled up in front. Randi looked out to see Danya's Jetta. Nicki came up the walkway with a white paper bag, her spiky black hair turning midnight blue as she passed into the shade of the house. "The tacos are here!" she called through the screen door. "Oh, hi, Randi, you're back. How about something to eat?"

CHAPTER TWENTY-THREE

Sunday afternoon Kim showed up at Pinkie's to find a crowd there. There were free appetizers making the rounds and streamers of pink, white and red crisscrossing the ceiling. Randi's friend Gareth was flitting about in a Cupid costume—a pink bikini and sparkly bow with a paper arrow glued to it, a garland of paper hearts on his head. He danced by Kim and aimed his arrow at her mischievously, drawing a spontaneous laugh.

The music playing was Bette Midler singing old romantic standards. A few couples were dancing slow. Minnie and Blair were at the bar. Seeing Blair was a little awkward, considering how they had last parted, but Blair came over, took her by the arm and walked her up to the bar, saying, "I'm so happy you came. I was hoping you would." To Jeff, she yelled, "A glass of white wine for Kim!"

"No," Kim objected, her voice raised toward Jeff. "I think I'll have iced tea today."

Blair made a pouty face. Kim wasn't going down that road again. The memory of that night still stung. Perhaps, Kim thought, looking at Blair, I'm destined to fall into nothing but awkward scenes with these Yuma women during my stay here, just one nutty misstep after another. At least the prospect of walking away in a couple of months hung out there on the horizon like an absolution. Perfect opportunity to make a fool of yourself when you could walk away like that.

"Hi, you guys," Randi said, approaching the bar. Her friend Danya was right behind her.

Jeff placed a tall glass of iced tea on the bar in front of Kim. Danya looked a little more presentable today than she had yesterday when they had apparently rousted her out of bed. Kim had recognized the smell of marijuana in Randi's house and wondered if that was as much a surprise to her as it had been to Kim. She had looked taken aback. But who was this Danya anyway? Kim wondered. And what was she doing living at Randi's house?

"What have you been up to since I saw you last?" Blair asked, shifting Kim's attention away from Randi.

"Just working, mainly," Kim said.

"Oh, what a shame. I hope that's not all you're planning on doing while you're here."

In order not to have to shout, Kim moved closer to Blair and said, "I'm not interested in romance. Just here to have a little fun."

Blair grinned. "Then we're on the same wavelength, aren't we? I just want to have a little fun myself."

Hopeless, Kim decided, shaking her head.

Minnie suddenly grabbed hold of Blair's hand and pulled her onto the dance floor. Randi went to dance with one of the guys. Kim recognized the song as an oldie from the Fifties, something by Jerry Lee Lewis. Randi and her partner Tony stepped through some highly coordinated moves of a Fifties-era dance.

165

"What is that they're doing?" Kim asked Danya, who was standing next to her at the bar.

"Jitterbug."

Kim nodded. "Oh, sure. I should have recognized it. I've never done it, though."

"Randi loves those old dances. She knows 'em all. The Fifties dances are her favorites."

Kim drank her iced tea, watching Randi and Tony dance. They were fast and smooth, and fun to watch. The music changed again and suddenly Randi was leading, twirling and dipping Tony. The guys at the table nearest them hooted. Kim felt her face stretched into a wide smile.

"Boy," Danya breathed, "that reminds me of the old days! It's great to see her dance like that again."

"You and Randi know each other pretty well?" Kim asked.

"Oh, yeah. We've known each other forever. We were a couple, you know, back in Phoenix."

Kim struggled to keep astonishment out of her voice. "Oh?"

"Sure. I'm so glad we were able to reconnect and get back together. She's the best, really. I just love her to death."

This time Kim made no effort to disguise her surprise. "You mean, you and Randi are together?"

Danya nodded. "Didn't she tell you that?"

"Oh... no, she didn't."

"Well, we are." Danya's voice was firm, her look severe. "For good, this time. I made some mistakes the first time around, but it won't happen again."

Kim realized she was disappointed to hear that Randi and Danya were a couple. The depth of her disappointment, in fact, took her by surprise. She'd gotten the impression, yesterday, that Danya was simply a houseguest. All the time that Kim had been spending trying to talk herself out of being attracted to Randi was wasted after all. Randi wasn't even available. Not that Randi had ever given her any encouragement at all. Maybe the reason for that was now clear. Maybe there were a lot of reasons, but this one reason was plenty all by itself. It's better this way, Kim told herself, trying to push her disappointment aside. With only two more months in Yuma, I have no business getting involved with Randi anyway.

Kim stood observing Danya for a few minutes, trying to imagine why Randi would be attracted to her. Maybe it had something to do with the good old days, their first time around. That was a powerful draw for a lot of women. Hard to give up old lovers.

Danya moved off and Kim noticed that Minnie, who had reappeared at the bar, stared after her with obvious dislike. "Do you know her?" Kim asked, moving closer.

"No. She just turned up out of nowhere."

"They knew each other before, I guess, in Phoenix."

"Randi's such a soft touch, taking in that mongrel. She's bad news, I can just feel it."

Kim felt a little sympathetic toward Minnie, whose bitterness wasn't the least bit disguised. She recalled again the inexplicable scene she'd witnessed the night that Randi had tossed Minnie down the bar. Was there any way to explain that that could justify Minnie's feelings?

"You think Randi's a soft touch?" Kim asked.

Minnie screwed her face into a what-are-you-nuts expression. "Yeah!"

"But she can be tough too, right? Maybe even sort of mean on occasion?"

Minnie looked perplexed. Love is blind, Kim thought. Maybe even deaf and dumb. She was about to ask something more specific when the song finished and Randi stumbled up to the bar, out of breath.

"Jeff, hit me!" she said.

Jeff poured her a Diet Coke, which she immediately guzzled down to about half. There was a bead of sweat running down her temple. Danya stepped between Kim and Randi and wiped the sweat off Randi's temple with a napkin, tenderly, in a gesture of ownership that left Kim feeling like she was watching something private.

Embarrassed, she turned impulsively to Blair and asked, "Want to dance?"

"Sure," Blair said with a delighted smile.

Blair held her tight and close as they moved to Bette Midler's "Tenderly." Kim's view directly in front of her was of Blair's lovely bosom, which was pressed up against her own. Her recollection of touching that silky skin with her lips was a pleasant one. She couldn't remember everything about that night, but she did remember the sensation of Blair's body on hers, flush with passionate desire. The woman was smoldering.

About halfway through the song, Kim felt Blair's hand move down past her waist to the seat of her jeans. Kim reached behind her and lifted it back up. She glanced over at the bar and saw Randi facing the dance floor, leaning against the bar, watching them closely. *What's she thinking?* Kim wondered. Then she thought, what difference does it make?

It might be nice, Kim thought, to have a spring fling while she was in town. Blair was certainly game for it. If ever there was a time and place for a no-strings affair, this was it. She would probably never be in this town again, never see any of these women again. Blair's getting to me, Kim realized. She's going to wear me down if I let her. That didn't seem like such a bad idea at the moment.

Kim smiled encouragingly at Blair, who slid her hand back down to her ass. She let it stay this time. Blair pushed her hips hard up against Kim's and whispered in her ear. "I want to lap you up like a kitten with a bowl of cream."

Oh, damn! Kim thought, her stomach turning a flip. There's really no reason to resist, she told herself. This is bound to be sweet and it wouldn't hurt anybody. As Blair's body moved suggestively against hers and she imagined taking this dance to Blair's bedroom, Kim grew hotter and hotter. Another few minutes, she thought, and I'm going to suggest we get out of here.

At the beginning of their second dance, Randi walked up and tapped Blair on the shoulder, cutting in. Blair frowned and went back to the bar. Is she trying to save me again, Kim wondered, as

Randi took hold of her hand. She didn't hold her close like Blair had, but she was a better dancer.

"Blair's really into you," Randi observed. "Looks sort of mutual."

"She's a sexy girl," Kim answered.

"True. There's hardly a woman in Yuma who hasn't found that out for herself."

"Oh, Randi," Kim said, "that's catty."

Randi didn't answer. She just applied a little more pressure against Kim's back and led her through the dance.

It's none of your business if I'm interested in Blair, Kim wanted to say, especially since you're with someone else. Randi seemed to think she was in charge of everything. But Kim wasn't going to make the mistake of offending her again, so she said nothing.

As the song ended, Kim turned to leave the floor. Randi grabbed her hand and pulled her back. "Let's try a faster one," she said. "More my style."

The new song was one of those old rock 'n' roll tunes. Randi twirled her and held her hand as they danced apart. Kim started to have fun, watching Randi stomping in her cowboy boots, her head bopping as she pulled Kim close and then spun her away again. Definitely more her style, Kim thought. She's really good at this. Kim got spun around so many times, she felt a little dizzy by the end of the song.

"Gotta take a break," she told Randi.

Randi nodded and released her hand.

Kim made her way through the other dancers and out the open back door to the courtyard. Standing with her back to the doorway, a woman was talking to a man who was seated at the redwood table. Kim easily recognized Blair's reddish gold hair and shapely legs. The man's face was obscured from view by Blair's body.

"Yes, it was unbelievable," Blair was saying. "She just came charging into my bedroom while we were making out and abducted her. Just dragged her out, literally right out from under me, and took off with her."

"Did she want Kim for herself?" the man asked.

Kim stopped where she was at the mention of her name, realizing that neither of them could see her.

"No," Blair said. "I'm sure nothing like that was going on. After all, Minnie went along, so they weren't alone. I have no idea why she did that. It was the most bizarre thing! You can be sure it isn't going to happen again. Kim is mine tonight and Randi will have nothing to say about it."

"You sound pretty confident."

Blair laughed. "I would place bets on it. That volcano is already spitting lava. My bedroom is going to be erupting tonight."

Randi would appreciate a metaphor like that, Kim thought as Blair twirled around like a ballerina, caught sight of Kim, and stopped in mid-twirl.

"Hey, Kim," Blair said, trying to look casual. "Have you met George?"

The man in the chair stood, revealing that he was tall and big like a bouncer. "Hello, Kim," he said. "I think I'll go get another drink."

George seemed anxious to escape this awkward scene. He went into the bar, leaving the two women alone. Blair approached and took hold of Kim's hand. "How long were you standing there spying on me?" she asked.

"About a minute," Kim said. "Long enough to know you were talking about me."

Blair nodded. "Yes, I *was* talking about you. I was telling George how much I like you and how much I hope we can see more of each other." Blair moved closer. "And by see more of each other, I think you know what I mean."

Kim didn't so much mind being talked about, but Blair's attitude did bother her. Listening to her talk to George, Kim realized just how impersonal this seduction was for Blair. Just the new girl, a potential conquest. Blair didn't even know her. In fact, Kim recalled, Blair's interest had begun the moment they met. Blair not only didn't know anything about her, she didn't care to know anything. There was nothing very flattering about that. And although Kim never had imagined that this was about love, hearing Blair talk like that made it seem detached and perfunctory. It had been fun to think about it for a while, to imagine this kind of passionate interlude with an attractive woman who wouldn't ask for anything but physical pleasure. No emotional complications. But I'm not really made that way, Kim told herself, for this kind of fun, even if I am going to walk away from here in two months.

"Come home with me," Blair said, putting her arms loosely around Kim's waist, her eyes turning green, her lips pursed. "Be my valentine."

Kim was unmoved. The spell was broken.

"I think I'll pass," she said. "No volcano's erupting tonight, Blair."

Blair released her, looking disappointed. "You're upset about what I said to George?"

Kim shook her head. "No. It just isn't what I want to do. I'm sorry if I misled you."

"Spoilsport." Blair pouted.

"Yeah," Kim said, "I guess so."

She headed for the door to the bar, thinking that sex was not really a sport to her. She had never been casual about sex and, as intriguing as it had seemed a little while ago, she thought she probably never would be. There had to be something more than just physical attraction for her. Still, she felt some disappointment walking away from that sizzling magma chamber.

As she returned to the dim room where classic rock music was still playing, she saw that nobody was dancing. They were all standing or sitting with their eyes on the bar. Kim turned to look, then gasped. Minnie was lying face down on top of the bar where Randi had a firm grasp on the seat of her pants.

Oh, my God! thought Kim, alarmed. This isn't happening! She couldn't believe what she was witnessing, but there was little doubt that Randi was about to fling Minnie down the bar again, and there was no one else close enough to stop her. Kim lunged toward Randi, grabbed hold of her shoulder and spun her around.

"What the—" Randi said, releasing Minnie and stumbling sideways.

Kim took hold of Randi's shoulders, pulled her away from the bar, and then shoved her with all her strength. Randi stumbled backward, fell against a table, then rolled off, her arms flailing. Just before she hit the floor, her hand caught the back of a chair, which came down on top of her.

Minnie jumped down from the bar with surprising agility. "What the hell?" she hollered at Kim.

She ran over to Randi and moved the chair away as Randi rolled over, holding a hand to her nose. Minnie helped her into a sitting position as a crowd gathered around her. Danya came running, kneeling beside Randi with her right fist clenched.

"Deck her!" Danya said through her teeth, obviously poised for a fight.

Oh, shit, thought Kim, imagining getting pummeled into a quivering bloody pulp by Randi. But the look on Randi's face, as she recovered her senses and looked in Kim's direction, wasn't rage but bewilderment.

Kim hadn't moved, standing dumbfounded, startled by both her own actions and everyone else's response. Jeff, who had come out from behind the bar to stand beside her, said calmly, "Lover's tiff?"

Kim didn't know what to say. Was everybody in this town a lunatic? Most of all Minnie, who was sitting beside Randi on the floor, stroking her face and cooing at her. Randi climbed uncertainly to her feet, pressing a hand protectively against her rib cage, and faced Kim with a questioning look.

"What was that for?" she asked.

"I—" started Kim. "I thought you were going to throw her down the bar."

Randi looked at Minnie and then back at Kim. "I was," she said. "So what?"

Randi still looked confused. Suddenly, Minnie burst out

laughing. Randi's expression gradually changed to amusement, but Kim was still in the dark.

"Come here and sit down," Randi said, taking a seat at the table she had fallen over. Kim sat beside her. "George," called Randi. "Why don't you demonstrate? I think my nose is broken and I'm not up to it."

George approached the bar and lifted Minnie onto it effortlessly. Kim watched as he flattened her out on top of the bar, which Kim now noticed was completely clear, and flung her down the length of it. Minnie went sailing, tucking herself into a tight ball just before hitting the wall. She bounced off the wall and to the floor, rolling twice, and then hopping upright. She held her arms up in a triumphant stance. Everyone else clapped and whistled.

"It's her thing," Randi said. "She's a stuntwoman. She's practicing for the movies."

"Let's do another one," Minnie said to George. "Throw me through the doorway."

Nobody was paying any attention to Kim now as George picked up Minnie and prepared for this new trick. Randi was grinning.

"I'm so sorry," Kim said. "Are you badly hurt?"

"Just bruises. I think I should get some ice for my nose, though."

Kim put together an ice pack with a towel and brought it to Randi, who placed it gently over her nose, which was visibly swelling.

"Do you want me to take you to a doctor?" Kim asked.

"I don't think it's broken after all," Randi said, her voice sounding a little nasally. "Damn, I thought my days of bar fighting were over. Maybe I'll just go home, take an aspirin, and relax a little."

"I'll drive you," offered Kim.

"No, thanks. I can drive."

"I can drive," Danya interjected.

"You stay here and have fun," Randi told her. "You can catch

173

a ride home later."

"No, I'll come with you and make sure you're okay."

Danya glared at Kim, who followed them outside, apologizing again.

"In a way," said Randi, unlocking her truck, "that was an extremely gallant act, especially since Minnie doesn't even like you."

"Minnie doesn't like me?"

Randi looked momentarily alarmed, then laughed nervously. "Oh, no, that's not what I meant. Sorry, I'm sort of muddle-headed right now."

"You've probably got a concussion," Danya chimed in, taking the keys from her.

Randi climbed into the passenger seat and shut her door. "Are you going back in?" she asked through the open window.

Kim shook her head. "No, I don't think so. Too embarrassing. I guess I'll just go home too."

"Isn't Blair expecting you?" Randi's tone was slightly accusing. Her eyes looked especially dark with the sunset behind her.

It suddenly occurred to Kim that Randi was jealous. Everything made so much more sense that way, especially Randi's continuing attempts to deflect her from Blair. Kim had thought it was Randi's sense of responsibility that had been motivating her, a natural, if misplaced protectiveness. But apparently it was more personal. What right does she have to be jealous of Blair? Kim wondered. But at the same time, a cozy warmth spread over her with the idea that Randi had those kinds of feelings for her.

"No," Kim said. "Nobody is expecting me. I'll be home. If you change your mind about the doctor, call me. I'll be happy to go with you."

Randi smiled, a bit crookedly due to the pain in her face. "In just a matter of days, Tilley, this is going to be a funny story. And I can guarantee you that you have now made a legacy for yourself at Pinkie's."

CHAPTER TWENTY-FOUR

"Calling in sick on a Monday isn't like Randi," Steve complained to everybody in general and Kim in particular when she showed up at the BLM office Monday morning. "I hope to God she didn't fall off the wagon. She's come up with some cockamamie story about some woman attacking her at Pinkie's and nearly breaking her nose. Ridiculous. I've got to say that I've never known Randi to lie before."

"It isn't a lie," Kim stated.

Steve stared at her. "What do *you* know about it?"

"I'm the woman who attacked her."

Steve stared some more, his mustache twitching almost imperceptibly.

"It was a misunderstanding," Kim explained. "I definitely didn't intend to hurt anyone. But she did take a nasty fall."

He shook his head, as if trying to clear it out, then lowered himself slowly into his desk chair. "Okay," he said at last. "*You* were at Pinkie's Valentine's party?"

Kim hesitated for a second, then said, "Yes." There was something liberating about being in a place temporarily. She didn't have to worry about what people knew about her or what they thought as a result. She could be herself in a way she wasn't accustomed to. She liked it.

Steve took a deep breath. "I see. Is there something that I don't understand about you female scientists? Is there some kind of rule or something that you have to be gay?"

Kim smiled. "Yes, it's a requirement."

"That's a shame, at least from my point of view." Steve sighed melodramatically. "I hope there's no bad blood between you two, though."

"No, not at all," Kim assured him. "We've become great friends."

"Good," he said, but then looked at her suspiciously.

He's a funny guy, Kim thought, leaving the office. She called Ramon and told him that she wouldn't be going to the site after all, that she had office work she wanted to do today. Then she went out and bought a get well card and a cheerful bouquet of daisies. Outside the flower shop, she sat in her truck and wrote a friendly message in the card. As she was about to sign her name, she changed her mind and signed "Tilley" instead.

Arriving at Randi's house, Kim carried her gift to the door and rang the bell. She could hear Breeze inside barking, and then heard Randi call his name. But it was Danya who opened the door. Her greeting, "Oh, hi," was cold. She stood with a hand on her hip, her expression challenging.

"Hi," Kim said. "I've brought a peace offering for Randi. How is she doing?"

"Bruised up. Ribs tender. Face a mess." Danya reached out to take the flowers, then said with finality, "I'll tell her you dropped by."

Kim was about to object when she heard Randi from the back of the house call out, "Who is it?"

"It's your assailant," Danya hollered back.

Randi appeared then, approaching the door. She was wearing blue pajama bottoms and a T-shirt, her feet bare, her hair in a ponytail instead of the usual braid.

"Hi, Tilley!" she said.

Kim was relieved to hear the friendly tone, but she was alarmed to see the black and blue discoloration across the top of Randi's swollen nose and across one cheekbone. Kim winced at the sight.

"Looks worse than it is," Randi assured her. "Nothing broken."

"When I heard you'd called in sick," Kim said, "I felt pretty bad and thought I'd bring you something cheerful."

"Thanks. Pretty bouquet. I'm sore in a couple of places. Mainly ribs. Should be fine by tomorrow. Except this, of course." She indicated her bruised face. "Don't know what I'm going to tell my students this week. No matter what I tell them, I'm sure they will come up with their own wild explanation anyway. Although getting beat up in a gay bar is wild enough, I guess."

"I wouldn't say you got 'beat up.'"

"No, you're right. Maybe sucker punched."

Danya carried the flowers inside and Randi took the card from Kim. With a ponytail and wearing pajamas, Randi looked softer than she usually did. She didn't look anything like a cowgirl today, just a girl, a very pretty girl with a bruised face.

Randi pulled out the card and read it, then looked up. "Thank you. Very thoughtful."

They stood looking at each other silently. Kim felt an affection toward Randi that she hadn't felt before, something that went beyond just the physical attraction. It wasn't just that she felt sorry for messing up her face. Things had changed since yesterday. She wondered if Randi knew that, if she felt it too.

Danya reappeared, inserting herself next to Randi in the doorway, a near-snarl on her face.

"Uh," Kim said awkwardly, "I hope you feel better soon. I'm really sorry."

Randi nodded and smiled reassuringly.

177

"If there's anything I can do—"

"Naw, I'm fine. And, you know, Danya's here."

"Right. Well, then, I'll be going. Bye."

Kim went home, feeling at loose ends. She had been expecting to be invited in, to be able to do something useful, to spend some time visiting. But Danya was extremely possessive and Kim had felt her bristling like a cat against an intruder as they had faced one another in the doorway. Assailant, indeed, Kim thought with irritation. Even if Danya hadn't been there, though, Kim didn't know if Randi would have welcomed her. Kim was frustrated.

Just like Minnie, she did not like Danya. Also like Minnie, her feelings had their roots in jealousy. Danya represented an impediment. Minnie had more right to those feelings than she did, though. She knew it was an inappropriate attitude, but feelings have a way of bypassing intellect.

She spent the rest of the day working in her trailer, listening to music. She found it hard to concentrate because she kept thinking about Randi and her swollen nose. She ended up accomplishing very little.

Tuesday, Ramon was clearly distracted and seemed unhappy. When they stopped for their lunch break, Kim asked, "Is there something wrong?"

He shrugged and didn't look at her. "I'm just thinking about things."

"Things?"

"Sophie. We had a fight."

"Oh. A serious fight?"

"Maybe. She wants to get married, have kids, you know."

"And you don't want to?"

"I wouldn't mind getting married, and eventually having kids, but I've been thinking about maybe going to a university, you know, like we talked about."

"She has a problem with that?"

He shook his head. "She says her life is here. And mine too. My friends, they say the same thing. They ask me why I'm pretending to be a big shot, hanging out with you, thinking I'm somebody."

Kim was taken aback. She didn't really know what to say. This was a situation she had never encountered and never imagined.

"You *are* somebody," she said. "Why shouldn't you have a dream and pursue it?"

"I don't know. It seems so unrealistic. A few months ago my dream was an A.A. degree and a job with the city. The other is something I can barely imagine."

"That's the thing about dreams. Why bother if you don't have one that's just a little bit out of reach?"

He was looking at the ground again.

"If Sophie can't see what you're capable of, you've got to persuade her. Make her see your dream, Ramon. Make it her dream too. Make her want it."

He looked at her sideways. "How do I do that?"

"By being positive and confident, by painting a picture for her."

"That's not so easy to do. Even my parents are trying to talk me out of it."

"Why? Why would they do that?"

"Nobody in my family has ever gone to college. I'm the first. They only agreed to let me because I could show them the job I was after. They thought it was a realistic goal, and it was only two years. I finally had them convinced about that, that it was worthwhile. Now they think I'm just in love with school, that I'm indecisive, and I'll be one of those guys who goes to school till he's thirty and has nothing to show for it. I can see their side. This is so different to them. They can't imagine that I would actually be able to do it. And I don't know if I could."

Kim saw a tear fall to the ground at his feet. She had had no idea what he was going through. She herself had come from a family with two college-educated parents who had insisted she go to college and had paid for it. She knew of people who struggled, who did it on their own, and she admired them. But for parents to discourage a college education, that was something

179

else entirely. She wasn't familiar with that position.

"They just don't want me to waste my life," Ramon explained.

"At least we all agree about that! I think it's time you invite me to dinner, Ramon. Time I meet your parents. I want to thank your mother personally, anyway, for all of the fabulous lunches. Speaking of which, what did you bring today? I'm starving."

Ramon's face brightened as he opened the lunch tote and offered her a fat beef enchilada with a smoky red sauce.

CHAPTER TWENTY-FIVE

"That city girl sure did a number on you," joked Dolly when Randi showed up at the restaurant for lunch. This was the refrain around town and Randi was getting tired of hearing it, but she smiled good-naturedly anyway. She also didn't like it that her tough-guy reputation was marred by the incident. Everybody was making it seem like there'd been an actual fight and she had lost. After a few attempts, she gave up trying to explain. Let them have their fun, she thought, even if it is at my expense.

The restaurant was crowded, so Randi took a stool at the bar. "Hey," she boasted to Dolly, "you should see *her*!"

"I have seen her," Dolly said. "Last night. Not a mark on her. So what'll ya have?"

Randi sighed. "How about a cheeseburger?"

At least Kim had been properly remorseful. Poor thing. Lovely bouquet she had brought over. Danya was more jealous than ever. It was all she could do to put the flowers in a vase without smashing them. That wasn't totally unreasonable, Randi thought, remembering how crazy she had felt watching Blair dancing with Kim at the Valentine's party. Did they have to dance that close? Randi didn't know how it had happened, but somehow Blair had lost her chance with Kim that night. For that, Randi was relieved. She liked Kim more and more and was finding it harder to come up with reasons not to like her. Her original assumptions had turned out to be mostly false. There was still the ambition thing. That appeared to be true at least. There was nothing inherently evil about that, though. Wasn't even a negative thing, really, as long as it was done honestly without stepping on anybody.

After several years of holding herself at a distance from love, Randi knew that getting involved with Kim would be disastrous. Having almost always made bad choices in lovers, she had resolved to do it right next time. This was her new life, her responsible, respectable, sober new life where she made right and honorable decisions and didn't subject herself to unnecessary emotional turmoil. For these reasons, Danya had no chance to win her back, though obviously Danya didn't believe that. And Kim was just one of those if-only or might-have-been things. Neither a short-term nor a long-distance relationship was acceptable. Nope, Randi thought firmly, Kim had to be avoided.

Dolly slid a cheeseburger and fries onto the counter, again clicking her tongue in dismay at Randi's bruises, then grinning like a mischievous child. Randi gave her an exaggerated frown. Looking down the bar to locate a ketchup bottle for her fries, she was surprised to see Flynn, a glass of beer in his hand, talking loudly to an old man she didn't know, possibly one of the wintering snowbirds.

"They all said it was a lot of damned nonsense!" he was saying, sloshing his beer. "Said it was just a story. But I knew. I knew it was the real deal all along."

Randi left her plate on the counter and approached him.

"Flynn!" she said loudly, getting his attention. "I didn't know you were coming to town today."

He lifted his glass to her and slid off his stool. "Randi Girl! I found it! Hey, what happened to your face?"

"Never mind about that. What did you find?"

"The gold! The Wolff gold!"

"Flynn, you're drunk."

"Hell's bells, girl!" he said. "Of course I am. That's what I came in here for, to celebrate. But I still found it."

"Sure, sure," Randi said, humoring him. "So where'd you find it?"

"Wouldn't you like to know," he said, evasively.

"You didn't find anything," she said, "except in your dreams."

Flynn slammed his glass onto the bar and looked indignant, a scowl on his face. He put his hand in his pocket, groping for something, then slapped a small object into Randi's hand. Randi looked at it for a second before closing her hand over what was undeniably a genuine gold nugget the size of a grape.

"There!" he said. "What do you think of that?"

Randi grabbed him by the arm and dragged him roughly behind her through the crowd.

"What the heck are ya doing?" he hollered, stumbling along.

She pulled him out the front door and around the corner of the building into a side street, where she pushed him onto a wooden bench. Then she sat down beside him and opened her hand to look more carefully at the nugget.

"It's real," he said.

"Where did you get this?"

"Didn't I just tell you that? I found it just where he said. It was there the whole time."

"Hendy Wash?" she asked, knowing that he would think she meant the phony Hendy.

He shook his head. "Nope. That part was wrong, but the rest was just like it was supposed to be."

"Where?" she pressed. "Was it the wash that runs by Black Point, then?"

His eyes widened in surprise.

"That's it, right?" she asked.

He pursed his lips and stared hard at her. He wasn't going to answer, but his expression had given it away. If he was telling the truth, he'd found the gold in the *real* Hendy Wash. But how could he have known to look there?

"Now, Flynn, if this really is the Wolff gold, you know it doesn't belong to you."

Still he said nothing. While they spoke, Randi kept an eye out for anyone within hearing, but they were off the main street and, at the moment, safe from being overheard.

"So where is it now?" she asked.

"Safe. I took out a couple of nuggets and buried it back where I found it. It's been safe there for a hundred and fifty years, hasn't it? It'll be safe there a while longer."

"I'll tell you what. I'll buy you dinner and then you can have a nice comfortable sleepover at the Lamplighter. Tomorrow you can show me where the gold is buried. Chances are, I can get you a reward. Okay, that's settled, then."

"Hey, give me back my nugget."

"I'll give it to you tomorrow when you're sober. Wouldn't want you flashing it around to anybody else tonight."

He frowned, but didn't argue. She didn't really know if Flynn had found the buried treasure or not. It hardly seemed likely, but he had found something because the nugget she put into her pocket was the real thing. Once he was sober and rested, he would either come clean with the real story or lead her to the treasure. Flynn wouldn't run off with it, she was sure of that. What he wanted more than anything was the notoriety.

She took him to the steakhouse where they both had a steak and baked potato, then a slice of boysenberry pie for dessert. As Flynn sobered up, he stuck to his story, but refused to tell her anything. Instead, he launched into old tales of youthful adventures, most of which she had heard before.

She left him at the Lamplighter in a clean room with a hot shower and a soft bed, hoping a night of civilized pleasure would put him in an agreeable frame of mind.

"I'll see you in the morning," Randi told him. "Don't talk to anybody else about this. Some damned fool is liable to believe you."

CHAPTER TWENTY-SIX

It was close to nine o'clock when a cloud of dust came barreling up the road and the white BLM truck sped past the site without slowing down and without the customary honk of the horn.

"Randi?" asked Ramon.

"I suppose it is. Early for her to be out here, though. And sort of odd she didn't stop to say hello."

"Maybe she's mad at you for breaking her nose." Ramon grinned.

"So you heard about that."

"Uh-huh."

"I didn't break her nose. Just bruised it."

"I heard you punched her out in a jealous rage over some woman named Blair."

"What?" Kim said, indignantly. "That is a complete fabrication. It was nothing to do with Blair."

"Oh, so there is a woman named Blair. Not a *complete* fabrication, then."

"You know, you're getting a little cheeky."

He grinned again. Now that Kim had met his family, they seemed to be on a more familiar footing. She had spent the previous evening at his home over a fabulous meal and some interesting conversation with his parents.

"What did you bring for lunch today? I'm already hungry. Any of that chicken enchilada casserole from last night?"

"No, there was none left. You finished it off, remember?"

"That was a memorable meal. Memorable evening too. I like your parents. Sensible people."

"They liked you too. We had a talk after you left. My father said you were very persuasive."

"Really? Are they on board, then, with the university plan?"

"They are if I can get a scholarship." Ramon was beaming.

"Fantastic! Are you happy?"

Ramon nodded vigorously. "Thanks to you. Hearing you explain about archaeology in terms of careers really helped. I didn't even think about all those things myself. I mean, it made an impression for all of us when you said the district archaeologist at BLM was retiring this year and there was an opening right here in Yuma. I thought I'd have to be a college professor if I was an archaeologist."

Kim raised an eyebrow at him.

"Oh," he said, quickly, "nothing wrong with that. You just gave us other things to think about, that's all."

"Good. So keep filling out those scholarship applications."

Ramon nodded, then put his headphones on to return to his work.

Surrounded by Ramon's parents and siblings at dinner, Kim had found herself defending her profession as a practical choice for someone like him. It wasn't all Indiana Jones. In fact, for most people, it was nothing like that. It was scientists working for the federal and state governments—in Flagstaff, Tucson, even Yuma. That's where the example of Matt at the BLM office had come in. Removing the romantic, fantastical misconceptions had helped them see this as a possibility for their son. It must have helped too that she praised his enthusiasm and dedication. She wanted them to dream large for Ramon, to believe that he was capable of going further than their original plan and beyond their own accomplishments, the perpetual dream of parents.

Less than an hour after Randi had gone through, a sheriff's car came by, heading in the same direction as the BLM truck.

"Something's up," Kim said as the dust cloud moved off in the distance. "Let's go check it out."

They ran back to the truck and drove to the only other destination along this route, Flynn's shack.

Sure enough, the BLM truck and sheriff's car were parked outside next to Flynn's green pickup. Randi emerged through the doorway of the dwelling and simply looked at Kim without expression. Something was obviously wrong. Breeze was sitting in the passenger side of her truck, his eyes intent on Randi.

"What's happened?" Kim asked, approaching her. She noticed that the bruises on her face had lightened from purple to green and her nose no longer looked swollen. "Is Flynn okay?"

"He's not here," Randi reported. "He's missing. And his place has been trashed, big time. They even ripped up the floorboards."

"They? What do you mean they? Who?"

Randi shrugged. "I have no idea. Somebody. Somebody looking for the gold."

"Gold? What gold?"

Randi frowned, looking slightly annoyed. "He was in town yesterday boasting around that he'd found the Wolff treasure."

"Really? Just boasting, though, right? I mean, he didn't find it?"

"I don't know. He had this." Randi fished something out of her pocket and held it in her open palm.

"Is that real gold?" Kim asked.

"Yes, it's real."

"Could he have gotten it out of his own mine?"

"Probably not." Randi tucked the gold back into her pocket. "He pulverizes quartz for dust. Nothing like this."

"So where did he get it?"

"He's sticking to his story. If it wasn't for the nugget, I'd think he was just talking, like he does. He was supposed to come back here with me this morning. I guess he decided to ditch me. He left town before sunup. Obviously, he came home because his truck is here."

The sheriff's deputy, a lean-faced man holding a shotgun loosely at his side, came out of the shack. "Whoever did this was thorough. I wonder if they got what they were looking for." He looked at Kim and said, "Who are you then?"

Randi introduced Deputy Nelson, explaining Kim's work.

"Did you see anything this morning?" the deputy asked. "Anybody come out here?"

"No, not until Randi came by. I got here about eight thirty. Flynn must have come back earlier than that."

"We need to find him," Randi said, impatiently. "I'm going to send Breeze out."

"Whoever did this," Deputy Nelson warned, "could still be out here."

Randi nodded and let Breeze out of the truck while the deputy radioed back to the sheriff's office. Kim, feeling useless, sat on her tailgate next to Ramon. Breeze was soon running this way and that sniffing for Flynn. Randi stood leaning against her pickup. Kim noticed she was holding an eight-by-ten photo, the corner of which was torn off. Kim recognized it immediately as the one she had given to Flynn.

"I shouldn't have trusted him," Randi said, not looking at them. "Should have known he would ditch me."

"Why did he?" Kim asked.

"Maybe he was considering keeping the gold. He's been looking to hit it rich all his life. It's been his one dream. If he did find it, he probably felt like he deserved to keep it. I can't really

189

blame him. He knew I would take it away and turn it over." Randi held up the photo. "You took this?"

"I did," said Ramon.

"Found it on the floor," Randi said. "Must have been hanging up, though. There are nail holes in the corners. Pretty good picture of him. At least we have a picture if we need to give one to the police or something."

I never imagined that, Kim thought, when I gave it to him.

Deputy Nelson, finished with his call, walked over to the group. "We'll have a team out here in an hour," he said. "We'll find him. He can't have gone far without his vehicle."

"If he's here, Breeze will find him," Randi said confidently.

But Breeze didn't find Flynn. All he turned up was a jacket in the mine shaft, a jacket that had apparently been left there for when Flynn was working in his mine. It was obvious that Randi was disappointed. Kim could see how worried she was and she felt helpless, having no comfort to offer.

When the sheriff's party arrived, Randi put Breeze back in the truck. "You should get back to work," she told Kim. "I don't think there's much we can do here."

"What about you?" Kim asked.

"I'll drop Breeze home, then go into the office."

Kim and Ramon went back to their site. They resumed working, but Kim's mind was preoccupied with the drama that was unfolding nearby as the sheriff's team searched for Flynn. The phrase "dead or alive" attached itself to that thought at some point, causing her to shiver. It wasn't out of the question that Flynn was dead. People got killed for a lot less than a treasure like this. Somebody had apparently believed his story, somebody who had overheard his claims.

As Kim sat working in the shade of the outcrop, she tried to imagine what had transpired this morning before she and Ramon had arrived. Someone had come out here and ransacked Flynn's hut, that much was obvious. Was that before Flynn arrived? Had Flynn come home and caught the marauder in the act? Had a fight ensued? Was Flynn killed? Or maybe kidnapped? If they didn't find the gold, they might have kidnapped him to torture him. Right now he might be in some old warehouse or basement, half-conscious and bloodied, stubbornly refusing to talk. After all, if he wouldn't tell Randi, why would he tell the bad guys? Kim realized she was imposing scenes from television onto her thoughts. She had no idea if such things happened in real life. But if they did, she thought, this would be a likely place for it.

She lived in a very different world. Randi would probably say she lived in an ivory tower, far removed from the grit of human existence. For the most part, that was true. People like Flynn and the man or men who had kidnapped him were not people she knew or ever had known. These kinds of people frightened her. They didn't seem to frighten Randi. She moved comfortably among many types of people. She had some experience, Kim decided, on the wrong side of the tracks. In this environment, with all of these characters living outside the law, that experience was valuable.

Kim couldn't help feeling that she would be relieved when she got home to California where the most threatening moment of her day would be an irate driver giving her the finger on the freeway.

For Randi's sake, as well as Flynn's, Kim hoped he would turn up safely. If he didn't, Randi was obviously prepared to blame herself. The tenderness that Kim had begun to feel toward Randi the day she'd knocked her down was deepening. She didn't want to see Randi unhappy. In fact, she thought that Randi's smile was about the prettiest thing she had seen since arriving in Yuma, especially when it was directed at her.

CHAPTER TWENTY-SEVEN

Kim sat across from Matt at a picnic table in the BLM demonstration garden. She had spread some photos out between them so they could talk about specific petroglyphs. Matt seemed like a congenial, easygoing man. She sensed none of the resentment from him that Randi's behavior had led her to expect. He was relaxed, casual and had slipped immediately into a mode of convivial colleague with her. His long career in the desert had marked his face with well-defined creases that joined with his deep-set eyes to give him the appearance of a wise man.

"I'd agree with you about this one," he said, pointing to a faint anthromorph wearing a headdress. "Anasazi, that's what I've always thought. Not too many of those, but there are a few. And the rest, like you say, Hohokam, mainly. The Patayan angle is harder to pin down because even the Hohokam glyphs are not quite what we expect. The two cultural groups seem to have been living close enough in this area to develop a style that incorporates elements of both. That makes this site interesting, of course, if not unique."

"Definitely interesting," Kim said. "I appreciate your opinion. I was also wondering if there are any we've missed, some that might be removed from the main groupings."

He brushed his fine silver hair back from his forehead. "There's a small spiral about a hundred yards west of the main site, your Site A here."

"Oh, yes, we've found that one."

"Have you found the handprint?" he asked, his light eyes twinkling.

Kim, intrigued, said, "No. No handprints. Is there a handprint?"

"Yes, there's just one. Not too common around here. Not a print, of course, but somebody traced the outline of his hand and then scraped it clean with a hammer stone."

"Where is it?"

"The main site. If you're on the west side, just about where you see a series of four antelope about yay big." Matt held his fingers three inches apart. "Lie down on the ground and scoot yourself right up against the panel and look up with a flashlight. There's a crevice there where two rocks come together."

Delighted, Kim said, "Thank you!"

He nodded. "There are still a few secrets out there waiting to be discovered."

"Can I ask you a personal question?" Kim asked.

"Shoot."

"Why haven't you ever done a formal survey of any of the artifacts in the area?"

He shrugged. "I suppose there's a little part of me that just doesn't like the idea. I like to think of them as wild and untamed. What you're doing is a kind of domestication like the capture of a wild horse. A horse that's been broken is diminished. That's why they call it 'broken.'"

"Rock art isn't alive."

Matt smiled a little mischievously. "Not to you."

"Point taken."

"Whatever the reason the ancestors drew those symbols, they didn't do it for tourism. I like the idea of somebody walking along in the desert and just stumbling across them. No parking lot, no BLM sign listing all the rules about no touching, no trashing. Just lying out there under the sky like they were when they were made."

"I guess that's where Randi gets her point of view."

He laughed. "Randi's a little less realistic than I am. I'm glad you're here doing this. It needs to be done. As I said, a tiny part of me wants to keep them wild. A bigger part of me is just not interested in that sort of work. I'll sit there and look at them and think up stories about them. You do all the details and report writing."

"Not a desk job sort of guy, huh?" Kim asked, smiling.

"Right. One of the great things about this job is that it kept me in the field a good part of the time. A few years back I was offered the District Manager job. Turned it down. They gave it to Steve instead. He's much better suited."

"It was a promotion, wasn't it?"

"Depends on how you look at things. It was more money. But you've got personnel issues to deal with, all the reporting, budgeting, on and on! I figure you're in the workforce for thirty-five years. It's not like you can afford to wait until your career is over to have a good time. I managed to have a good time all along. I don't believe in putting off your life, spending it working *toward* something, some pie-in-the-sky dream. Six years of that, to get you through college, that's okay, but not thirty-five!"

Kim nodded.

"I just wasn't ambitious," Matt added. "Once I got to a place that suited me, I stopped. Like the ancestors. Very practical, economical people. They didn't build a skyscraper just to say they had the tallest building. If they built up high, it was to protect themselves from something down low. They didn't resist and struggle against nature. They went along with it as much as possible."

"Yes. That's something we assume when we try to understand why they did what they did. Why they settled in a particular spot or why they moved on. You know there was a good reason for it."

"Let me tell you a story. This is about my great, great, about twenty times great-grandfather. He was a tribal chief in the Four Corners area. He was very tall and had black hair that came down to his waist."

Kim, confused, said, "So how do you know that?"

Matt touched his forefinger to his forehead. "Memories," he said. "Ancestral memories. Why do you think the ancestors had no written language? They didn't need to write anything down. Their children and their children's children remember what happened."

Before her eyes, Matt seemed to take on the guise of an ancient as he proceeded to tell her a story about a long-dead Indian chief with a deep scar across his left cheek and a wife with mysteriously light-colored eyes.

CHAPTER TWENTY-EIGHT

Deputy Nelson called Randi late in the day to report that nothing had been found. Flynn was still missing. She had been worried and frustrated all day, unable to concentrate on her work. She stared at the photo of Flynn that she'd been carrying around since he disappeared. He was grinning widely with his gap tooth visible, standing in front of the petroglyphs, his clothes loose and worn, his face lined and leathery.

"Where the hell are you?" Randi asked the photo quietly.

Obviously, someone thought Flynn had found the gold. She was still skeptical. How could he have found it when the clues they had were so useless? On the chance she had missed something, she went to talk to Bill, the BLM botanist, a transplant from North Dakota, fair-haired, fair-skinned and often pink from the

Arizona sunshine. He never went outside without sunscreen, a wide-brimmed hat and long sleeves. His complexion was hardly suited to his locale, but after more than twenty years of peeling sunburns, his knowledge of desert flora was incontestable.

"Do you know any place around here where there might be palm trees," Randi asked. "Wild ones, I mean?"

He rubbed his hand over the reddish stubble on his chin. "Yeah, those palms in Kofa Wildlife Refuge."

"Other than those. Anything near the Gila, up in the feeder washes?"

Bill shook his head. "No, no palms there. The thing about palms—they're pretty good indicators of a freshwater source, like a spring. They're practically required for an oasis. So we know where they are. We've known for hundreds of years where the water is in the desert. Any people living out here knew where to find water. They couldn't have survived otherwise. Even artificial water sources, like the rock tanks the early settlers built, appear on the maps. You're not going to find any palms out there we don't know about because there aren't any water sources we don't know about."

"What about a hundred and fifty years ago?" she asked.

Again, he shook his head. "You're not the first person to ask these questions, Randi. It's not like I haven't been through this before. If there were palms in any of those washes back then, they are long gone and any evidence of them is also gone. I suppose the soil would still retain the plant material, chemical evidence, but you'd need to know where to test in the first place to verify it. You're not going to just stumble on the right spot by chance."

"I'm just trying to figure out if there's any way Flynn really could have found it."

"The whole town is buzzing with this story," Bill said, looking sympathetic. "I don't see how he could have found it, though. But, hey, I hope he's okay."

Bill had merely confirmed what Randi already suspected. It didn't seem possible that Flynn had found the Wolff gold with no new information to go on. No, he had probably found that one nugget and presented it as evidence that he'd found the treasure. He was the man who cried Wolff, Randi thought, and, if she had not been so downcast, she might have found that amusing. For his indiscretion, it was possible that he had gotten himself killed. The only hope Randi had was that no body had yet been found.

The one thing that troubled her about this likely explanation was that Flynn had been so insistent, even after she told him she didn't believe him, that he had found the treasure. Yes, he was a kidder and a boaster, but he wasn't quite a liar. Maybe he was delusional. He wanted to find that treasure so badly for so long, maybe he'd finally gone over the edge. She didn't really believe that either, though, so she was left with a puzzle.

Randi was on her way out of the building after work when she saw Kim and Matt seated at the picnic table in the demonstration garden. Matt was talking too quietly for Randi to hear, gesturing with both hands. He looked like he was telling one of his stories.

Randi approached the table as Kim said, "That's quite a story. Very amusing."

"Oh, hi, Randi," Matt said jovially. "Kim and I were just talking about Black Point. Sounds like she's got a good handle on it. Knows her stuff."

Kim glanced at Randi with a look of inquiry, as though she expected Matt's statement to be contradicted. Randi wasn't about to do that. On the table between them were some photographs of the petroglyphs.

"I'm glad there's finally going to be a survey of these sites," Matt said. "I was telling Kim here about that archaeologist, Fordham, who came through here back in the Seventies. If I can dig up his book, there's a chapter in it about the rock art near the Gila with some black-and-white photos. That missing panel, the one that was stolen, could be in one of those photos. That book has been out of print for decades and I haven't looked at it in quite a while myself."

"I'd love to see it," Kim said, eagerness on her face. "I've seen references to it, but haven't found a copy of the book anywhere."

"That was probably the first thing written about them," Matt continued. "And you know about the later work. But I have to say that the sketch Nellie made is right on. That's pretty much what they looked like."

Kim nodded, then looked up at Randi with a concerned expression. "Anything about Flynn?"

"No," Randi replied. "Nothing."

"Now that's a nasty bit of business," Matt said. "It makes me wonder if you should even be working out there right now with somebody out there tearing up property and who knows what else. That area is funny that way. The more people there are around, the more dangerous it is."

"The sheriff is out there patrolling," Randi said, "at least for the time being."

"And I don't have much choice," Kim said. "If I don't get this job done by April, it isn't going to happen until next winter."

"Maybe you should get off your can," Randi suggested to Matt, "and go out there and help. Nobody knows more about Black Point than you do."

He leaned back and laughed. "No thanks. Gotta use up my sick leave and I have to do it by June. I gotta get out of here. That's what I promised my wife. Not one more summer in this town. I don't think she ever did get used to the heat and we've been here for thirty-five years. By July, we're going to be sailing out into the Pacific with an ocean breeze, pelicans and the setting sun."

Matt's impatience to leave Yuma seemed a betrayal of sorts. He seemed almost euphoric thinking about his escape. "We've got a setting sun here too," Randi said, realizing that she was saying nothing. Her feelings were not rational, she knew. But Matt was her friend and she had been missing him already since he went on leave. He was a big part of why she had so quickly become one with this place. His sense of identity with the land had infected her and she didn't understand how he could so easily leave it behind.

"I'm going to expect to see you," Matt said, "over there.

199

You come anytime and we'll go sailing. Maybe we'll go whale watching even. Besides, it sounds to me like Kim has everything well under control. She doesn't need some old guy telling her what's what." He winked at Kim.

Kim gathered her photographs into a neat pile. "Thank you for the background," she told Matt. "It's very helpful."

"I'll dig out that book," he said. "I'll leave it here at the office for you when I find it."

Matt clambered out of the picnic table and pulled a baseball cap over his thin silver hair. "See you later," he said, then walked over to his car.

"He's entertaining," Kim said.

Randi smiled. "Yep. He is that."

"Hey, I can't see any bruises on your face. How's your nose?"

"All better. Just about fully recovered."

"Good. You're off work for the day, I guess."

Randi nodded.

"Would you like to go to dinner?" Kim stood, looking at Randi with a hopeful smile.

So she still hasn't given up on that, Randi thought, hesitating. She's still trying to be friends. What's the point? She's going to be leaving soon. What does she want from me? she wondered, feeling ambivalent. She did want to go to dinner with Kim. She wanted more than that, even, but under the circumstances, there was just too much at stake. She couldn't afford to let her guard down. She knew she had been giving Kim mixed signals since the day they met. Must be confusing for her, but didn't she see that they had nothing to offer one another?

Seeing Randi hesitate made Kim add, "It's not a date, you understand. I'm not suggesting...I mean, I know that you and Danya are together."

"What?" Randi asked, confused.

"Uh," Kim started, "you and Danya. That's her name, right? The woman who's living with you, the old flame from Phoenix."

"Yes, that's her name. What makes you think we're a couple?

Just because she's staying at my house for a few weeks, you don't have to assume that."

"Oh, it isn't an assumption. She told me herself at the Valentine's party."

"She told you what exactly?" Randi asked with an ominous feeling.

"She told me the two of you had resumed your old relationship. Gotten back together."

Kim was beginning to look and sound uneasy. Randi was beginning to get angry. She found herself shaking her head involuntarily. "No," she said. "If she said that, she was lying to you. We're just friends. I mean, we were more than that once, a long time ago, but there is absolutely nothing like that going on now."

"Oh, okay."

"No, really," Randi insisted.

"Yes, I get it. I guess I misunderstood."

Kim was just trying to be polite now, Randi could tell, pretending that it had been her mistake and not Danya intentionally misleading her.

"Sorry. I need to get home," Randi said, turning toward her truck, wondering what excuse Danya was going to come up with this time.

"Bye," Kim called, her voice tinged with confusion.

"She misunderstood," was Danya's response when Randi confronted her. "I was talking about the past."

"I don't think so. I think you told her we were together now."

"Why would I say that?"

"That's what I want to know."

"So who are you going to believe? Your oldest friend or some stranger from California?"

Randi took a deep breath. "To be honest, Danya, I believe her. And I want to know why you told her that."

"What difference does it make?"

Randi felt herself losing her temper. "What difference does it make? It's a lie!"

"I mean, why do you care what she thinks? Are you interested in her after all? You wanna get in that girl's pants, Rocky?" Danya's expression was an accusing sneer.

"That's none of your business," Randi said, suppressing an old, familiar rage.

Danya moved closer. "Oh, so that's it. You like her. Isn't that cute? You think you have a chance with a woman like that?"

"I—" Randi began.

"Other side of the tracks, Rocky. She's uptown. I bet she's never been busted for so much as shoplifting a pack of cigarettes. A fucking university professor! Just because you teach at a community college in this dump of a town doesn't mean you're in her league." Danya stood next to Randi, talking low but emphatically so that Randi could feel her breath on her cheek. "You're one six-pack away from being somebody she'd step over in the gutter."

Randi glared, feeling her right hand tighten into a fist.

"Are you going to hit me, Rocky?" Danya taunted.

"You'd like that, wouldn't you?" Randi said, willing her hand to relax. "You'd like to see me brought down. Why is that, Danya? So I'd have nothing but you? So I'd need you? Just you and me, wallowing in one another's self-pity, just like the good old days. Is that it?"

Danya took a step back, her expression blank.

Randi took a deep breath and felt her composure returning. "Pack your things and get out," she said calmly.

"What?" Danya looked stunned. "You're kicking me out for telling a tiny, harmless lie to your girlfriend?"

"I'm kicking you out for wanting to destroy me."

"Oh, come on, Randi, that's so melodramatic. I'm not trying to destroy anything. I just wanted to keep her away from you, you know. I was hoping for a little more time. Maybe I could show you it could work between us. Things are different now. We're both older and wiser."

"This isn't about Kim," Randi said. "It's about how you make me feel about myself and how you want to go back, to have things like they used to be. Things were fucked up back then, Danya. I was fucked up! You were fucked up! Why do you want to go back there?"

"Those were my good times, Rocky," she said, lowering her gaze. "Yours too, right? It doesn't look like you're having so much fun here."

"Yes, well, fun isn't really what I'm going for anymore."

Danya looked up, her eyes sad and, Randi thought, a little scared. "Are you really kicking me out?"

Randi nodded, steeling herself.

"Where am I supposed to go?"

"I don't know. Visit your mother. I'm sure she'd like to see you."

"My mother! Are you nuts?"

"I don't care where you go. You have to leave here, though. You're not good for me. I need to take care of myself."

Danya pursed her lips, her lank body slumping in resignation. "Randi," she said, "you aren't as weak as you think you are. You've really made it, you know? Please don't make me leave. Not yet. Just a couple more weeks. Time to get something figured out."

Danya had a pathetic look on her face like a dog in an animal shelter.

"I won't cause you any more trouble," she promised. "I'll even go apologize to Kim if you want."

"You stay away from her!"

"Okay, whatever you say. I haven't been sober very long. I really need your help."

"I'll give you two more weeks. You find yourself a job. Or you find someone else who will take you in. I think your mother would be happy to see you, especially without the booze. I can call her for you if you want. Your mom always liked me."

Danya grabbed her arm, her look desperate. "No!" she said. "Don't call my mother."

"Okay," Randi said, confused by Danya's agitation.

203

Danya released her, forcing a smile. "You don't need to do that," she said, more calmly. "I can call her if I decide to go there. Two weeks. I get it, Rocky. Don't worry. I'll get my shit together and be outta here by then."

Randi was still angry at Danya when she fell asleep. She was determined to stick with the two-week deadline, even if at the end of it Danya was still penniless, friendless and homeless. Even without the booze, Danya was still trouble, and Randi felt a new urgency to be free of her.

CHAPTER TWENTY-NINE

Site A contains at least two hundred and thirty distinct images, Kim typed on her laptop, *representing three discrete styles and multiple temporal periods. Most are almost certainly from the Ceramic Period, presumed to be Hohokam. These reside alongside an older set of images with occasional superimposition and light repatination. The older images exhibit characteristics of the Archaic period and are presumed to be Anasazi. Many of these are too faint to distinguish.*

When her phone rang, Kim glanced at the clock. It was still early, only nine o'clock on a Saturday, but she had already been up for three hours working.

"Hi, Tilley," said Randi on the other end of the line. "I thought I'd let you know that Matt dropped that book off for you at the office yesterday afternoon, the one by that guy, Fordham. I took it home. I thought you might want to look at it over the weekend."

"Oh, yes," Kim said, "I definitely do. I was just working on my site report. I'm hoping to get quite a bit done today."

"So you're not going to the festival?"

Kim remembered hearing something about a weekend event from Ramon, but she hadn't paid that much attention. "Festival?"

"It's Yuma Crossing Day. Big deal here. Everybody goes."

"Are you going?"

"Sure. I'm just on my way out. I was going to drop the book off on my way."

"What kind of festival is it exactly?" Kim asked.

"Oh, you know, just a shindig to honor the various groups who came through here back in the day—Native Americans, Spanish, pioneers, Forty-Niners. Right up your alley, I would say, especially since that's the whole point of the petroglyphs, right, the old crossroads."

"Yes, I suppose so."

"I'm going to be working the BLM booth from ten until one o'clock, so I need to get going. Shall I drop the book off?"

"Yes, if you have time."

As soon as she was off the phone, Kim made up her mind to go to the festival. She yanked on a pair of jeans and a clean shirt and ran a comb through her hair just as Randi's pickup coasted up to her door. She was outside and opening the door to the passenger side before Randi had time to cut the engine. She hopped in.

"Hey," Randi said, looking confused.

"I need a lift to the festival."

Randi raised one eyebrow, then shifted into drive.

"Thank you," Kim said, noticing that Randi wasn't accessorizing her uniform with the cowboy hat today. Apparently, being on call to meet the public, she was being well behaved. But she did have her cowboy boots on.

On their way downtown, Randi asked, "How are you getting back home?"

"I'm sure I can find a ride if, as you say, everybody is there.

And if not, you can take me when you get off duty."

A small smile appeared on Randi's face, as if it manifested itself against her will, then she drove downtown where a throng of people milled around streets lined with booths with white canvas covers.

"Hey," Randi said, "we can catch the end of the parade before I have to start my shift."

Kim followed Randi at a fast clip to a sidewalk along the parade route. City officials in cars passed by, waving. People dressed as Spanish Conquistadors, miners and pioneers walked past. There was one covered wagon, drawn by horses, complete with a pioneer family spilling out the back. A sizable troupe of Native Americans in traditional clothing followed the Yuma High Band on foot and horseback. Kim was startled to recognize Nellie driving her colorful cart, a burro in a straw hat pulling her along. Today she was dressed in fringed buckskin with a many-stranded turquoise necklace on her chest, looking more than ever like her First Nation ancestors.

Kim grabbed Randi's arm to get her attention, pointing out Nellie as she approached. Randi stuck two fingers in her mouth and let out a shrill whistle. Nellie looked their way, then waved enthusiastically.

"I've got to go," Randi said in Kim's ear. "The BLM booth is right at the corner of State Street if you need to find me."

Kim watched the end of the parade before setting off on her own. As she began to smell food, she realized that she hadn't eaten anything since a six o'clock piece of toast. She followed her nose to a booth where she stood in line to order the specialty, Indian tacos. That was Arizona's state dish, she was told by the man who handed her a paper tray of Indian fry bread topped with beef, lettuce, tomatoes and cheese. Kim found a bench, folded her taco and ate while watching people pass. She didn't expect to see anyone she knew, but while she was eating, Darlene and Trina came by.

"Oh, hi," Kim said, wiping grease off her chin.

"Did you see the Indian artifacts for sale?" Darlene asked.

"There are some nice pieces there. Might be of interest to you."

"I haven't seen anything yet," Kim said. "Haven't been here long."

"Down that way," Trina said, pointing. She then peered with interest at Kim's lunch. "That looks good. Hey, babe, let's go find something to eat."

"See ya," Darlene said as Trina grabbed her hand to lead her to food.

When Kim had finished her taco, she spent some time at a booth displaying fossils and minerals, hovering momentarily over a beautiful piece of malachite. She considered buying it for Randi, but decided against it. She had seen only a few pieces of Randi's rock collection and had to assume there was more to it. She had no idea what she had, what she liked. But the main reason was that she realized that an expensive gift would be awkward and might even damage the tentative friendship they had managed to forge. For whatever reason, Randi was keeping her distance and Kim needed to respect that.

Even so, she had not been able to help the relief she had felt over learning that Danya and Randi were not romantically involved after all. She had been so delighted, in fact, that soon after hearing that, she had actually danced in the tiny space between her trailer walls as her microwave dinner cooked. It hadn't been a rational response. Even if Randi didn't belong to Danya, she also didn't appear to be available to Kim. And since she had only a little over a month left in town, that was for the best. So she resisted her urge to buy Randi a gift, as she had been resisting so many urges toward Randi lately.

Eventually she reached the tables with the articles of her main interest—tools, baskets and pottery of native peoples. Her collection of pottery was not large, but it was selective. She looked often, but she rarely bought a piece. She didn't expect to buy anything today, but she did enjoy browsing. Perhaps more than this, she liked looking at the display pieces that collectors brought to show off, items not for sale at any price. While she was admiring an impressive Zuni pot, a short, stocky man in jeans, boots and a brown Stetson suddenly appeared at her side. He had one lazy eye and yellow teeth.

"Mornin'," he said, looking her up and down.

"Good morning," she replied.

"Nice piece, isn't it?"

"Extremely fine."

"I got that in Nuevo Mexicano," he said, hooking his thumbs in his belt loops and puffing out his chest. "Anything special you're interested in?"

"I go mainly for pottery. In particular, I'm always looking for polychrome ware by the Gutierrez family of the Santa Clara Pueblo."

"You know your stuff. I don't have anything right now by them. But I do have a few pieces from Santa Clara. Lois Redbird."

"Yes, I saw them. They're beautiful, but I prefer the more traditional patterns. By the way, the black wedding vases you have over there are counterfeit."

"Oh, no!" he objected. "All authentic. I go right to the source."

"Nevertheless," Kim maintained, "not everything here is the real thing." She reached over and picked up a bowl with a faded black-and-white design and a jagged hole through the center. "This, for instance."

"Mimbres," he said confidently. "You be careful with that. One of a kind."

"A replica."

"No way! That was found in a burial site on private land. Legal and authentic."

Kim shook her head, turning the bowl over in her hand. Too bad it wasn't the real thing, she thought, admiring the design. She would have bought it on the spot. There weren't that many of these around outside of museums. "The color is off," she said. "And the weight isn't right."

"Now how would you know that?" he asked, skeptical.

"It's lovely, but it isn't genuine. It's not even a decent copy."

He took the bowl from her and set it back in place. "Damn! I

209

guess I've been had." He grinned, showing off his yellow teeth.

Kim looked at him sideways and said, "I guess. You might want to lower the price on that or somebody might think you're trying to pass it off as an original. Could get you into some serious trouble."

He narrowed his eyes at her, then said, "Aren't you that archaeologist?"

"I'm an archaeologist, yes. Kim Gatlin."

"Working out at Black Point, right?"

"How do you know that?" Kim asked, noticing that he didn't bother to introduce himself.

"It's my business, isn't it? Cultural artifacts. Word gets around. You found anything out there other than the rock art?"

"Some obsidian flakes. Charcoal stain. No pottery shards. Nothing like that."

"That's what I figured. Good luck with your glyphs," he said, dismissively, then turned toward another customer.

Kim took one of the business cards from the display table and stuck it in her back pocket, then moved on.

After a couple of hours, she headed toward the BLM booth where Randi slouched in a metal folding chair with her feet perched on the edge of the table. The BLM insignia was prominently displayed on the front of the booth and brochures were neatly arranged across the table. Randi smiled easily at Kim and offered her a chair.

"Having fun?" she asked.

"Sure. Lots of interesting stuff."

"You've picked up some of it, I see," Randi said, indicating Kim's shopping bags.

Kim took out one of her purchases and unwrapped the tissue paper to show Randi an ammonite fossil. "This is for one of my nephews."

"Very nice," Randi said, taking it in her hand. "Pyrite. Good choice."

"Thanks." Kim took the fossil back and wrapped it carefully. "I got one similar for the other boy. I'm sure they would both rather have me bring them a velociraptor, but I think they'll like these."

"It sort of goes with the territory, doesn't it, animal fossils and hominid bones. I mean, your profession makes you sort of an expert in other types of fossils."

"Sure. You and I had to learn a lot of the same things in school."

"How did you memorize the Paleozoic eras?"

Kim laughed. "Oh, wow! Let me try to remember."

"Come On, Suzie," Randi chanted, "Dance, My Pretty Princess."

"Oh, I've never heard that one. How cute."

"I'm still using those in my night class. I have the students make up their own. They get a kick out of it. Did you remember one?"

"Yes. How about this? Clever old sages die mouthing poetic passages."

"Oh! I like it!"

Simultaneously, as if they had rehearsed it, they both said, "Cambrian, Ordovician, Silurian, Devonian, Mississippian, Pennsylvanian, Permian." Then they both laughed.

Kim put the fossil back in its bag and sat in the folding chair beside Randi. "So how are you doing?" she asked.

"I'm watching the clock. When I get off here, I'm heading for that little cantina down the way for a cold drink and a plate of carne asada."

"I'll be glad to bring it to you," Kim offered.

Randi's face lit up. "Oh, that would be great."

Heading for the cantina, Kim felt happier about her chore than was warranted, as if she had won some victory by being allowed to wait on Randi. She felt a little silly about that. A few minutes later she brought the food back and handed it over, saying, "Lunch is on me."

Randi shrugged and said, "Thanks," sitting up in her chair to eat.

"Who's going to relieve you at one?" Kim asked.

"Bill."

Kim pulled the business card out of her pocket and set it on the table next to Randi's plate. "Do you know this guy?" she asked.

Randi read the card. "Lucas Thornton? Nope. Why?"

"He's not quite above board. A bunch of his stuff is counterfeit and I wouldn't be surprised if a lot of it is also black market. He gave me the creeps."

"Bound to be some of that here," Randi said. "Same thing with fossils. You really have to know what you're looking at." She sopped up the sauce in her plate with a tortilla as a boy shoved a rolled-up poster in her face, wordlessly indicating that he wanted to buy it.

"Six dollars," she said. "Tilley, can you take his money, please?"

Kim conducted the transaction, noticing that the poster was an artist's conception of life in the Sonoran desert from the burrowers under the ground to the birds in the air and teeming mammals, reptiles, insects and plants in between. The same poster hung at the back of the booth. It was colorful and busy. By the time the boy had gone, Randi was tossing her plate in the trash and it was one o'clock.

Bill arrived right on schedule, so Randi and Kim went off to look at mineral displays.

Randi didn't seem to even see the beautiful piece of malachite Kim had thought of earlier as a potential present. Instead, she went directly to a gray hunk of rock that she identified for Kim as wolframite. Kim smiled to herself. She should have known. A geologist saw a different kind of beauty in rocks, a beauty that had nothing to do with bright colors or sparkle factor. Kim imagined it had something to do with the crystal structure or the particular composition of a piece. The beauty of a rock for a geologist was influenced by the much greater depth of knowledge of how and under what circumstances it was formed. It wasn't much different from any other discipline. A deeper appreciation of a thing often came from a deeper understanding. That could even be said of people sometimes.

"Exceptional," Randi said, holding the wolframite firmly in her palm, feeling the heft of it. Then she replaced it and turned to move on. One of her students appeared at her side, wanting to engage her in a discussion of the various rocks on display. While Randi was talking to him, Kim turned the wolframite over to check the price. It was expensive, more than she had guessed. Maybe as a thank you gift when she left Yuma, it would be okay, wouldn't arouse any suspicions or create awkward expectations. Kim paid for the mineral and tucked it into her tote bag, then caught up with Randi a few feet further on.

Kim spent the next hour at Randi's side as they made their way among the booths, stopping frequently to speak to friends and acquaintances of Randi's. Kim knew a few of these people already, but most were strangers. It did seem as if everyone in town was out for the event and that just about everybody knew Randi.

When Kim attended a festival in Sacramento, no matter what kind, like the Jazz Jubilee or something smaller, it was very rare for her to run into someone she knew. Everything was just so much larger there. And because of that, less personal.

They made very little progress moving through the street due to the constant stopping to greet friends. Kim found herself being introduced repeatedly as, "This is my friend, Kim." The first time Randi introduced her that way, she was surprised. She had expected, "This is Dr. Gatlin from California." The "my friend" part made her feel grateful. Again, she felt a little silly for being so desperate for a shred of goodwill from Randi. It had just been so long coming.

"Hey," Randi said, taking Kim's elbow and turning her toward a food booth, "have you ever had a date shake?"

"Date shake?" Kim said. "Sure. I've had a date shake, shiver, quiver and moan."

Randi laughed loudly, then shook her head.

Kim shrugged and said, "No, I never have."

"Then come on. You have to have one once anyway."

Randi ordered her a shake and Kim sipped it tentatively. It

was cold, sweet and delicious. Randi smiled at her as she nodded appreciatively.

It was just after three o'clock when Randi said, "I'm ready to head home. You want me to take you back?"

Kim nodded and followed Randi to her pickup. "Thanks for getting me out," Kim said. "It was fun. And informative."

"It's nice to learn a bit about the place you're living in," Randi said, starting the truck, "even if you're only living there a few months."

"This place sort of grows on you," Kim said, thinking about her initial impression of the town back in January. "It definitely has a personality. Not necessarily a pleasant one, but a distinctive one anyway."

Kim was getting used to sitting in the passenger seat beside Randi, watching her drive, her right hand at the top of the steering wheel, her left arm resting on the door frame. Her driving posture was relaxed, confident.

"No word about Flynn yet?" Kim asked.

"No. Nelson said they've found nothing. They're still patrolling out there, but no more foot searches."

The drive to Kim's RV park was a short one. "Thanks for the lift," she said, hopping out of the idling truck in front of her door.

Randi nodded. The strong, silent type, Kim thought, not for the first time. As she unlocked her front door, the pickup rolled away.

CHAPTER THIRTY

Randi hadn't even made it out of the trailer park before she saw Matt's book on the backseat. They'd both forgotten about it. She looped back around to Kim's trailer and took the book to the door.

At her knock, Kim's face appeared in the little window toward the front of the trailer. "Come in," she called through the window.

Randi opened the door and stepped in, holding up the book. "Oh, thanks!" Kim said. "I'm glad you remembered that."

Kim immediately opened to the index at the back of the book. "Here it is, Black Point!" Then she turned several pages before stopping abruptly, looking up and catching Randi's eye. "Oh, sorry. Just curious."

"That's okay," Randi said. "Enough fun for today, right? I guess you're anxious to get back to work."

"Uh, no, not if you're interested in doing something." Kim looked flustered. She squinted at Randi. "Are you? I mean, did you want to go out? Catch a movie? Dinner?"

Randi was amused by Kim's discomfort. Why was she so nervous? Sexual tension? There was no denying it was there, had been there all along. Randi herself wasn't the least bit nervous, though. Having spent the afternoon with Kim, she was feeling relaxed and comfortable in her presence. Being here with her felt familiar, like it would be the most natural thing in the world to reach out, take this lovely woman in her arms and kiss her. She had already had this feeling so many times, and each time had pushed it away. It just wasn't a good idea. There was no way it could turn out well. Even if they were great together, there was no time to find out, and the potential for pain was so great that it just wasn't worth it.

While Randi was talking to herself, trying to persuade herself to turn away, it was already too late. Her arms were around Kim and their lips were touching. And then their bodies were touching and Randi was exploring Kim's mouth more deeply.

Kim was compliant, eager, pressing herself in tightly. Randi felt lost in long, luxurious kisses that reached deeper and deeper into her, moving a powerful wave of desire closer and closer to the surface. She felt Kim's hands at her back, pulling her shirt free from her slacks. She had a momentary thought that she shouldn't be making out in her uniform, and then thought, "What a fucking stupid thing to think!" But the knowledge that her uniform was now askew had a distancing effect on her, taking her far enough out of the moment to regain her reason.

She released Kim's mouth as Kim reached for the buttons on her shirt. Randi grasped her hands in both of hers, holding them fast. Kim, breathing hard and obviously on fire, looked at Randi with distracted, questioning eyes.

Oh, God, she is so beautiful! thought Randi, already full of regret for what she was about to do. "Let's stop," she said,

216

swallowing hard. "I don't want you to get hurt."

"What are you talking about?"

"Why start something we can't finish?"

"It's okay," Kim said gently. "I know what the situation is. We both do. Don't worry about hurting me. I'm not expecting anything from you."

Randi spent half a second changing her mind and then changing it back before releasing Kim's hands and saying, "Okay, then, let me say it this way. I don't want *me* to get hurt. It's not worth the risk for me. Look, I'm sorry I kissed you."

"I'm not sorry," Kim mumbled.

Randi tried to smile, but felt her mouth resisting. "I've got to go."

She left in a hurry, afraid of her own ambivalence. She was sure Kim wouldn't understand because, as usual, she was giving mixed signals. Kim probably thought she was playing some manipulative game with her. And if Kim was angry with her, was fed up with her, so much the better. That would just make it easier to stay away from her.

When she got home, there was a note from Danya saying that she was out with Nicki and there was a roasted chicken in the fridge if she was hungry. Randi changed into shorts and a T-shirt, then took Breeze out for a long walk into the deep shadows of evening. She walked fast with long strides, far enough and fast enough to try to forget the eager insistence of Kim's mouth.

Her words, "I'm not expecting anything from you" told Randi what she had already surmised, that Kim was available for a no-strings romp. She had been looking to get laid ever since she arrived in Yuma. She had tried first with Blair and Randi had messed that up, so then she had turned her attention to Randi, correctly concluding, no doubt, that Randi was attracted to her. Ever since the night she had drunkenly asked Randi to kiss her, her eyes had had an open invitation.

And why not? Randi thought. Why shouldn't she find some pleasure here? Perfect opportunity for it. She was single with a finite stay, enough time to have some fun, but not establish any serious ties. Randi wanted to kick herself for not letting Blair have her. Blair would have known exactly how to take care of Kim. She would have fucked her brains out and sent her home satisfied. Nobody would have gotten hurt and Randi would not now be aching so badly to be with her.

Randi noticed that the sun was disappearing behind the mountains. She stopped and called to Breeze, who had run ahead. She turned to head home, realizing that she hadn't walked nearly far enough to walk Kim out of her mind.

CHAPTER THIRTY-ONE

Following Matt's directions, Kim lay down in the dirt under four antelope and scooted close in to the rocks with a flashlight pointed up. And there it was, just as he said, a single hand tracing. The hand wasn't much bigger than her own. It was well defined, etched deeply around the outer edge, then scraped clean inside. The person who made this would have had to have lain on his back exactly as Kim was doing now. He would have held his hand up against the surface of the rock, in shadow, and traced it with a sharp stone. Why had he put this in such a hidden place? Why hide it? And from whom? These were questions that would never be answered.

She pushed herself away from the crevice and called Ramon over so he could see it too. As he lay looking up at the image, he said, "Oh, my God, this is so cool!"

She handed him the camera so he could take some photos.

Then he emerged and sat up. "Congratulations on finding that!"

"Actually, Matt Mendoza told me where to look. After thirty-five years working out here, there are probably not too many secrets he doesn't know about. He's an interesting man. I'm sorry we weren't able to work with him."

Ramon stood and dusted off his shorts. "At least he told you about that."

"Yes. It's something, isn't it? One more mystery to add to our collection."

"I found a little mystery myself today."

"Oh? What's that?"

"A piece of licorice."

"A what?"

Ramon walked over to his station and then returned with a Zip-loc bag containing a rope of black licorice. "It was just lying here on the ground."

Kim took the bag. The licorice was dusty, but not old. "We haven't brought any licorice out here, have we?"

"No."

"Have you seen any other evidence of somebody being here recently?"

He shook his head. Puzzled, Kim set the bag aside and went back to work. She was keeping an eye out for Randi's truck, hoping she would come by. But the morning turned into afternoon and nobody came. Kim wasn't sure what was going on with Randi. But she did know that her kisses had been unselfconscious and full of longing, the sort of kiss a woman can't give you if there's no real feeling behind it. It had been a long time since Kim had been kissed like that, kisses that drew her whole body into the moment. And just when Kim had thought there was no turning back, Randi had stopped and fled like she had just remembered a kettle boiling on the stove. And her excuse? She didn't want to get hurt. Could that really be true? She didn't seem like the type who would be that vulnerable. She was a complicated woman.

Or just a wacko. Maybe she's a wacko, Kim thought. Damn good kisser, though, for a wacko.

Randi didn't come by the next day either and Kim wondered if she was purposely avoiding her. Randi had no business on this road, though, not since Flynn was gone, but that didn't seem like a reason to keep her away. She sort of expected Randi to come out and check Flynn's place every day, just in case he turned up.

Midmorning, Kim walked to the road to use the toilet and noticed that there was no toilet paper.

"Damn it!" she said to herself, then remembered that she had some Kleenex in the truck.

When she got back to the outcrop, she tapped Ramon on the shoulder to get his attention. He looked up, squinting into the sun, and removed his headphones.

"When you use the last of the toilet paper, you've got to replace it. Or at least tell somebody so we can get some more."

"I didn't use it. There was a new roll there yesterday."

"Are you sure?"

"Uh-huh. I remember getting it out of the truck and putting it in there."

Kim scanned the horizon pointlessly, as if she might see a toilet tissue bandit running across the desert. "We must have left it unlocked. Maybe a coyote got in there and took it."

"A coyote?" Ramon sprang to his feet. "Why would a coyote want a roll of toilet paper?"

"To play catch with the other coyotes? TP somebody's house? How should I know?"

"Maybe you should call Randi and tell her. You know what happened the last time somebody took some of our stuff."

"Uh, maybe."

If Randi didn't want to see her, Kim didn't want to intrude. One thing she knew about Randi, though, was that she would come if called. That could be a good thing this time because Kim really did want to see her.

"Okay, I'll call her."

She called Randi's cell phone, aware that her number would show up, tipping Randi off. If she didn't want to talk to her, she wouldn't answer.

"Hey, Tilley, what's up?" Randi asked casually.

"There's been an incident out here."

"Oh? What?" Randi sounded mildly alarmed.

"A tiny incident," Kim told her. "Probably nothing. I just thought— Ramon thought you should know. A roll of toilet paper disappeared overnight. From the Porta-Potti. Maybe some animal."

"Did you see any around on the ground?"

"No."

"So you're thinking a neat, dainty type of animal that could open the spring-loaded door and take a roll of toilet paper intact off to her den to build a nest or something like that?"

The sarcasm in Randi's voice was so welcome that Kim felt herself break into a wide smile. "Something like that, yes."

"Seen anybody around lately?"

"No, nobody. Do you think it could be another group of illegals?"

"I don't know. Are you afraid?"

"No, not really. I mean, we're fine, other than the fact that we have no toilet paper. Just keeping you informed, that's all."

"Okay. Well, thanks."

An hour after Kim hung up, she saw the BLM truck headed their way and her pulse quickened. Ten minutes later Randi was walking up wearing her white hat and sunglasses.

"Hey," she said. "I replaced your toilet paper and put a couple extras in your truck."

"Oh, you didn't have to—"

"I know, but it was no trouble. By the way, have you seen any coyotes around here wiping their butts with Charmin?"

Ramon laughed and Randi grinned at her own joke.

"On a different subject," Kim said, producing the licorice baggie, "we found this right over there."

Randi took the bag. "Today?"

"Yes. It could have been there a while, but obviously not weeks or months."

Randi looked confused. "Flynn loves these things," she said. "He has a perpetual supply of them."

"Oh. Then that's not so surprising. He was out here visiting a couple of times, you know. Must have dropped it."

"Yes," Randi said thoughtfully. "I suppose so. Damn, I wish something would turn up. I wish he would turn up is what I mean. Alive. But if he were alive, we probably would have heard from him by now."

Randi sat on a boulder, staring silently across the dusty landscape. A half a mile south two buzzards circled. Kim wondered if Randi was watching them, thinking that maybe they had zeroed in on something, not a dead rabbit, but the body of a man. Kim decided not to give voice to this thought.

"Pretty hot today," Randi said at last. "Your time's running out."

Randi sounded neither relieved nor disappointed, just matter-of-fact. Kim didn't know what to say. *Why did she even come out here?* she wondered. A lizard ran past Randi's boot and she seemed to have forgotten Kim, was just watching the lizard, so Kim sat in her beach chair with the laptop and returned to her work. Apparently Randi was just going to sit out here and be a distraction. After a few minutes, she started to whistle and Kim looked up from the computer to give her a dirty look. She stopped whistling, but stayed where she was.

After fifteen minutes of not being able to concentrate, Kim put the laptop down and walked over to Randi. "Look, maybe you should go," she said.

"Why?"

"You're bothering me."

"I'm not making a sound."

"No, but you're distracting me. I can't focus on my work with you sitting here."

"Oh, really?" Randi stood, grinning. "Can't get me out of your mind, huh?"

223

Kim glanced over at Ramon, who had his headphones on as usual and was facing in the other direction. "Randi," she said firmly, "why don't you make up your mind? Either cut it out or follow through."

Randi scowled. "Not in the mood for a little flirtation?"

"No. I think we've gone past that point."

Randi's expression relaxed into something passive and unreadable. "Yeah, you're right. See ya."

She turned and headed for the road. Kim sighed, realizing that she was glad she was going. It was true. She wasn't in the mood for flirting. She was merely annoyed by it. Once Randi had kissed her, she was ready for the real thing. It had been some kiss, had brought up feelings that had been lying dormant for a long time, and she couldn't help being disappointed that it hadn't had the same effect on Randi.

CHAPTER THIRTY-TWO

"Don't they ever get tired of that song?" Minnie asked, frowning and hooking the heel of her shoe on the brass rail along the bottom of the bar.

The boys were dancing to "It's Raining Men," which was blasting out of the jukebox. Minnie took a slow sip of her beer.

"Do you ever get tired of 'I Fall to Pieces'?" Randi asked, standing with her back to the bar.

Minnie raised her beer in a salute to Patsy. Despite her professed dislike of the song, Minnie was tapping the railing with her foot in time with the music. Darlene and Trina sat at one of the tables drinking red wine.

"If you want to dance," Minnie said after the music ended, "I can play one of those Fifties tunes. Maybe 'Ain't That a Shame.'

How about a little Fats Domino?"

Randi laughed. "A *little* Fats Domino. That's funny."

Minnie tilted her head and narrowed her eyes at Randi. "Do you want to dance or not?"

"No, I don't think so. Don't feel like it." She turned around to face the bar, then drained the last of her ginger ale. "Jeff," she said, "fill me up."

Nicki came in from the pool room and walked up to the bar. "Hi, Randi," she said. "Is Danya here tonight?"

"No. She's home."

"I think I found somebody who wants to buy her car. I'll just give her a call, then."

"Buy her car? She's selling her car?"

Nicki nodded. "Yeah. Pretty cheap too."

Nicki walked off, leaving Randi confused.

"Why are you letting that woman stay at your house?" Minnie asked.

"She's an old friend. Down on her luck. She needs help."

"You're such a big sap."

"She'll be gone next week."

"Good, because she gives me the creeps."

Hearing the squeak of the front door opening, Randi looked over her shoulder to see Kim coming in. She stopped just inside the door, looking around, her eyes lingering for a second on Randi.

"Oh, great, look who's here," Minnie said dismissively.

"Is there anybody you *do* like, Min?" Randi asked affectionately.

Minnie shrugged. Kim walked over to Darlene and Trina and joined their table. Randi turned back to face the bar as Jeff poured her another ginger ale and plunked some fresh ice cubes into her glass.

"Let's go out to the patio," Randi suggested to Minnie.

"Okay." Minnie unhooked her shoe from the railing. "Let me get another beer first."

Jeff had gone over to Kim to take her drink order. Trina went

226

to the jukebox and played El Debarge's "Rhythm of the Night." She crooked a finger in Kim's direction and Kim got up to dance with her. Randi stood where she was, watching them, watching Kim's body move in tight jeans and a silky, gold-colored blouse that sparkled under the lights of the dance floor. Randi watched for about a minute, then pulled her gaze away and faced the bar. She picked up her glass and knocked back a hard swallow. She noticed Minnie staring at her.

"That's ginger ale you're drinking there," Minnie said. "I don't think you're going to get the effect that you're trying for."

Randi sighed, then turned back to watch Kim and Trina dancing.

"I thought you wanted to go out to the patio," Minnie said.

"Right. I guess so."

"What's wrong with you tonight?"

Randi didn't answer. She couldn't stop watching Kim now. She looked like she was having a good time. One thing Randi was grateful for tonight was that Blair wasn't here. Even if she was going to let Kim drift out of her life, she didn't think she could take it if those two got together.

Minnie stood on her tiptoes to get closer to Randi's ear and said, "Why do I get the feeling that somebody around here is in love with that stuck-up, know-it-all bitch?"

Randi tried to smile. "I think I'll go home," she said.

"Randi, you can't let her do this to you. I've never seen you like this. Forget about her. She's not worth it."

"But she is," Randi said solemnly. "That's the problem. She's just so right for me."

Minnie stared up at Randi, looking serious. "If that's true, then why don't you go for it?"

"Because in a few weeks she'll drive out of here and I'll never see her again." She slapped Minnie lightly on the back. "Sorry I'm no fun tonight. See you later."

Randi made her way home, remembering, when she saw Danya's car parked at the curb, that it was for sale. Danya was in her room with a pile of laundry on her bed, folding clothes.

"Hi," Randi said in the doorway.

Danya turned and smiled. "Oh, hi. You're home early."

"Nothing much happening over there tonight. I ran into Nicki, though."

"Oh?" Danya turned a pair of socks inside out around each other.

"She said she has a buyer for your car. I didn't know you were selling it."

Danya turned to face Randi. "Yeah, I need the cash."

"How are you going to get around?"

"Bus. I'm going to go visit my mother after all."

"Oh, that's great. I'm glad." Randi felt a huge sense of relief, knowing that Danya had a place to go. But then the look on Danya's face made Randi wonder if she was telling the truth. It was always hard to know with Danya.

"I'll be leaving Monday morning."

Randi nodded. "Okay. I'll give you a lift to the bus station."

"No, that's okay. I have a ride. Nicki's taking me. Thanks for everything, though, Randi. You've been a lifesaver."

Randi felt uncomfortable and a little guilty. "Hey, you want some ice cream? I picked up a pint of strawberry this afternoon. I know it's your favorite."

"Okay, sure. Let me put these away and I'll be right out."

Randi returned to the living room where she noticed a flashing blue light circling the ceiling. She looked out the front window to see a patrol car on the street. It was parked behind Danya's Jetta. The cops were sitting in their car. Randi wondered if they were running the plates.

"Hey, Danya!" she called. "You got expired tags or something?"

Danya came out of the back and looked outside. "Shit!" she said under her breath, then stumbled backward away from the window, a look of terror on her face. Regaining her balance, she turned and ran into the bedroom. Randi went after her, finding her stuffing clothes into her backpack.

"What are you doing?" Randi asked.

228

"I've got to get out of here," Danya said, grabbing her wallet from the nightstand. She shoved that into her back pocket. "Stall them if you can. I'll go out the back door. Thanks for everything."

Danya kissed Randi on the cheek and then squeezed past her through the doorway. Randi ran after her, catching her in the kitchen, where she grabbed her by the shoulders and spun her around so they were facing one another. The backpack fell to the floor.

"Danya," she demanded, "what have you done?"

"Let me go! I've got to get out of here."

Randi held her tighter, insistent now. "What have you done?"

Danya twisted in vain against Randi's tightening hold.

"Dammit, Rocky, you stupid fuck! If you don't let go of me, I'm going to bust your nose again."

"I'm not letting you go until you tell me." Randi clutched Danya fast in both her arms, locking them together around her waist. Danya quit struggling when she realized there was no escape.

"I hit a guy," Danya said, breathing hard. "An old guy in a crosswalk. I hit him. I ran a red light. He went down."

Randi, stunned, loosened her hold.

"You hit a guy?" she asked, her voice subdued. "Was he killed?"

"I don't know. I took off. There were people there. He had help. They could call. I mean, I didn't leave him there with no help. I don't remember. I don't remember anything after that. I woke up the next day...there was blood on my car...the dent."

"When did this happen?"

"The day before I came here. In Phoenix. I didn't know what to do, where to go."

Randi suddenly understood. "You were drunk?"

Danya, standing now with her head down, nodded. Randi felt her knees buckle. She fell into a kitchen chair as lights swirled around the room, flashing red, blue and white, casting Danya's face alternately into dimness and starkness. She looked more desperate than Randi had ever seen her.

"Don't tell them about Nicki," she whispered, picking her backpack off the floor. "She's going to help me get to Mexico. A little sooner than we thought. Randi, don't look at me like that! I already have a DUI. I can't—"

There was a loud knock at the front door. Randi thought she could feel the vibration of it going through her torso as Breeze began to bark in the front room. She sat frozen in her chair, her mind suddenly empty, her body detached and unresponsive.

"Love you," Danya said, leaping toward the back door. She flung it open and ran through the doorway just as one of those blue lights passed by, bathing the door and Danya in a cool glow against the black of the night beyond.

As Randi watched, Danya stepped onto the back porch, seeming to move in slow motion, the strap of her backpack catching on the doorknob. She turned, a look of determination on her face, and yanked at the strap so hard that she reeled back on one foot when it came loose. She turned again, poised to run.

Randi heard a forceful male voice. "Stop! Police!"

Danya's figure, framed by a blue then a white light, quavered on the step for an indecisive second before she dropped her pack to the ground. Her hands rose slowly above her head.

CHAPTER THIRTY-THREE

"Did Randi go out to the courtyard?" Kim asked Minnie when she'd finished her dance with Trina.

Minnie scowled up at her with an unfriendly expression that left Kim perplexed.

"No, she went home."

"Oh." Kim was disappointed that Randi had left without speaking to her. Not even a hello.

"She wasn't feeling well," Minnie added, her tone suggesting it was Kim's fault.

Was she still angry over that Valentine's Day blunder? Kim decided to ignore her. She had had enough of these confusing Yuma women. They were all wackos, the whole lot of them. Something in the water, most likely.

But while she waited at the bar for Jeff to bring her a cola, Minnie turned purposefully toward her and said, "Do you have any feelings for her at all?"

Taken by surprise, Kim was about to tell Minnie to mind her own business, but the solemn look on her face caused her to reconsider. "Yes," she said, simply.

Minnie looked up at her for a moment, as if she were struggling with a thought, then said, "Then you should be together."

"But she—"

Minnie waved her hand between them. "Nope. That's all I'm going to say. You should be together."

With that, Minnie turned and walked away. Jeff placed a glass on the bar. Kim pulled the cap of paper from the straw and sucked on it absentmindedly, trying to make sense of Minnie's sudden altruism. Apparently Randi had said something to her. Kim had been rejected so many times by Randi already that she was reluctant to take heart from this exchange. But as she sat on a bar stool finishing her drink, the idea that Randi wanted her grew more and more insistent.

She paid for her soda and left the bar, then drove to Randi's house, not really knowing what she would do when she got there.

Despite all of the scenarios going through her mind, she was unprepared for the two police cars parked on the street in front, lights flashing. Kim slowed and rolled over to the curb of a neighbor's house. Between the flashing lights from the cruisers and the motion light on Randi's garage, the scene was as brilliant as daytime. Kim saw a uniformed policeman walking across Randi's front yard beside Danya, whose hands were cuffed behind her. Danya was stowed into the backseat of one of the police cars.

What the hell? Was this some kind of domestic violence situation? Had Danya hurt Randi? Kim started to panic. *Could Danya have killed Randi?* She shoved the door of her truck open and half fell, half jumped out of it. Running toward Randi's yard, she spotted Randi on her front porch talking to a female police officer. Relieved, Kim slowed to a walk as the officer turned and went back to the street. Randi stood in the doorway as the two cars pulled away, leaving behind a scattered group of onlookers in front of the houses on both sides of the street. These began to disperse as Kim approached the front door.

Randi looked at her, then turned and went inside, leaving the door open behind her. Assuming this was an invitation, Kim followed her in, shutting the door quietly. Randi slumped onto the sofa in the front room, put her face in her hands and started sobbing. Kim was shocked. The Lone Ranger doesn't cry!

Recovering from her surprise, she sat beside Randi, then tentatively took her in her arms. Though alarmed, Kim waited, keeping her confusion in check, while Randi sobbed with the grief of a woman suffering a deep loss. She held Randi gently with one hand on the back of her head, slowly stroking her hair. Breeze had come silently into the room and dropped down on a throw rug nearby, his snout resting on one paw, looking in their direction with what seemed to Kim a sympathetic expression.

After several minutes, Randi finally grew still and quiet, and at last she lifted her head and sat facing Kim, her eyes red and tragic.

"My God, you're a patient woman," Randi said, wiping the tears from her cheeks and attempting a small smile.

Kim smiled too, encouraged by the fact that Randi still had a sense of humor. "So, are you ready to tell me what happened?"

Randi took a deep breath and explained that Danya had been arrested for a hit-and-run incident in Phoenix in which she had struck a pedestrian, an elderly man who was still hospitalized with serious injuries. That was why she'd come to Yuma. She was hiding out.

"Why did she run in the first place?" Kim asked.

"Because she'd been drinking. And she blacked out. She didn't know he survived, even. I just now found out those details from the police."

"I see. That's bad."

"Someone got her license plate. They've been looking for

her ever since." Randi seemed to be talking to herself when she said, "That's why she couldn't go to her mother's. They would be expecting that. She was planning to run to Mexico." Randi sniffled, then blew her nose with a Kleenex.

"I'm very sorry," Kim said. "I guess she means a lot to you."

Randi shook her head. "No, that isn't it. I mean, sure, I'm sorry she's gotten herself in trouble. And I'm sorry someone got hurt. It's terrible. But, you know, we haven't really been friends for years. Too many bad scenes. Danya's always been a screw-up. We were both screw-ups together, in those days. I wasn't happy when she turned up here."

"But you seem to be really torn up about this."

"Oh, yeah, well, it's more selfish than that."

"I don't understand."

"I'm thinking of myself. I'm thinking that it could have been me being taken off to jail like that. It could have been me who ran over some innocent person on the road because I was a total loser wallowing in self-pity." Tears appeared in Randi's eyes again.

"Why are you saying that?"

Randi swallowed hard. "Because I'm like her. You don't know me, Kim. You don't know what a mess I made of my life back there. God, if you'd met me then, you wouldn't have wasted a hello on me. You don't know how much like her I am."

"Was," corrected Kim. "If even then."

"Maybe so, but it doesn't feel like there's much separating us. Like she said the other day, I'm just one six-pack away from—" Randi's voice faltered.

Kim touched her cheek, pushing away a tear with her thumb. "Randi," she said gently, "do you feel like having a drink now?"

Randi looked puzzled. "No."

"Then it isn't true. It's been a pretty crappy day and you weren't even thinking about it. I would say you're not anything like Danya. I think you're a very strong woman. You turned your life around. You've made it. About the only thing I can see in you that's lacking is belief in yourself."

Randi looked grateful and blew her nose again. She took a

couple of deep breaths, composing herself. "Sorry I lost it."

"It's okay."

"Bet I look like shit."

"I've seen you a little more together than this."

But it's kind of nice, Kim thought, to see the steely exterior discarded for a change. She now realized why Randi had been protecting herself so carefully, why it might even be true that she was afraid of being hurt. A vulnerable woman sat beside her.

"Let me get you a glass of water," Kim offered.

When Kim returned to the sofa, Randi had wiped her face dry. "I suppose I'll go down tomorrow and see how bad it is. What the charges are. What the bail is. And let her mother know she's here."

Kim nodded. "You're a good friend."

Randi shrugged, took a long drink of water, then set the glass on the table. Turning back to Kim, she said, "What are you doing here anyway?"

"Oh, right. Just passing by?" Kim laughed. "No, I . . . I thought you might want to see me."

"Really?"

"A mutual friend suggested that we might be missing an opportunity."

"A mutual friend?" Randi raised an eyebrow. "Short of stature? Sort of surly?"

Kim laughed. "You make her sound like the Travelocity gnome."

They sat looking into one another's eyes for a moment, Randi's expression serene.

"Come here," she said, finally, reaching one hand out to slide around Kim's neck.

Kim moved closer. "Aren't you afraid of getting hurt?"

"Yes. But I think it will be worth it."

Randi leaned in to touch her lips to Kim's, softly, lingering with a delicious uncertainty on her lower lip before committing herself to a deeper exploration. Kim closed her eyes as Randi's arms tightened around her, pulling her further into the kiss. She knew Randi wouldn't change her mind this time. She gave herself up to desire as their kisses grew more passionate and their bodies melted into one another, like to like.

Randi's hands moved over her blouse, stroking her through the cloth, wakening her senses.

As their mouths continued to take possession of one another, Kim felt Randi's hands on her skin as her bra went slack, caressing, teasing, pressing down on her, pressing her into the cushions, lying on top of her.

She threw her head back against the arm of the sofa as Randi released her mouth and moved her lips across her neck, grazing her skin, thrilling her nerves. Kim's arms strained to bring them closer yet.

As Randi's hand slid over the rough denim of her jeans, sensation shot through her, tingling down her thighs and up through her torso, taking her over, focusing her entire mind and body on that one spot. *Touch me again!* she thought, her breath suspended, her body poised and anxious. Responding to her unspoken request, Randi touched her again, and continued to touch her, through her clothes and then even more intensely against her bare skin.

As the night deepened, they lost themselves in relentless kisses and tangled limbs. Kim realized how much she had missed this, the soft touch of another woman's skin, the surging of desire in her core, the heady smell and taste of a woman's body. The hours slid by as they allowed themselves the unrestrained pleasures of physical passion, unaware or unwilling to acknowledge that the spontaneous longings of the heart and mind were rapidly keeping pace.

CHAPTER THIRTY-FOUR

The grin on Randi's face as she buttoned the shirt of her uniform said it all. Kim reluctantly rolled out of bed and covered herself in Randi's bathrobe.

"I'm running late," Randi said. "No time to make breakfast, but there is coffee. Sorry we couldn't hang around here longer."

Kim ran her fingers through her hair, trying to encourage it to stay out of her face. Then she stood gazing at Randi, at the uniform hiding that lovely body, remembering what she looked like without it. No one would ever guess how curvy she was. She had emerged from her clothes like a brilliant butterfly out of a tan chrysalis.

Randi buckled her belt and came over to Kim, pulling her close with a cherishing hug. Kim heard her sigh and felt the urgency of her embrace.

"See you tonight?" Randi asked.

Kim nodded. "Try to keep me away."

Randi smiled widely, then sat on the edge of the bed to pull on her boots. After Kim poured herself a cup of coffee, she kissed Randi goodbye at the front door. Randi opened the door to reveal Minnie standing on the front porch with her hand balled up in a fist, ready to knock.

The three of them, all startled, stood motionless for a moment before Minnie said with exaggerated sarcasm, "Just look at this. What a pretty little scene of domestic bliss."

"Now, look, Min, if you came over here to spy on us—"

Minnie waved a hand. "No, that's not why I'm here. You guys are old news, as far as I'm concerned. I came to find out if the other story was true."

"Other story?" Randi asked.

"The big story about how your houseguest got arrested last night, you dope."

"Oh! *That* story."

"Yeah, I realize you have something else on your mind this morning." Even Kim could see that Minnie's snarl was designed to hide a smile. "You guys make me wanna puke."

"Yes," Randi said, solemnly, "the story is true. I'm going over to the jail later. Look, I have to get to work. Tilley can fill you in."

Randi slipped past Minnie, giving her a pat on the head.

"I'm not jealous!" Minnie called after her as she ran for her pickup.

"Glad to hear it!" Randi called.

"How about a cup of coffee?" Kim offered.

When the two of them had settled in the sunroom with steamy mugs, Kim asked, "You're really not jealous?"

"Really," Minnie confirmed. "Oh, I was serious in the beginning about her, but after a while, once I realized it wasn't going to happen, I got over it. The last year, it's just been a flirtation thing, you know. Sort of a game. My way of making her feel loved. My heart hasn't been in it for a while, though."

The desert landscape sloped away through the expansive sunroom windows, cacti casting long morning shadows. A crow sat in a palo verde tree, cawing loudly.

"So tell me what happened," Minnie said.

Kim told the story in broad strokes, realizing that everybody probably already knew about Danya's arrest and would soon know about Kim and Randi's night of passion. No, there was no privacy in this town, but, in a way, that was kind of nice because it meant that there was a close-knit community of people who cared about you, mostly in a positive way.

"I knew that woman was here to cause trouble," Minnie said. "I can't even imagine how Randi ever got involved with her in the first place."

"She was a different woman in those days, I guess. Maybe both of them were. Young."

"Young, yes. *Young* explains a lot of things." Minnie laughed.

Kim started to think she could like Minnie, that they could be friends. She was sort of churlish, but good-hearted and loyal. She was the kind of friend you'd want to hang on to and she could see why Randi was so fond of her. I'd like to be a part of this, Kim thought, this community of women. There was nothing like this back home. There were friends, old college chums, colleagues, people she rarely saw. They weren't really a part of her day-to-day life. Why is that? she wondered. What's so different here that lives are so much more connected?

"So I guess I'm responsible for this," Minnie said, vaguely waving toward Kim.

"You mean me being here?"

Minnie nodded.

"I suppose you can take the credit, although I suspect we would have managed it on our own at some point."

"Oh, sure! Left up to your own selves, the two of you would have been playing hide-and-seek right up until you went back to California." Minnie laughed good-naturedly. "God, some women are just so hard to get into bed!"

They sat quietly for a few minutes, drinking coffee, enjoying the morning, until Kim's cell phone rang. She grabbed it from the side table. It was Ramon.

"Where are you?" he asked. "It's nine thirty."

"Oh, shit!" Kim said. "I'm sorry, Ramon. I forgot. I had kind of a rough night."

Kim saw Minnie roll her eyes.

"What do you want to do?" Ramon asked.

"Why don't we take the day off and have a long weekend?" Kim said.

As she hung up, Minnie stood. "I think I'll be going. I have to be to work too and I know you need some time to yourself to recover from your *rough* night."

At the front door, Kim said a heartfelt, "Thank you."

Minnie shrugged with mock indifference before stepping out into the heat.

Left alone, Kim stood inside the house for a moment with her eyes closed, images of Randi's body drifting in and out. She roused herself from this daydream, cautioning herself to keep it all in perspective. A temporary diversion, she reminded herself.

CHAPTER THIRTY-FIVE

Friday night merged into Saturday morning and Saturday night as Kim and Randi continued to get to know one another. Kim felt herself sliding into the most affectionate of gestures and thoughts with alarming ease. This romance was only a couple of days old, but already she had developed an automated response to Randi's touch. Randi's body felt familiar and comfortable, all of her curves fitting so nicely into Kim's hollows.

By Sunday morning, as they lay in bed after making love, the words that came to her mind were frightening. It had been a long time since she had felt or spoken those words, and she knew better than to speak them now. She was a scientist, after all, and the facts all pointed in a different direction.

"They think Danya's a flight risk," Randi said, nuzzling her face against Kim's shoulder.

"Not surprisingly."

"Her mother's coming tomorrow."

"Then you'll be out of it, don't you think?"

"Yes. Her mother's a practical woman. She can take care of things. She's hired a lawyer. She's so disappointed in Danya, but, ultimately, she'll do whatever she can to protect her. So, yes, I'm out of it."

Kim wove her fingers through Randi's. "Do you think this will be the thing that does it for her, that gets her sober for good?"

"I don't know. If she goes to prison, she won't have a choice, of course. I'm guessing she's going to have to serve some time. It's surprising what it takes sometimes, to make a person finally stop drinking."

"Was there something like that for you?"

"Nothing so dramatic, no. Thank God!" Randi kissed Kim lightly on the lips. "What do you want to do today?"

"I need to spend a few hours back at my place. Do some chores."

"How about meeting me for lunch later?"

"Dolly's?"

With that plan in place, Kim went to her trailer and sat down at the computer to catch up on answering e-mail while a load of laundry washed itself at the clubhouse. She sent a photo of Randi to her brother Jack and was surprised to see him IM-ing her almost immediately with the question, "Who is she?"

"Her name's Randi," she typed back.

"Cute," came the response. "Is it something?"

"Yes."

"☺" was his reply.

"She's adorable," Kim typed.

"Are you bringing her back with you," asked Jack.

"No."

"☹"

"I know!"

Those emoticons pretty much sum it all up, Kim thought.

By the time she met Randi for lunch, she had a few clean clothes and no important business left undone. Since it was Sunday, Ramon was waiting tables at Dolly's. He brought them their lemonades, then looked suspiciously from one to the other of them. He said nothing, however. After he left, Randi giggled and said, "I think it shows."

"It's that goofy grin on your face."

"It's been quite a weekend," Randi said, grinning even more goofily.

Kim was absentmindedly coloring in the Wild West scene on her paper placemat with an ink pen.

"Do you want me to get you some crayons for that?" Randi asked, impishly.

"No, thank you. I'm just doodling."

When their cheeseburgers arrived, they both quit talking for a few minutes, focusing on the food. Kim held her burger in her left hand and continued doodling in the margin of her placemat with her right, drawing geometric designs.

"He must have been lying," Randi said.

"Huh?" asked Kim. "Who are you talking about?"

"Flynn. He said the gold was just where it was supposed to be, under a palm tree. Since there aren't any palm trees, he had to be lying."

Now that the Danya incident was over, Randi's mind was back on Flynn. Kim wasn't listening very closely, which didn't matter, because she was mostly just thinking out loud. The thing that Kim was obsessed with was different. It had to do with Randi and the countdown in her head to the day they would say goodbye.

"I might let Ramon go in a few days," Kim said. "I won't need him anymore. The survey is pretty much complete."

Randi looked at her and then dropped her gaze to her plate. Kim hated to bring her down, but there was no point trying to avoid reality.

"I'll stay a while longer myself. There's quite a bit of writing and research I can do, most of which could be done back home. Doesn't require being on site. But I don't have to leave just yet. I mean, I don't *want* to leave just yet."

Randi looked up again. "I'm glad to hear it." She reached over and took hold of Kim's hand. "I'm going to miss you when you do go, really badly."

"Me too. It's going to be a bittersweet memory for a long time, I think."

Kim saw that Randi's eyes were welling up. Tough girl with a soft heart. "Hey," she said, "I haven't gone yet!"

Randi smiled half-heartedly. "Right. Let's have as much fun as we can while you're here."

"Absolutely."

Randi released Kim's hand and narrowed her eyes at the doodles. "What is that you're drawing?"

"Oh, just some of the glyphs from the site. They run through my brain, you know, because I've spent so much time looking at them and thinking about them."

"So what is that?" Randi pointed to one of the sketches. "An umbrella?"

Kim laughed. "Not very likely, now, is it? I don't think the Hohokam had umbrellas. These two are together on one of the panels. The other symbol, this circle with the spokes, is sometimes interpreted as the sun. The umbrella, which is about three inches below it, is a little less obvious. It's what we unimaginatively call a forked line. Since it has these four downward-trending lines around the center, upright line..."

"Is it a palm tree?" Randi asked.

"No." Kim shook her head. "Trees are drawn completely differently. This could represent the four corners of the earth. The upright line would be the axis on which the earth rotates. It's odd, though, that they would think of the earth in rotation if they also saw it as flat, but..."

Kim looked up from her placemat and saw Randi staring at her, eyes wide, as if something momentous had just happened. "A palm tree?"

"It might look like a palm tree," Randi said, "to an untrained eye. The upright line is like a trunk and the four downward lines are like the palm fronds."

They sat motionless, staring at one another. Then Kim turned to her doodles again with a different eye. Looking at these two glyphs that she had seen so often on the basalt, she saw, for the first time, the image of a sun over a palm tree.

"Where is this?" Randi asked, her voice quavering.

"Site A, Hendy Wash. The old, original Hendy Wash."

"My God!" Randi said. "Could Flynn have seen this?"

"He did come out to the site a couple of times. It's right there toward the front, visible enough, but not very obvious, really, unless you've got your nose in it like we've had. I mean, there are dozens of other images all around it. It doesn't stick out like a signpost." Kim hesitated, thinking back over Flynn's visits, trying to remember if they had ever talked about these two symbols. "Wait a minute. You know that photo that Flynn hung up in his shack? The one Ramon took of him?"

"Yes, it's in my truck. I've been carrying it around ever since the day he disappeared."

"Let's go take a look at it," Kim suggested.

They went to the parking lot and Randi took the photo out from behind the seat. In the background, behind Flynn, the sun and "palm tree" glyphs were distinctly visible, located just to the left of his leg.

Randi and Kim looked at one another with a silent mutual understanding. "Let's stop by my house and get a shovel," Randi said.

CHAPTER THIRTY-SIX

Kim sat in the middle next to Randi, giving Breeze the window seat. It was too hot to have the window open, so he sat with his nose pressed against the glass. After they'd turned off the highway, Randi said, "There's somebody behind us."

"Following us?" Kim asked.

"I don't know."

After several miles, Randi turned down their usual side road. The vehicle behind kept going straight. Randi sighed and said, "I'm just paranoid, I guess."

They continued to the petroglyph site and didn't see anyone else. The wildflowers were gone now. The burst of energy and color that the desert put forth with such enthusiasm was short-lived. It was also getting oppressively hot some afternoons.

Unfortunately, they had arrived at the site at the hottest part of this afternoon, but neither of them would have considered waiting even a couple of hours to find out if this hunch was correct.

Randi carried the shovel, Kim the water bottles and Breeze ran ahead. Kim showed Randi where the spot was, a petroglyph of the sun over a shape that someone might interpret as a palm tree, about six inches above the ground. Randi sank the shovel into the ground underneath, and it went in easily.

"This ground has been turned recently."

Kim assumed that Randi was thinking the same thing she was, that the mystery was about to be over, that Flynn had dug up this spot and found the gold and, if he had been telling her the truth, it was still here. Kim's heart was pounding furiously as she watched Randi remove the gravel and dirt shovelful by shovelful, digging down about a foot and a half before she hit metal.

At that sound, Randi stopped abruptly and looked up at Kim with disbelief. Then she tossed the shovel aside and knelt at the hole, moving the dirt with her gloved hands until she could grasp the edge of an old iron lid, the top of a small Dutch oven. She worked her fingers around the edges of the pot until she was able to lift it out of the hole. Kim knelt beside her as she pulled off the rusty lid. Inside were three buckskin bags, each tied with a leather strap. Randi removed her gloves. Kim saw that her hands were shaking as she untied the strap from one of the bags. Kim moved aside to let the rays of the sun illuminate the contents. The gold dust in the bag sparkled as the light hit it.

"Holy shit!" Randi said, then let out a high-pitched whistle between her teeth.

She retied the bag and opened up the other two in turn. One of them contained nuggets of varying sizes. The other contained dust and flakes. She returned them to the pot, then stood. They were both speechless. So it was all true. The treasure had been here all along.

Just as Randi got to her feet, they heard the sound of crunching gravel and both of them turned toward the noise as a man holding a large handgun emerged from behind the outcrop.

247

He was aiming the barrel of his gun right at them. He wore a cowboy hat low over his forehead and a bandana over his nose and mouth like an old-time bank robber. All they could see were his eyes, but Kim recognized him almost immediately as the Native American art dealer, Lucas Thornton. It was that one lazy eye that gave him away.

"I knew you girls would lead me right to it," he said, stepping toward them. "Don't do anything stupid. All I want is the gold."

He stopped walking when he had come within twenty feet. "Move over there," he said, motioning toward his left.

Randi and Kim slowly moved away from the pot at their feet. Thornton stepped toward the gold, keeping his eyes and his gun trained on them. "Is this it, then?" he asked. "This is really the Wolff gold? That old fool was telling the truth after all."

"Looks like it," Randi said. "And you must be the guy who tore up Flynn's shack."

Thornton looked up from the pot at his feet. "Yeah, that would be me. I thought he took it home with him. But he was smarter than that, leaving it buried."

"Where is he?" Randi asked.

"No idea. Last time I saw him, at his place, he threw a log at me and knocked me down. By the time I got up, he was gone. Been watching his place ever since. No sign he ever came back. Been watching you too. Figured he told you all about it that day in town. Hell, he was telling everybody who would listen. And you did seem awfully anxious to get him off to yourself."

Thornton knelt down to the pot and held one of the bags in his hand briefly, feeling its weight before dropping it back in. He stood again.

"So who are you?" Randi asked.

He laughed. "You think I'm going to tell you that?"

Kim wished she could tell Randi that she knew who he was, but that was dangerous. In the movies, if the bad guy thought you could ID him, he'd have to kill you. Let him go, Kim thought, trying to communicate telepathically with Randi. Don't do anything heroic.

"I'm going to take your vehicle so you can't follow me."

"You didn't walk out here," Randi observed.

"No, I didn't. I'll drive your truck to mine. It's parked about two miles east. I'll leave your truck there with the keys in it. Gonna have to bust your radio, of course. By the time you reach it and get back to town, I'll be long gone. Nobody gets hurt, so long as you cooperate. Give me your keys and your phones."

Randi reached into her front pocket and lifted her keys out slowly, letting them dangle in front of her.

"Okay," Thornton said. "Just toss them gently here at my feet."

Kim was just as surprised as Thornton was when Randi threw the keys hard and screamed like a lunatic, a high-pitched, crazy-ass scream. Thornton jumped back against the wall of rock as the keys whizzed past his head.

"What the hell!" he said as the keys hit the ground. "You crazy?"

He had taken one careful step toward the keys just as Breeze came charging up from the wash behind him. Randi pointed at Thornton and yelled a command. Then, as Kim saw Breeze lunge at Thornton, Randi leapt at Kim and pushed her to the ground, landing on top of her. The gun went off twice. Oh, God! Kim thought, desperately, why the hell do you have to be a hero? She couldn't move with Randi on top of her and she couldn't see anything because her face was smashed in the dirt. She could hear Breeze growling ferociously and Thornton hollering, so she knew that the two of them were still alive. *Randi*, she thought, *if you're dead, I'm going to kill you.*

But in that second Randi rolled off. When Kim turned over, she saw Randi picking up the gun from the dirt while Breeze tore into Thornton's arm. He was screaming in terror and pain, desperately swatting at Breeze with his other arm. The handkerchief had slipped off his face in the struggle.

Randi aimed the gun at him and called out a "Heel!" to Breeze, who immediately let go of Thornton and came to her side. Thornton lay on the ground, his arm bleeding, long scratches across one side of his face. Randi turned to look at Kim, who was getting to her feet, then she looked back at her prisoner.

"If you move," Randi said, "I send my dog back at you."

He sat where he was, sullenly cradling his bleeding arm.

"Are you okay?" she asked Kim.

"Yes, I think so," Kim said, spitting dirt.

"Call nine-one-one."

They waited for forty minutes, sitting in silence, until the sheriff arrived, driving off-road right up to the petroglyph site, which made both Kim and Randi cringe. Thornton was handcuffed and put in the vehicle. Once they could relax, Randi opened up one of the leather bags again and she and Kim peered at the gold nuggets.

"It's something, isn't it?" Randi said.

"Very beautiful stuff," Kim agreed. She took a couple of photos of Randi holding the bag of gold.

"I'll take that," the sheriff said, taking the bag from her. He put it back in the pot and had a deputy carry the pot to the truck. "You two come into the office and fill out a report."

Randi sat on a boulder while the sheriff and deputies drove off in a thick cloud of dust.

"Easy come, easy go," Randi said as silence prevailed once more. Then she stared at Kim and laughed. "You should see your face."

"And whose fault is that?" Kim asked, wiping at her nose with her hand.

"Here, let me clean that off."

Randi stood and pulled a handkerchief out of her pocket. Just as she began wiping the dirt off of Kim's cheeks and chin, Breeze suddenly started barking in the direction of the wash. As Kim turned to look, she saw Flynn climbing up over the edge of it and walking toward them. He too was covered with dirt. A licorice rope hung from the corner of his mouth.

"Oh, you girls are making such a ruckus over here this afternoon!" he called, sounding disgruntled.

"Flynn!" Randi hollered, running over to him. She stopped

short of a hug. "Where the hell have you been?"

"Hiding. Been holed up in an old mine just over yonder." He pointed vaguely toward the west.

"What mine?" Randi asked.

"Not even you know about this one, Randi Girl. My secret bunker. Keep a few things there, just in case. Like a squirrel, burying nuts here and there. Came in handy this time, that's for sure. I was waiting for things to cool off. That jackass would have killed me."

"You're damned right he would have killed you," Randi said, her voice cracking with emotion. "You stupid old fool. I thought you were dead."

Flynn smiled affectionately at her, then stepped over to the hole where the gold had been buried.

"You girls figured it out too, eh? Pretty good puzzle, wasn't it?"

"You should have told me where it was," Randi complained. "We all could have been killed."

"Glad you weren't, though," he said, grinning.

Randi gave him a crooked smile. "You don't seem too upset about losing your fortune."

Flynn shrugged. "What was I going to do with all that money anyway? Just you make sure they get it right in the paper. It was Flynn who found it, fair and square."

"Yes, it was!"

"Guess I'll go home now the coast is clear. Got some cleaning up to do. See you tomorrow, same as usual, eh?"

He winked at Randi, then started walking east with his familiar limp.

"Wait," Randi said. "We can give you a ride. You ride in the back, though. You're too dirty for the cab."

"Me?" He pointed at Kim. "Look at that one."

Randi laughed and handed the handkerchief to Kim. The three of them and Breeze headed for the road, casting long shadows as the sky dimmed toward night.

"Was it you who took that roll of toilet paper?" Kim asked Flynn.

251

"Uh-huh. Snuck out in the middle of the night for that. A man can live without a lot of things, but that ain't one of 'em."

The three of them laughed. Randi slapped Flynn on the back, sending a cloud of dust into the air.

CHAPTER THIRTY-SEVEN

Perched on the edge of a ravine as the sun became a red ball on the horizon, they finished the dessert they had taken from the restaurant after their farewell dinner. The walls of Rainbow Wash deepened to a brilliant shade of red as they watched. Beyond, on the flat desert floor, the teddybear cholla glowed with silver auras as the slanted light lit their needles.

"It's gorgeous," Kim said.

"This is one of my favorite places," Randi told her, taking her hand. "I come here a lot."

Kim put the last bite of cheesecake into her mouth. "Ummm. This is the best white chocolate raspberry cheesecake I've ever had."

Randi leaned over and kissed her briefly, tasting the sugar on her lips. "Yes, it's delicious."

They sat close, leaning against one another.

"What's that over there?" Kim pointed to a line of greenery in the distance.

"Colorado River. That's California on the other side." Randi wondered if the mention of California reminded Kim about her impending departure. The knowledge that this was their last night together was a thought Randi couldn't get out of her mind for a minute.

As if she could read Randi's mind, Kim said, "We can get together now and then. You can come to Sacramento. I'll come visit you here for Christmas break. It's only an eleven-hour drive. If you took off heading north and I took off heading south, in only five and a half hours we'd be together. Where would that be anyway, the midpoint?"

"Bakersfield, maybe, or Lancaster."

Kim laughed. "Bakersfield! Not many people would think of that as a romantic getaway spot."

Randi had to laugh too. It was a funny idea.

"Or we can meet somewhere easy for us both to get to, like San Diego or Phoenix," Kim said. "I'm in Phoenix quite a bit, actually. It'll be a lot more fun going there if I can meet you there."

"Yes, that sounds great. My parents still live there, so I go back now and then too. We should set a date before you go so we know it will actually happen."

"Okay. Come see me in July when it's unbearable here. Come visit for two weeks. How's that?"

Randi nodded. "I will."

"Good. I'll plan something fun for us to do."

Kim kissed her, smiled reassuringly, then said, "I have something for you."

After searching through her bag, Kim produced a colorful gift box. Randi took it, noticing that it was surprisingly heavy for its size. She opened the box to reveal a stunning piece of wolframite.

"Oh, my God," she said. "It's the same one, isn't it? The one we saw at the festival."

Kim nodded.

"You're very sly. Oh, I love it!"

"Good. Give it a nice spot on your rock shelf."

"I will," Randi said. "Place of honor. Thank you!"

"You're welcome."

"I have something for you too," Randi said, producing a small plastic cube from her backpack. Embedded in the center of the cube was a gold nugget. She handed it to Kim.

"A memento of our treasure hunting adventure," Randi said. "That's the nugget Flynn gave me."

"Wow, thanks," Kim said, holding it in her palm. "But doesn't this belong to the feds like the rest of it?"

Randi shrugged. "I don't know where that nugget came from. For all I know, Flynn dug it out of his own mine. I tried to return it to him, but he told me to keep it. I guess finding the gold was really all he wanted after all. Sort of makes him notorious. He's got the newspaper article tacked up in his place like a trophy."

"Yes, I know. I went out there yesterday to say goodbye to him."

"He's sorry to see you go too, I know."

It was dark now and the stars were popping out by the dozens as a cool breeze came up.

"Shouldn't we be going back?" Kim asked.

"Can't follow this road in the dark," Randi said. "We're going to have to stay here for the night and wait for the light."

"What?" Kim asked, alarmed.

Randi stood and took Kim's hand, helping her to her feet. "Come here."

She led Kim to the pickup and unhooked the cover of the bed, lifting it off. In the bed of the truck Randi had arranged a thick foam pad covered with a pair of sleeping bags and a couple of pillows. Kim looked startled and unsure.

"It'll be very comfortable," Randi assured her.

"You're serious? We're really going to stay out here all night?"

"Nobody will bother us. You'll love it."

They climbed into the back of the truck and settled into the spongy bed. As Randi lay in Kim's arms with the sky above a nearly solid shimmer of stars, she felt serene and happy. In just a couple of weeks, she had grown so used to having Kim beside her. It didn't feel forced or complicated. It felt right. The image in Randi's mind was of a slow-motion reverse-action film where the hundreds of slivers of a shattered goblet all come back together into a perfect whole. That's how she felt when she was with Kim—whole.

They embraced and kissed one another and slowly removed their clothes. Kim's body in the starlight was dazzling. They made love in the light of a rising moon and then, as the chill of the night overtook them, slipped inside the sleeping bags. The moon was three-quarters and had now risen to about eleven on the face of the sky's clock.

"I've never seen so many stars," Kim said. "Even with that bright moon."

"So, what do you think of this idea now?" Randi asked.

"You were right. I love it."

Randi was trying to make their last night special. She was actively committing memories to a permanent place in her mind. The silky sensation against her cheek as she brushed her face against Kim's back, the twinkle of starlight in Kim's eyes, the howl of a distant coyote—these were the details she wanted to remember.

"Are you sad?" Kim asked quietly.

"Sort of," Randi admitted.

"I'm glad we decided to go for it, even though it will be hard to say goodbye."

Hard is an understatement, Randi thought, saying nothing.

Kim fell asleep curled around Randi's back, the wind blowing around them, coyotes howling, the moon sliding by in the southern sky. At some point, Randi too fell asleep.

When she woke, the sky was beginning to pale, though the sun had not yet appeared on the horizon. Kim was asleep, looking like a beautiful, innocent child, strands of hair pasted across her cheek, her dark eyelashes resting at the top of her cheekbones, her left hand lying on the pillow beside her head, palm upturned and open. Randi lay with her face close to Kim's open hand and watched her breathing in the dim light. At the moment, the whole world seemed to consist only of this lovely sleeping woman and the velvety gray sky. Now that would be a world to live in, Randi thought sadly. This could have been the real thing.

There was no doubt in her mind that everything that felt best to her now would feel really bad later.

When Kim opened her eyes, Randi smiled and said, "Good morning."

Kim smiled too, and then stretched luxuriously, like a cat.

Randi reached for her and pulled her close in the sleeping bag, threading their legs together, filling her arms with Kim's warmth. They lay together watching the sun peek over the horizon, silently. Randi would have liked to have stayed like that for hours or days, but her stomach was rumbling loudly.

Before the sun had freed itself from the edge of the earth, they were making their way back to town to a hearty breakfast at Dolly's. Neither of them had much to say, though Randi was sure that both of them had a lot to say. There just wasn't any point in saying it.

Ramon was working today. He took their orders, then said, "Kim, I've got my application in to UA. I'm pretty sure I'll get in. Go Wildcats! Now I just have to pull out one of those scholarships."

"That's great. The fieldwork here should help a lot."

"And your letter of recommendation."

"Ramon, I know you'll make it." Kim clasped his hand warmly. "I want you to keep in touch and let me know how you're doing. Not just school. Life in general. Your family. Sophie."

He nodded. "I will. I'm so glad I got to work with you. You've changed my life."

"Oh, you're responsible for that. Don't blame me." Kim laughed.

When their breakfast arrived, Kim pushed the ketchup bottle across the table to Randi, a gesture she did automatically because she knew Randi would put ketchup on her eggs. That unconsidered gesture nearly brought Randi to tears.

If that's enough to make me cry, Randi thought, I am in bad shape. She forced a smile and Kim smiled in return, an affectionate, joyful expression.

"What a wonderful night that was," Kim said. "I'll never forget it. Just absolutely beautiful in every way."

Randi was glad that Kim had that memory to take home, that she would be able to look back on her visit so fondly. She herself was already hurting and it would only get worse. She desperately wanted to make Kim stay, but didn't know any way to do that. All she had were fantasies. She wanted to tell Kim everything that was in her heart, but if she did it would seem like manipulation and it would spoil Kim's perfect memories. They had both known when they started this how it would end and they had both agreed to the terms, so Randi kept her thoughts to herself.

CHAPTER THIRTY-EIGHT

The girl sitting in the uncomfortable visitor's chair in Kim's university office was cute, blond and shapely. She had the smooth, fresh face of youth and the inevitable arrogance that went with it. She'd come to argue over her grade in Survey Techniques, in person this time, thinking perhaps that it would be more effective than the e-mail arguments they had already had.

"I don't see why you couldn't just change it to a C," she protested.

"Because you earned a D," Kim said again. "And really, not on the upper edge of that."

"I offered to do extra credit. Remember that?"

"Yes. And as I told you then, 'extra' by definition denotes something in addition. Since you didn't do most of the assigned work, extra credit is meaningless. Besides, I don't give extra credit. It's a ridiculous concept."

The girl sighed in exasperation.

"I'm sorry, Brook, but I think we're finished with this discussion. I'm not changing your grade."

The girl stood, glaring at Kim. "This is so bogus," she said, then walked out.

Kim leaned back in her office chair, glancing at the screen of her computer where she'd been working on class schedules for the fall semester. Spring semester was over and they were still quibbling about grades from last fall. Nothing much had changed here.

On the one bare wall of this small space, crowded with filing cabinets and bookshelves, Kim had hung three new photos. One was of Flynn grinning with his gap tooth in front of the petroglyphs. One was of Kim with Connie Thompson showing off her projectile point. The third was Randi holding a bag of gold, looking triumphant and beautiful.

On the desk was the gold nugget encased in clear plastic, which she found herself picking up and fingering often.

She and Randi kept in touch by e-mail mostly and by phone some evenings. In this way, Kim had learned that Lucas Thornton was in big trouble, for not only was he being charged with his crimes against Flynn, Randi and Kim, but he was also being investigated by the FBI for shady dealings related to his art collection.

Kim had also learned that Blair and Minnie were now a couple, apparently driven together through their mutual feelings of rejection by Kim and Randi. And, as unlikely as it seemed, Blair appeared to have changed her ways and become a devoted partner. So something really positive had resulted from their spring fling, something more than the heartache Kim felt every day now. She knew that Randi felt it as well as they both struggled to recover from the sweetest episode of their lives.

For a while after returning, Kim lived for nothing more than the daily phone call or e-mail from Randi. Lying on her bed in the dark, the phone pressed against her ear, she had often said, "I wish you were here right now." And Randi might say, "I wish you'd been here today to see the sunset."

They were both pushing a bit to see if anyone was willing to make a change. At least that was what Kim was doing. But she knew it wasn't going to happen. Randi loved the desert and she had fashioned a fulfilling life there. She belonged there in a way that Kim had never belonged anywhere. Kim didn't really expect or even want her to give that up.

The news items coming in from Yuma cheered Kim's days. There were people there she knew, people she felt a kinship with. When Randi wrote her about driving out in the desert and visiting with the desert people, Kim could imagine being there, and wished she was there. She had lived a lot of life in those few months. Not unlike those spring wildflower blooms that burst forth in such lavish exuberance for just a brief moment—brief, but brilliant. In the desert, mediocrity didn't play much of a part. The odds were against you, whether you were a flower, an animal or a person. It took something special to survive there, some remarkable skill. You didn't get a free ride.

One thing that had begun to seem absurd to her was why she and Randi had agreed to meet again in July. Why so long? Why not May? Or June? If it had been June, they could be together right now, making love on a Sonoma Coast beach. When you're living in April, looking directly into her eyes, maybe July seemed like just around the corner, but when you were living apart, it was another story entirely. She clung desperately to the promise of that visit.

Another thing she missed about Yuma was how you could walk into the grocery store, a restaurant, the post office, and there was someone you knew. In fact, all you really had to do was drive through town to see someone you knew. The same people seemed to go to the same places, like Dolly's and Pinkie's. You knew you could go there and find someone to talk to. She didn't have a place like that, not one, in Sacramento. She wasn't a part of any community. The closest thing she had was the faculty at Davis, which was something valuable, but very different. For one thing, it was homogenous, composed of well-educated professionals whose politics were all similar. She didn't interact much with people who were different from her. The others were out there, somewhere, in their neighborhoods. The community of Sacramento or Davis, the towns, didn't need her, didn't know her. There were so many people like her here, she wasn't a special commodity. Even in the short time she was in Yuma, she had felt more special. Certainly Randi had found that to be true.

She was feeling disillusioned about her life, her academic life. She had enjoyed getting her hands dirty for a while, not just because of the actual dirt. She'd loved everything about her time in Yuma, especially Randi. She desperately missed the touch of Randi's skin and the sweet softness of her mouth.

She had thought—hoped, actually—that once she was back in her own world, everything that had happened in Yuma would dissipate like a dream, leaving just a few vague, pleasant images. But her memories weren't anything like a dream. They were acute. They hung together in a picture that remained so real it seemed she could simply step back into it.

She heard a knock and looked up to see Trish in the open doorway. "Do you want to run over to the cafeteria and see what's for lunch today?"

"Actually, I'm meeting my brother for lunch, but thanks for the invitation."

"All right. I'll catch you another time."

Observing Trish's warm smile and intelligent eyes, Kim wondered for a moment if there could be anything between them, if they could fall in love and make a go of it. That would definitely be convenient. Why was the heart so uncooperative? Why did it always seem to defy the brain?

"How's it going, by the way?" Trish asked.

"Okay, though I've been having a little trouble working up sufficient interest to finish any course plans for fall."

"Not too surprising, is it? Your head's still out there in the desert."

My head? thought Kim, amused. "Yes, but I've just about wrapped that up. God, Trish, you should have seen that place, the remoteness, the beauty, the sheer reality of it. It's like a dangerous woman, irresistible and deceptively innocent looking. Gets under your skin."

Trish grinned. "A dangerous woman, huh? I like the sound of that!"

Kim hadn't told Trish about Randi. There was no particular reason other than the difficulty of talking about her. She didn't know Trish that well, not intimately enough to reveal that kind of emotional vulnerability.

"Did you run into any dangerous women out there, then?" Trish asked good-humoredly.

"Yes, actually, we did. There was this old woman with a gun who came after us one day. I thought she was going to blow our heads off."

"That's not the kind of dangerous I meant."

Kim nodded. "Yes, I know."

"Okay, then, keep your secrets." Trish smiled and said goodbye.

Randi was the most dangerous kind of woman there was, far more dangerous than Nellie and her rifle. The kind of woman who could throw your whole world into a tailspin and take away everything you thought you knew about yourself.

Kim's thoughts drifted once again to the last time she had seen Randi, the day they said goodbye at the RV park, the day after that delicious night in the desert. Randi had come over to help her finish packing and hook up the trailer. When everything was ready, Kim got in the cab and put the window down. She'd glanced in her side mirror to see Randi standing there beside the trailer, in some ways looking just like she had the first time Kim had seen her on that road outside the BLM office. But that day, C. Randall had just been an interesting-looking woman in a white hat. This day, that same woman looked like the most important person in the world to Kim. Don't cry yet, Kim had cautioned herself as Randi approached the open window, leaned in and kissed her.

263

"I'll see you in July," Kim said softly. "Don't you dare change your mind."

Randi forced a smile. "Call me . . . a lot."

Kim started the truck, touched Randi's cheek gently, then pulled away. Randi waved. Kim waved back and drove slowly down the street, looking back in her side mirror. Randi stood in the street, waving. Kim put her arm out the window to return the gesture as she turned a corner and lost sight of those long legs and white hat. That's when she had let her tears go.

Kim shook her head, trying to focus on the outline she was working on. A familiar ding told her she had new e-mail. Since coming home, she was not able to ignore e-mail like she had before. She opened her inbox and clicked on the new message from CRandall@blm.gov.

I finally did it. I stayed out all night at Rainbow Wash and photographed the Queen of the Night. It was worth it! I wish you'd been there. See attached photo. Love, Randi.

Kim opened the attachment. A gorgeous white bloom, illuminated by a camera's flash, filled her screen.

Wow, she thought. That thing wasn't much to look at for three hundred and sixty-four days of the year, but this one night, it was fabulous. It was like the century plant that took twenty-five, thirty years to bloom once before it died. It had this one glorious shot at brilliance. Were people like that too? she asked herself. Was there a moment so full of possibility, so singular that it could appear only once in a lifetime? If so, wasn't it worth waiting for, watching for and then grabbing at when it arrived?

She took another long look at the flower on her computer screen, then logged off and left the office to make her lunch date with her brother.

When the waitress had left with their orders, Jack held up his cell phone to show Kim a photo of a white cockatoo. "Check this out," he said. "Mom's new baby."

"Oh, you're kidding!" The bird had a yellow crest like a duck-tail hair style from the 1950s. "It's really funny that she fills her empty nest with birds."

Jack laughed. "I met him yesterday. Name's Mitchell. Mitch for short."

"He's cute," Kim said. "He'll keep her distracted for a while."

Jack snapped his phone shut and leaned back into his chair. "Is there something on your mind, sis?"

"No, no, just thought it'd be nice to have lunch. We don't get together that often."

He gazed silently across the table at her, his expression noncommittal.

"Okay," she said, "there is something on my mind."

"Or *someone*."

"Or someone, yes, smart-aleck. Of course, someone. You know, I thought I could just walk away. But this is so hard."

"Then don't walk away. If you love each other—"

"It's not that simple. Love's not enough if you have to make too many sacrifices for it. It's not enough if you have to give up your dreams for it."

He nodded. "Yes, all right. You're right, of course."

Their lunch arrived, foccacia bread sandwiches in red baskets, surrounded by a rainbow of red, purple, yellow and orange vegetable chips.

"And the dream you'd have to give up," Jack said, continuing their conversation, "is your career, I assume. There's no university in Yuma and no other town close enough to commute. Quite a sacrifice for someone like you. You've spent your entire adult life going in this certain direction. Very successfully, too. Like nobody else I know, you've always seemed to know exactly what you wanted to do. You were going to be an archaeologist before I could even pronounce it. Remember how I used to bury little trinkets in the backyard for you to dig up?"

Kim smiled and took a bite of her sandwich.

Jack dug a sweet potato out of his chip medley. "Mom always thought she was losing her mind because she'd end up with all of those single earrings."

Kim laughed and wiped her hands on her napkin. "It may have looked like I knew exactly what I wanted to do. Being an archaeologist was definitely right. The teaching, though, that may have just been the default."

"Really?"

"Yes. It's the model you see when you're a student. You go out on digs with professors who spend their summers in the field and the school year in the classroom. Teaching is one of the usual ways of making a living in this profession. Unless you're an heiress or something, you can't really spend all your time in the field. You don't make money that way."

"That's kind of a shame, isn't it?"

"Yes, it is. I don't think I ever considered any other way, honestly. All of my role models were professors. It was the same thing for my student helper, Ramon. He had this idea that if he got a degree in archaeology, he'd have to be a college teacher. But like I told his parents, it isn't the only option. Timely discussion, though, because BLM in Yuma has an opening right now for an archaeologist."

He shook his head. "It's a huge decision. Maybe you should take more time to think about it. You can visit her there. She can visit you here. You don't want to just toss off your entire career plan for a girl you don't know very well."

"It's not just Randi. This, the career path I'm on, was never really *my* plan. I was just following the course of my mentors. It was the path of least resistance, like a river flowing to the sea."

Jack looked at her thoughtfully. He wasn't trying to influence her, she knew. He was playing devil's advocate. He would want to support her in whatever she decided.

"Not every river flows to the sea," Kim said quietly.

She stared at the grease stain on the waxed paper in her basket, thinking about how hard it was to be this practical. Her heart, mind and body all just wanted to rush down to Yuma and fling themselves at Randi whatever the consequences.

"Randi once told me about this test they use to decide if a mining claim is valid. Called the prudent man rule. As in, what would a prudent man do in this situation. I've been thinking a lot about that lately. What would a prudent woman do in this situation?"

"What would she do?"

"I have no idea!" Kim laughed. "I know what a *reckless* woman would do."

Jack smiled and nodded understandingly. Kim was grateful for Jackson today. He always made a good sounding board.

"And I want to be at least a little reckless for a change. But I just haven't been able to persuade myself that it isn't a dead end or that the summer heat wouldn't kill me."

"So you're actually considering taking the job?"

"Yes. I've become attached to the petroglyph site, if nothing else. It feels like mine now. Next winter they're going to open it up to the public. Their archaeologist would do tours, give talks, that sort of thing. Look over it. Protect it. And, you know, there's a lot of wild land down there, full of discoveries to be made. The other guy, Matt, he hinted to me that he knew a lot of secrets about that place and I believe it. I could find them too, in my own time."

"It sounds like maybe you fell in love with more than a woman down there."

Kim nodded. "Oh, Jack, I loved being out there! Such an incredible, rugged beauty and everything is alive with a tremendous, pulsing life force. I can't describe what it feels like."

"You're doing a pretty good job. No need to rush into this decision, though, is there?"

"I can't just wait and make up my mind some day in the future. They have only one archaeologist on staff there and the job is open now. I called the District Manager the other day and asked him about it. He said they've hired someone, some kid fresh out of school, but if I wanted the job, he could make it happen. He said he was tired of Randi moping around and he'd even let me wear whatever damned kind of hat I wanted with my uniform if I'd take the job." Kim laughed, then waved a hand. "Never mind.

That's an inside joke."

"What did you tell him?"

"I told him I needed to think about it a few more days. I asked him not to say anything to Randi. No point getting her hopes up, you know. I'm under contract at Davis. I have a full load of classes scheduled for fall. Changing directions like that, it just isn't so easy for me. It isn't even easy for me to imagine."

"So why don't you talk her into moving here? Better weather."

"She'd hate me within six months. She belongs there. She's happy there. I couldn't ask that."

Jack smiled sympathetically. "Whatever you decide to do, I know it will be a sound, rational decision."

Kim sighed. "Oh, how I wish I weren't so rational!"

CHAPTER THIRTY-NINE

The air was heavy today and too hot for being outdoors. Randi caught a whiff of her sunscreen and was immediately transported to a moment with her nose pressed against Kim's cheek, a lazy, luxurious moment. Kim always smelled of sunscreen. With that smell came all of the associated emotions of lying close and touching Kim's body. Randi made a mental note to change to some other brand. This smell was now just a reminder of what she had lost.

She drove through the desert with her air conditioner on full blast, passing the road to Rainbow Wash. She wouldn't be going there today, hadn't gone there for a while. That night she'd gone to photograph the Queen of the Night had been the only time since Kim had left. And the only reason she'd been able to do it that night was the knowledge that she would be able to show the flower to Kim the next day and share the experience. That spot had become their place now. Being there alone was just too painful.

There were so many things like that, places that reminded her of happy days and nights with Kim. Although Kim seemed to be looking forward to Randi's impending visit with great anticipation, she wasn't really of the same mind. She was even considering canceling. She was afraid that it would be too agonizing, like ripping off a Band-Aid really, really slowly. Honestly, their romance was over. Visiting one another now would be sweet, but it would also take place under a cloud of doom with the constant dread of parting and the certainty that each such visit could be the last one. One of them would eventually find someone else, someone in proximity. And the other one, who Randi always assumed was herself, would be left in mourning. That's how she saw it, a prolonged period of mourning, starting with Kim's departure a couple of months ago. Why drag it out?

For the first time in her life she thought she had gotten it right in so many ways. Kim was the appropriate age, compatible in temperament, complementary in background and personality. It was so much fun being with her, so sublime waking up next to her.

In her mind, Randi relived the short, sweet journey of her romance with Kim over and over, from the day Kim showed up with her fancy Tilley hat to the day she drove away, and all of the precious moments in between. She'd tried to talk herself into moving to Sacramento almost every other day. Part of her believed that if she gave up everything here she loved, she would arrive in that alien California place with nothing of her own, relying on one thing only, her love for Kim. And what if that didn't last? What if it wasn't real? Then she would be left with nothing at all.

Minnie told her she was overthinking everything. Minnie said she was a dope, that she should just go. Just go, she said. This may be the best thing you ever find. Minnie was tired of Randi's moping. At least Minnie was happy now. Randi liked visiting Blair's ranch, seeing the two of them together. There was such a strange transformation in Blair. She seemed totally devoted to Minnie, as though Minnie had cast some sort of spell over her. She was a changed woman and a joyful one. They both were. Randi was happy for them.

She looked at her Blackberry screen. No e-mail from Kim. She'd gotten this device after Kim left so they wouldn't be out of touch, even when Randi was out in the desert all day. It didn't always get a signal out here, but it often did. She was disappointed. No messages from Kim today at all.

Maybe she was out with that Trish, the art teacher. That's how it would be—one day Kim would call her and say she was involved with someone else, Trish. Probably Trish. That was the only woman Randi knew about who might take Kim away from her. And she would have to stand by helplessly letting it happen.

So she needed to call Kim and tell her that maybe the visit was a bad idea after all. There wasn't much time, as it was now July. Kim would be really upset, but it was better this way. She would call Kim tonight and cancel the visit. It would be the end. Their spring romance would not spill over into summer after all. It was finished. It was time to move on.

Just as she hit the paved road, Steve came on the radio. "Randall, come in."

"Go ahead."

"Can you come back to the office? The new guy is here and I want everybody to be here to give him a proper Yuma welcome."

"You mean like this hundred and eighteen-degree day you ordered up?"

"You're on your way, right?" Steve asked.

"Sure," she said. "Be there in a few minutes. Out."

She turned around and headed toward the office. The "new guy" Steve was referring to was the archaeologist they had hired to take Matt's place. Randi had met him already, during the interview process. He was a young, skinny twerp with no experience. Very little, anyway. Barely qualified. But the applicant list had been short. Randi tried to remember his name, but couldn't. It hadn't registered with her at all.

She knew she'd been disagreeable lately. And she knew that Steve knew why, and, to his credit, he was treating her with extra leniency. He was a good guy. In a couple more months she would be back to herself again, she knew, and he knew it too.

Randi's cell phone rang as she cruised through the middle of town unimpeded. No traffic now. Even the locals were not out on a day like this. She glanced at her phone to see Kim's mobile number displayed, and felt a sense of relief.

"Hi," she answered, slipping on her earpiece.

"Hi, yourself," Kim said. "Can you talk?"

"For a minute. I'm on my way to the office. The new archaeologist is here and I have to go put on a happy face for him."

"Oh, too bad. I know how much you're going to hate that, not to mention how lousy you are at it."

"I just don't see much point in pretending." Randi turned down the dirt road to the office, briefly remembering the day she'd driven up here to find Kim helplessly blocking the road in her RV. "I'll be in the office in just a minute, so I'm going to have to turn you off soon unless you want to listen in."

"I'd get a kick out of that, listening to you pretending to be friendly."

Randi grunted. "So what kind of day are you having?"

"Not bad. I got a new outfit today."

"Business or casual... or bedroom?"

As Randi said this last word, she thought about how she was going to have to quit the flirting if she really was going to tell Kim it was over.

"Business," Kim said. "But not without a certain seductive quality. At least that's my take on it. Hard to say what you would think."

Randi pulled into her usual parking space and stepped out of the truck. The outdoor heat slapped her in the face. She couldn't imagine anybody wanting to stay here if this was his first taste of the place. The new guy would probably be gone in a week.

She noticed a late-model four-door sedan with California plates parked amid all the pickups and SUVs. The guy was from Los Angeles, she recalled. What kind of a vehicle was that for a college kid? Very sedate. Very girly, as a matter of fact, especially in a town where even the straight girls drive butch vehicles.

She pulled open the door to the building. "I wish I could see you right now in your new outfit, although why you would choose something even remotely seductive for your students is a little odd."

"It's not for the students," Kim told her.

"So who's it for, then," Randi asked, heading through the office, "this seductive new outfit?"

Randi pushed open the door to Steve's office to see him standing just inside the doorway. Leaning against his desk, facing the door and wearing a BLM uniform was Kim, her phone open against her ear.

"It's for you," she said. Then she smiled triumphantly and closed her phone.

Randi, feeling like her legs were about to give way, froze in place, momentarily stunned.

Steve pushed her gently out of the doorway so he could get past her. "Randi," he said, his voice full of joviality, "I'll let you and the new guy get acquainted. She's going to need some help getting settled and finding a place to live. Maybe you can give her a hand with that." He left, closing the door behind him.

"Tilley!" Randi said, grabbing her firmly and hanging on. "My God, this can't be real."

"It is," Kim said, her eyes full of emotion. "Are you happy?"

"I'm ecstatic."

Randi kissed her and then just stood looking at her. The familiar uniform looked so unfamiliar on her. "I'm sorry, but I just can't get over it. I can't stop looking at you. How is this possible? You quit your job?"

"Yes. Caused quite a stink, really, but they let me go in the end. So here I am, your new archaeologist."

"What happened to the kid from L.A.?"

"They found him a spot at the Barstow office. He preferred that, as it turned out. Closer to home."

"You gave up your career for me?"

"Oh, absolutely not." Kim laughed. "I didn't give up my career at all. Just shifted direction a bit."

Kim flung her arms around Randi's neck and kissed her passionately, then pulled back and sighed. "God, I've missed you!"

Randi just swallowed, trying not to cry.

Kim's expression relaxed into an affectionate gaze. "Like Steve says, I'll need a place to live. Any ideas?"

"I think I know just the place."

She grabbed Kim's hand and pulled her out of Steve's office, yelling over at him, "I'm taking the rest of the day off."

"Not surprised," he hollered back.

"I'm going to help the new guy move into her new place." Turning to Kim, she said, "Where's your stuff?"

"I have a suitcase in the car with some clothes. A trunk full of stuff too. My brother is driving down in a few days with the rest, once all the details are settled."

"Details?"

"You know. Where I'll be living, for one thing. I wasn't going to presume—"

They stood in the public reception area, alone except for the coyote staring at them through the glass of the diorama.

Randi faced Kim, holding both of her hands. "You know, I'd be happy if you did presume." Randi felt awkward. "I mean, I want you to— You do know how I feel about you, don't you?"

Kim squeezed her hands. "Tell me all that later," she said, "when we're home alone."

Randi smiled gratefully. As they left the building, a wall of heat pounded into them.

"You know," Kim said in a perplexed tone, fanning the air with her hand, "it's hot here."

Randi laughed, feeling lighthearted, certain that Kim would never regret this decision. I'll make sure she doesn't, Randi thought, unable to control the huge grin she knew was spreading across her face.

Publications from Bella Books, Inc.

Women. Books. Even better together.

P.O. Box 10543 Tallahassee, FL 32302 Phone: 800-729-4992

www.bellabooks.com

TWO WEEKS IN AUGUST by Nat Burns. Her return to Chincoteague Island is a delight to Nina Christie until she gets her dose of Hazy Duncan's renown ill-humor. She's not going to let it bother her, though...
978-1-59493-173-4 $14.95

MILES TO GO by Amy Dawson Robertson. Rennie Vogel has finally earned a spot at CT3. All too soon she finds herself abandoned behind enemy lines, miles from safety and forced to do the one thing she never has before: trust another woman.
978-1-59493-174-1 $14.95

PHOTOGRAPHS OF CLAUDIA by KG MacGregor. To photographer Leo Westcott models are light and shadow realized on film. Until Claudia.
978-1-59493-168-0 $14.95

SONGS WITHOUT WORDS by Robbi McCoy. Harper Sheridan's runaway niece turns up in the one place least expected and Harper confronts the woman from the summer that has shaped her entire life since.
978-1-59493-166-6 $14.95

YOURS FOR THE ASKING by Kenna White. Lauren Roberts is tired of being the steady, reliable one. When Gaylin Hart blows into her life, she decides to act, only to find once again that her younger sister wants the same woman.
978-1-59493-163-5 $14.95

THE SCORPION by Gerri Hill. Cold cases are what make reporter Marty Edwards tick. When her latest proves to be far from cold, she still doesn't want Detective Kristen Bailey baby-sitting her, not even when she has to run for her life.
978-1-59493-162-8 $14.95

STEPPING STONE by Karin Kallmaker. Selena Ryan's heart was shredded by an actress, and she swears she will never, ever be involved with one again.
978-1-59493-160-4 $14.95

FAINT PRAISE by Ellen Hart. When a famous TV personality leaps to his death, Jane Lawless agrees to help a friend with inquiries, drawing the attention of a ruthless killer. No. 6 in this award-winning series.
978-1-59493-164-2 $14.95

A SMALL SACRIFICE by Ellen Hart. A harmless reunion of friends is anything but, and Cordelia Thorn calls friend Jane Lawless with a desperate plea for help. Lammy winner for Best Mystery. No. 5 in this award-winning series.
978-1-59493-165-9 $14.95

NO RULES OF ENGAGEMENT by Tracey Richardson. A war zone attraction is of no use to Major Logan Sharp. She can't wait for Jillian Knight to go back to the other side of the world.
978-1-59493-159-8 $14.95

TOASTED by Josie Gordon. Mayhem erupts when a culinary road show stops in tiny Middelburg, and for some reason everyone thinks Lonnie Squires ought to fix it. Follow-up to Lammy mystery winner *Whacked*.
978-1-59493-157-4 $14.95